061002

Cohen, Jamey.

Dmitri

DATE			

DMITRI

DMITRI

JAMEY COHEN

Seaview Books

NEW YORK

Grateful acknowledgment is made to Harcourt Brace Jovanovich, Inc. for permission to reprint from "Burnt Norton" in *Four Quartets,* copyright © 1943 by T. S. Eliot; renewed 1971 by Esme Valerie Eliot.

Manufactured in the United States of America.

FIRST EDITION

Designed by Tere LoPrete

Library of Congress Cataloging in Publication Data

Cohen, Jamey.
    Dmitri.   91 - B811

    Bibliography: p.
    1. Dimitriĭ, Saint, Cesarevich of Russia, 1582-1591—Fiction. I. Title.
PZ4.C67699Dm   [PS3553.04243]   813'.54   79-67610
ISBN 0-87223-583-1

To Do and Jerry

Time present and time past
Are both perhaps present in time future,
And time future contained in time past.

—T. S. Eliot

Prologue

Bitter wind rattled the huge courtyard gates behind the boy. Despite the fierce northern chill, the impediment of his bulky clothing, and the scarce light of the not-yet-dawn, he worked with assurance.

He already had completed two snowmen. Awkward-looking, but snowmen. Now, as he shaped a third, his hands moved swiftly, if gracelessly, inside his weighty gloves. In his gestures he reflected none of boyhood's customary enchantment with this, the winter's first snowfall. Instead, his small figure projected a purposefulness uncharacteristic of one so young. His body twitched angrily as he heaped snow on the icy image and clawed it into a semblance of the human form.

The two completed snow figures watched him from irises of stone, their eye sockets gouged in faces which he had carved crudely with a pointed stick. Little red candies, stolen from the great house, served as mouths—mouths that neither smiled nor expressed disapproval.

The boy's eyes sparkled as he jammed a head of packed snow on the third figure, patted it into place, and roughly formed a face. Only after he finished did he assess the rude sculpture. He shrugged indifferently; it was not the artistry of his work that he cared about, but something infinitely more significant in the scheme of his life. Walking along the row of coarse figures, he poked each with his sharp-tipped stick and wrote a name on each chest: Feodor. Bitiagovsky. Godunov.

He paused before the last snowman, the figure lettered "Godunov," and breaking the stick in two, jabbed its ends deeply into the head of the white image. Like horns.

The boy clenched his jaw and moved his right hand to his hip. He slowly pulled a *nagaiskii* dagger from its sheath, his eyes moving intently from snow figure to snow figure. Even through his gloves, the boy felt the knife's sharp edge. He held the weapon aloft, brandishing it in the thin rising morning sun, and sliced the air.

Then, as if on signal from a secret force that was his alone to know, he leapt forward. With a wraithlike swiftness he charged the snow figures and slashed at them savagely, heedless of where his blows fell.

Snow flew as he plunged the dagger repeatedly into the three torsos, stabbing at putative hearts, throats, heads. He attacked wildly, mercilessly, piercing frozen exteriors and amputating snowy globs.

The boy flailed until all that remained of the snowmen were three mounds in the courtyard. The stone eyes lay scattered. Small patches of snow, smeared red by the dissolving candies, glistened in the light like droplets of blood.

The boy sank to his knees, his fury spent. He pressed a handful of snow to his lips, sucking the welcome moisture and spreading it across his hot, flushed face where it mingled with beads of sweat. Thrusting the dagger into the ground, he fell on his back. His body shook with laughter, each burst expelled within the cloudy domain of a frosted breath. The laughter grew loud and uncontrolled and he hugged himself with a frenzied, almost maniacal delight.

Meanwhile, unbeknown to him, his revelry had reached the ears of an inhabitant of the great house. An expressionless pair of eyes, veiled behind gossamer curtains, watched the courtyard pantomime with interest and with the knowledge that the boy's imaginary arena would, in the near future, be cloaked in reality. An arena built not of mud and thatch, nor of brick and mortar, nor even of concrete and steel. But of sordid ambitions and the shifting gales of power.

Far above the courtyard, the tower bells pealed. The new day had begun.

MONDAY, MAY 10

Chapter One

She loathed the rain and what it suggested: a disruption of her splendidly ordered existence. Marina, the quintessence of organization, a woman functioning as if driven by the sweep of the second hand. She rose at eight, retired at midnight, and structured the interim into a routine of uncanny precision. Before John had arrived in her life, his whimsical nature in tow, she had meted out even her leisure like beats of a metronome. But John, ah, John. He played havoc with her orderliness just as surely as did this inexorable rain, an inconvenience which she sensed—with that impeccable feel she had for the dislikeable—would deluge the campus for the remainder of the afternoon.

They had met scarcely a month into the school year. She, a first-year graduate student learning the ropes, and he, a college senior following those same ropes to the end of a conspicuously lackluster academic career. It was not fate nor first-glance love that had brought them together, but a dull October party at which he had made a drunken pass that she had drunkenly accepted.

It was not the stuff, she'd once thought, on which a lasting relationship was based. Especially one begun with such an uncharacteristic lack of inhibition on her part. And yet, seven months later, she was wholly committed to John and his unpredictability. For although she seldom admitted it, a lusty streak of romanticism flourished within Marina's compartmentalized life. Hell, she would even welcome this lousy rain if it evoked a little of the mystery, the romance, so fashionable in Gothic novels. But the pellets that whipped the air around her were bereft of Gothic ambiance. Simply raindrops, nothing more.

Standing in the cafeteria archway, she felt her stomach gurgle appreciatively as it digested lunch. She had plied it with an obscene amount of food, and its muted rumble harmonized with the intermittent thunder. Timorously, Marina placed a hand beyond the protection of the door frame. The piercing rain needled her flesh. She shuddered and retreated into the dry security of the archway.

This was California?

A cavalcade of yellow slickers and umbrellas passed by, flapping under the onslaught of water, followed by a lone bicyclist. He looked miserable. His glasses were streaked with trickles of rain and he swiped futilely at the lenses, smearing them. It was foolhardy, Marina thought, to risk cycling today. Brakes that wouldn't work on wet pavement. Tires that wouldn't grip; pedals that invited slippage.

Someone was bound to get hurt.

Her watch crystal fogged and she strained to read the time. Damn. One-fifteen already. She dreaded the watery trek to 130–B and the hour's lecture that awaited her. Her last classroom had smelled of damp wool and plastic, a combination she intrinsically associated with stormy weather, and the stiffness in her fingers had made her handwriting illegible. She sighed and pulled the hood of her poncho snugly around her brown mane.

One thought cheered her: John would be there. "The Psychology of Hypnosis" was the first class Marina had ever shared with him. His history major left him little time for electives. When he did take one, it usually fell into the category of a "mick"—a course requiring little mental rigor—such as "The Structure of Social Encounters," the university's answer to basket weaving, in which students groped for each other while blindfolded.

Marina was miffed that John had classified "Hypnosis" as a mick, but she wasn't surprised. He considered psychology a "fuzzy study," one without focus or applicability. When she tried to defend it, he insisted that her arguments were exactly what one expected from a person who'd spent the last three years ringing bells and watching dogs salivate.

She considered skipping today's class, but suddenly recalled that in lieu of the lecture a demonstration of hypnosis had been planned. John was to be one of the subjects. Already he'd participated in several of Professor Sloane's experiments, his susceptibility to hypnosis having been ascertained through a simple test given at the beginning of the quarter. Marina had never seen him hypnotizd and didn't want to miss her chance.

She lingered a moment longer under the archway, and then, bracing herself, stepped onto the sidewalk. Her poncho stopped at knee length, and she cursed as the faded blue of her jeans turned indigo from the splashing water. There were puddles everywhere—a virtual obstacle course of them—and she sidestepped each with little success. The tissue wedged in her left shoe expanded as it absorbed the incoming water.

Marina's feet were two different sizes, hence the necessity of the tissue. It wasn't merely a matter of the toes of one foot being longer. The actual bone structure and shape of each foot were distinct. One was appropriate for the

body of a pudgy adolescent; the other seemed a vestige
of an extinct species of hominoid. A Frankenstein's monster from the ankles down, Marina nevertheless had no
trouble coordinating the two. But the soggy tissue, squish-
ing as it did with every step she took, was a source of
much exasperation.

Lightning reflected in the math building's windows as
she reached its overhang. Gathered there with students
alien to her own field of psychology, she waited, hoping
the downpour would subside. It did not. Resigned to the
upward march of dark blue on her jeans, she plodded
across the gravel courtyard to a covered corridor.

Though she was late, Marina walked slowly across the
yard, having witnessed too many rainy-day accidents in
her year as a graduate student. Around the corner, a
bearded man pumping the pedals of his bike was also pro-
ceeding carefully on a slick bikepath. And yet, for all
the good intentions on both parts, for all the caution, the
impending collision could no more have been avoided than
if Marina and the man had been clumps of seaweed propelled toward each other by the sloshing tide.

The people under the overhang winced as they saw the
bicyclist, his head bowed, careen around the corner and
snag Marina's poncho on his handlebars just as she crossed
the bikepath. She saw the flash of his slicker and heard
the ripping canvas before being thrown sideways. Like
a marionette with her strings severed, Marina landed
soundly on one knee, scattering books and papers.

The bicyclist stopped some twenty feet away. You son
of a bitch, she thought, I'm going to kill you. Rivulets of
black ink streamed down the wad of papers she clutched
in her hands. Her paperbacks were littered across the
courtyard, and her hair, released from the confines of her
hood, plastered itself against the sides of her face. The
cone of the hood began collecting water. She sat in a two-

inch pool and debated which profanity to scream first.

"Jesus, I'm sorry. You were on the bikepath." The biker bent over her. "Are you okay?"

She didn't bother looking up at him. "What does it look like, clown? I'm on a scavenger hunt?" She snatched a pen before it floated downhill.

"I'm really very sorry. I slowed down when I saw you."

"Right." Like hell, she thought.

"Here, let me help you up." He put his arms under hers.

"That's okay." She sloughed off his assistance. "Much as you did your damnedest to crush me, I'm still ambulatory." She felt an ache in her knee as she stood. "Why don't you grab some of my books before the bushes eat them?"

"Sure."

As he collected her belongings, his bike, precariously balanced on its kickstand, wobbled and crashed to the ground, spilling the contents of his briefcase. He swore and ran to it. The front wheel was bent. "Goddammit," he said again.

Marina had retrieved the last of her books and started laughing. Revenge was sweet. She walked over to where he stood. "Aw, gee, tough break. Lemme help you."

The man grunted. She stooped and picked up the book nearest her. *The Psychology of Hypnosis*, the textbook used in her next class.

"Whatta-y'know? Do you realize that we—" She handed the man his book and looked at his face for the first time. "Professor Sloane! I had no idea! I didn't mean to . . . it's just that. . . ." She thrust the book into his hands: "Here. Yours."

"Thanks," he said grimly, with water dripping off his nose. "You're a big help." As Marina hovered about anxiously, he repacked his drenched briefcase. Finally he turned to her, and said with an odd smile of malicious glee, "Y'know something? You've got mud all over your face."

He departed, wheeling the crippled bike up the bike-path.

She watched him enter the hallway leading to 130–B.

By the time she had washed herself off, class was already in progress. Professor Zugelder, the co-teacher for "Hypnosis," was on the stage, and he spoke so softly that Marina, standing just inside the room's rear entrance, could barely make out what he was saying. Acoustics in 130–B were lousy. She quietly closed the door.

The room, a small auditorium really, was far too large for the class of fifty students, but it was the only room in the psychology building available for the time slot. It was also too cold. To offset the heat radiated from the three hundred bodies attending the class before Marina's, the custodians lowered the thermostat in 130–B. The fifty psychology students shivered under their jackets. Marina's nose ran.

Professor Sloane was sitting in the left-hand side of the auditorium, listening intently to his colleague onstage. Normally classes were taught by a single professor, but Sloane and Zugelder shared an interest in hypnosis and had agreed to split the teaching chores. Marina understood that they were collaborating on another project as well.

She walked briskly through the lecture hall, dripping a trail of water on the carpet, and scanned the rows for John. She spotted him in an aisle seat. The wrong aisle, unfortunately. To get to him she'd have to cross a congested row of students almost as bedraggled and sodden as herself. She coughed and decided to backtrack to an empty row when, to her horror, the student on the nearest aisle seat, interpreting her cough as a signal to pass, politely stood. Committed now to this row, she began arduously wading through its ten fold-up desks, two umbrellas, and innumerable pairs of legs.

There is a real art to climbing past a row of people. One tries to be as inconspicuous as possible, but only an exceptional individual can preserve any semblance of grace or agility. Marina was not exceptional. She tripped and stumbled as she plunged through knotted feet, the wet laminated canvas of her poncho adhering to the backs of the seats in the row ahead. She suppressed a smile as an umbrella she dislodged gouged the leg of an uncooperative young lady in maroon.

"I give you a five on technical skill and a ten on originality," John said as she sat down and stripped off her rain gear.

"Thanks a lot. You would choose to sit all the way over here." She pulled up her desk and opened her notebook. "You going to clue me in on what's gone on so far?"

John slouched in his chair and rested his feet on the back of the seat in front of him. "Oh, Sloane spent the first five minutes hypnotizing some guy using the active form of induction. That's why that exercise bicycle is onstage. Seems you don't have to have a calm, passive person to induce hypnosis."

Marina jotted down a few notes. "So what did Sloane have him do?"

The young man smiled. "Well, that's where he ran into a few minor problems."

"What do you mean?"

"See that dial below the seat? The big white one?" He pointed to the bike. "It controls the amount of pressure that the rider needs to exert to get the wheel moving. Now, if you were a marathon biker, you'd put it at five. If you or I were riding, we'd put it at two and a half."

Marina's eyes glimmered. "Let me take three guesses."

"You got it. Sloane had it on eight, and that jerk"—he

indicated the student on the extreme left of the stage who was sweating profusely—"didn't have the courage to speak up until he practically gave himself a hernia." He laughed. "You should have seen him crawl off that bicycle."

"You sadist."

John responded good-naturedly. "Probably. Needless to say, he never got hypnotized. Instead of concentrating on Sloane's suggestions to feel alert, he was totally absorbed with getting the damn pedals to turn. That woman there"—he pointed to the slender brunette on the stage—"was put under with the standard 'Your eyes are getting heavier and you're sleepier and sleepier' induction. Sloane used her to show how hypnotism can affect the senses."

"How so?" Marina chewed on the end of her pen.

"In this case Sloane screwed up her sense of taste. He gave her a jelly bean and told her it was a clove of garlic. She spat it out. Then he gave her an onion and told her it was a big, juicy apple. She ate the whole goddamn thing, licking her lips and everything. Of course, when he woke her, she turned slightly green."

"That all I missed?"

"Um, yeah. Except for the first part of Zugelder's lecture. He's been talking about the history of hypnosis. Devoted about one minute to Mesmer, one to the last four centuries, and the last five minutes to his own personal theories. One of your more balanced, objective surveys. When he finishes, it'll be my turn to go onstage."

"You nervous?"

"Nah."

"I know you told me before, but I forgot—what have they got lined up for you?"

"Age regression."

"I thought that guy Steve was demonstrating that."

"He was—until the accident last week."

"What accident?"

"They age-regressed him to . . . I guess it was age two. Anyway, he started clapping his hands and giggling, looked real happy, and then urinated right there on the floor."

"You're kidding!"

"Nope. Rather surprised the professors, I imagine. Seems little Stevie wasn't potty-trained until he was three."

"How embarrassing."

"Yeah. Steve wasn't too keen on participating in the experiments after that, so they've been using me for age regression."

"How's it been going?"

"Okay, I guess. They tried regressing me to before I was seven, but . . . well . . . I just came up blank. You know."

John started doodling and Marina turned her attention to her throbbing knee. Gingerly she pulled up a leg of her jeans. The knee was only slightly discolored, but she felt a sizeable lump. Examining it further, she found nothing more than a few faded scars, remnants of her days as a social-climbing eight-year-old. Marina grimaced at the memory. In the third grade, jumping rope and popularity were inextricably interwoven. If a girl in Missouri in the early sixties couldn't do double dutch, she was a pariah. So Marina's scars remained, like the cauliflower ears of a boxer, to tell the story. She rolled the leg of her jeans back down.

". . . and so there are many factors that correlate with hypnosis," Professor Zugelder continued. "But the key word in determining hypnotizability is 'involvement.' Take a person who likes to read. The person who allows himself or herself to become involved in the book, who identifies with the characters or gets swept away in the plot, is much more likely to be hypnotizable than a person who is an objective, passive reader. The hypnotizable reader is one who savors the text, who cherishes the experience of the moment, who suspends reality testing— who will, moreover, let the author's values become his own for that limited time.

"But enough said. I believe we're ready for our next demonstration. Professor Sloane?"

Sloane jumped on the stage and stood with his hands in his back pockets, a roguishly good-looking man of about thirty-five. He'd recently grown a scruffy beard and mustache—to compensate, Marina thought cattily, for his thinning hair.

"Okay, where's our third subject?" he asked. "John?"

Marina slumped in her chair, turning her head to the wall so that Sloane wouldn't notice her as John stood. Zugelder and the two hypnosis subjects filed off the stage, and John came up and sat in one of the vacated chairs.

"Now, with John we're going to try a nonverbal induction. This is a little trickier to pull off than your standard verbal induction but it achieves the same results," said Sloane. "It is, as the name implies, a method of hypnotizing the subject without speaking to him or her. There are many different nonverbal techniques. Often the subject concentrates on an object—say, a dangling watch—until he or she is relaxed and in a trance state. Rasputin supposedly had people stare into his eyes to hypnotize them. The same held true for Count Dracula. He didn't need to speak to his sub . . . well, in his case, victims . . . in order to hypnotize them. He did it nonverbally."

Sloane crouched next to John's chair. "All right, I want you to sit back and relax. . . . Fine. Now just shut your eyes and breathe normally. . . . That's it. Don't worry about the audience. Just ignore them."

Sloane picked up John's arm and held it in the air for a

few minutes. The young man continued to breathe deeply and regularly. Neither spoke. Occasionally Sloane checked John's eyelids. When they began to flutter lightly, he released his grip on John's arm. It remained suspended. Sloane reached over and guided the arm down to John's lap.

"Good. Now what depth are you at?"

"Five."

"That's fine."

Depth, Marina knew from her limited experience with hypnosis, is the method of measuring the extent to which an individual is hypnotized. During hypnosis, the hypnotist periodically will ask the subject at what depth, or stage of hypnosis, he is. If the subject replies "zero," the induction has not been successful. "Two" means the subject has entered a light state of hypnosis. "Five" represents a moderate trance, and "ten" indicates a deep trance. The scale, Marina recalled, is purely arbitrary, and an experimenter is free to use any variation he desires.

She made a few notations in her notebook. Although she doubted she would ever use hypnosis in her study of psychology, it wouldn't hurt to familiarize herself with the procedure.

"John, I'd like you to imagine, if you would, that you've just stepped into an elevator and that you're riding it down to the ground floor."

Sloane shifted his weight from one knee to the other and paused a fraction of a second to let John's mind grasp the image.

"You're watching the lights that tell you what floor you're on, and as you pass each level, you find yourself sinking deeper and deeper into hypnosis. You're starting to descend. There goes ten . . . and there's nine . . . eight . . . seven . . . two . . . one. Deeper and deeper. Okay, what depth are you at?"

"Nine."

"That's excellent." He touched the young man's leg. "I want you to listen carefully to me. In a short while I'll be waking you, but when I do, you'll no longer be the college student you are now. I want you to go back in time to any day you wish—any happy day that you recall—when you were nine years old. Maybe it's your birthday, maybe you just spent the afternoon with a best friend. Any pleasant event that sticks in your mind."

Marina studied the scene onstage. John seemed to be in perfect repose, as he was on those mornings when she woke before him and watched him sleep.

It was strange knowing that—within a few seconds— she would have a glimpse into John's life as a child. Although Marina was not jealous by nature, she sometimes felt twinges of envy when John and his old friends reminisced about the past. It was a part of John she would never share. A segment of his life that had always been closed to her. Until now.

She could hardly wait to see what he actually had been like—not just what she'd heard about, but what traits of his had continued into manhood. It was, she supposed, the closest she would ever come to being with him in his past. Hypnosis—a time machine of sorts. Not the Wellsian version that offered a large overall picture of the world, but one that gave a smaller, more intimate picture of a single person, of the child within him and the seeds of his maturity.

She listened closely to Sloane's words and stifled a yawn. His soothing monotone was infectious.

"I'm going to count backward from five to zero, and when you awake you'll no longer be twenty-one years old. You'll be a nine-year-old boy and feeling refreshed and relaxed. Five, four, three, two, one, zero."

The boy opened his eyes.

"How are you?" asked Sloane.

The boy made no reply but was clearly surprised to see Sloane. He mumbled to himself.

Sloane spoke more distinctly, abandoning the hushed, almost conspiratorial tone with which he had performed the induction.

"Did you want to say something?"

No response. Like those around her, Marina had closed her notebook and was sitting back in her seat waiting for something to happen. The sounds of rustling paper and the shifting of crossed legs filled the room.

John fidgeted in his chair, and Marina began to notice the subtle transformation. Although he had not yet spoken a word, his physical mannerisms were already those of a younger person—of a boy. As if pumped with a superfluity of boyish energy, John tapped his foot and squirmed in the chair. Marina felt a surge of excitement, but at the same time, the metamorphosis bothered her. Though she reminded herself that John was merely reliving an episode in his childhood, she sensed that he was no longer in control of the body onstage. The strange feeling did not fade.

Suddenly he spoke, calling out a single name. "Vasilisa!"

Vasilisa? Marina did not recognize the name. It must be someone from his boyhood that he didn't talk about, she guessed. As she stared at him, the stage grew lighter. His figure seemed illuminated, bathed in a ray of hazy golden light. She raised her head and examined the fluorescent tubing in the ceiling. Someone must have flipped another switch.

"You don't have to be afraid, you know." Sloane spoke calmly to John, in the tone a parent uses to placate an upset child. "I just thought that since we were both here we could talk a little."

The boy glanced to his left, away from Sloane, as if looking for someone. Sloane moved to the other side of the chair. As he resumed his crouch, his shirttail jerked from his belt and his fumbled attempt to tuck it in conveyed a mild exasperation with himself. He loosened his tie and sat back on his knees, intimating to the class that the boy's reticence to talk puzzled him.

"I tell you what, I've got a litle something in my pocket that might interest you." Sloane pulled out a handful of jelly beans.

Laughter erupted from the audience.

"I swear to God that man has more uses for jelly beans," Marina overheard one student tell another. "Just think what a marvel he'll be if he ever discovers gumdrops."

The boy made no move toward the candy. Professor Zugelder spoke up from the front row.

"Dustin? Maybe you ought to take him back and try to regress him again. Looks like he may be so deeply hypnotized that he's finding it an effort to communicate."

"That's probably it. All right, John, I'd like you to close your eyes." Sloane gazed at the floor, contemplating his next few sentences. "You're still under hypnosis, only now you're skipping a few years to the time when you were thirteen. It's your birthday and you've just woken up—"

Sloane was interrupted by laughter. He quickly raised his head. The boy had risen from his seat and was surveying the floor, stopping here and there for a closer look. He ignored Sloane. Marina, leaning forward in her seat to hear better, was baffled by John's behavior.

Sloane arose sheepishly.

"I don't mean to keep interrupting, Dus," said Zugelder, "but John may have had hearing problems as a child. Judging by his reaction to your suggestions—rather, his lack of reaction—that could be the case."

"Funny. He never mentioned it to me before." Sloane placed his hands on his hips and faced the audience. "It's worth a try, I suppose."

The professor circled around the now-kneeling boy, and as the boy stood, Sloane loudly clapped his hands.

An immediate reaction set in. The startled boy whirled around and angrily spat out a stream of words.

But not in English.

"*Čto ty delaješ? Sad von tam.*"

Marina was stunned. John was hopelessly inept at foreign languages; he butchered both French and Spanish beyond recognition. But the language now was not French or Spanish. And the voice was not his. It was high-pitched, boyish. Yet it contained undercurrents of complete control and authority. Even menace. She was disturbed by the dichotomy.

Sloane stepped backward, startled by the foreign speech and by the boy's obvious tone of contempt. Abruptly the child's voice softened and he gave Sloane a bemused look. The class fell silent, as if numbed by a bolt of electricity shot through the room, a current whose conduit was this voice.

Sloane laughed, but his hands moved nervously at his sides. He, too, felt the surge of energy pulsating in the air.

"Well, Cy, that's one explanation we didn't think of." Sloane interlaced his fingers and spoke to his colleague in the audience. "Strange that John failed to mention earlier that English wasn't his native language. What does it sound like to you? Russian? Not that it matters. He'll still understand us."

Marina was bewildered by Sloane's remark. How could John understand Sloane's English if, as a nine-year-old, he'd spoken only Russian? she queried her neighbor.

"Translogic, that's how," the student explained. "John'll be able to understand English for the same reason that a hypnotized person can have a double hallucination. In both cases the person processes information from two levels—the real and the hypnotic. For example, you can hypnotize a person into seeing two of you and he won't think there's anything wrong with it, whereas if an un-hypnotized person saw two of you he'd freak out. Logic would tell him that it was impossible. The hypnotized person, on the other hand, has two dissociated streams of thought. One belongs to the objective world and one is tied to the subjective world of hypnosis. Both streams can operate simultaneously. So although John is *subjectively* reliving his childhood by talking in his native language, he will continue to understand English since his knowledge of that language is an *objective* fact of the present. Got it?"

"I think so. It's pretty confusing." Especially since she knew that John didn't speak Russian.

"It's important stuff, though. Comes up in a later chapter on the Hidden Observer phenomenon. We'll be covering that next week."

Marina nodded silently, not really sure she'd understood a word the young man had said.

"Got you to talk, huh?" Sloane was grabbing something from the moveable chalkboard and offering it to the boy. "How'd you like to do me a favor? Take this chalk and write your name and the date on that board over there. It's okay, you can use a different color if you want."

The student next to Marina tapped her shoulder. "Now, the reason that Sloane asked him to write his name is because—"

"I know, I know. I *did* read part of the chapter, you know."

Marina realized she was being too defensive. The young man only wanted to help. "Sorry. He asked for the sample because if John has truly regressed, his penmanship may appear childish. Or he may use a younger version of his name. Like 'Johnny.' And the date should corroborate his behavior. Am I right?"

"Yeah." The student quickly buried his nose in his notebook.

The boy onstage turned the chalk over in his hand. With a mixture of distrust and bewilderment, he threw it at the professor and spoke again, rapidly, his words running together. Words that Marina, to her surprise, understood.

Sloane was caught off-guard. Half to himself he murmured, "If I didn't know better, I'd say this kid hasn't understood a word I've said."

Marina heard her voice ring out before she was able to control it. "You're right. He hasn't."

"Ah, a resident expert." Sloane tried to find her in the sea of faces.

Marina blushed and wished she could pretend she hadn't spoken but knew he would discern her position. She rose hesitantly. If he recognized her from their collision in the courtyard, he gave no indication of it. She launched into an explanation.

"He just said that if you don't start making some sense he's going to call one of the guards and have you tossed out on your . . . um"—she fumbled for the word—"rear."

The laughter from the audience broke the tension. Sloane's voice lost its condescending edge.

"So I take it you understand him. Why not enlighten us and tell us what he's speaking?"

"Russian." Marina twisted the silver ring on her finger. "It's Russian. Only it's kind of . . . uh . . . formal."

She sat down quickly. She hated being the center of attention.

Sloane would not let the matter rest. "Formal?"

"Yeah." She stood again. "Y'know, a lot of stilted language and combinations, in Slavic form. No slang."

"Oh." Sloane paced the floor. Marina sat down again.

He spun around abruptly. "Now, Ms. ——?" Sloane tried to locate her once more.

"Kuryev."

"Kuryev, fine. Ms. Kuryev, would you mind coming up to the podium? It's a little difficult to keep track of you."

Marina's palms started to sweat. She didn't want to go up to the podium. She didn't want to keep conversing with Sloane nor did she particularly relish having to squeeze past the row of people again. But she had to find out what was happening to John. Something was wrong. Undeniably wrong.

"Of course not. I'd be happy to," she lied.

She folded down her desk, ignored the retributory jab from the young woman in maroon, and circumnavigated legs and umbrellas for the second time.

Sloane had stepped off the stage to Zugelder's seat on the auditorium floor, and Marina stood by awkwardly as the two professors conferred. Sloane remounted the steps and motioned her to follow.

"How well do you speak Russian?" he asked her.

"Well enough." She was relieved that he hadn't recognized her. "My father's Ukrainian and we occasionally speak it around the house."

"How do I ask 'What is your name?' "

Marina rattled off a few Russian words.

"Can you repeat that a little more slowly?"

Before she could get the words out of her mouth the boy had answered.

"Dmitri."

Chapter Two

The silence that suffused the auditorium after the boy's reply was eerie. There was no conversation nor movement in the rows. Simply fifty faces all turned toward the same spot. Fifty people arrested by the simple utterance of a boy. For all had caught the special quality of his voice, of the way he pronounced his name. As if there were no other name quite as wonderful, quite as magical. As if he were special.

Marina had jumped involuntarily. The boy had surprised her, and she felt the same combination of shock and anger that accompanies the betrayal of an intimate trust or the discovery of an eavesdropper in one's midst.

If this is John's idea of a joke, I'm going to kill him, she thought. But when her eyes met his, she knew John was no longer there. Someone else controlled that steel-blue gaze.

She wanted to yell at him and wake him. To slap him. To wipe that blank look off his face. A look that said he'd never seen her before. A look that tried to deny all that had passed between them.

He spoke to her. "Who are you and what do you think you're doing?"

Marina felt the boy's eyes penetrate her own, suspicion in his voice. She nervously cleared her throat. This is ridiculous, she thought. There's an explanation for this. I've just got to play along, that's all. Just play along.

"Marina. Marina Kuryev." As if you don't know, she almost added. "I'm . . . I'm just here because he asked me to come." She pointed at Sloane.

"What did he say?" Sloane touched her arm.

Marina whispered out of the side of her mouth, her eyes riveted on the boy. "He asked me my name and what I was doing."

"So he's with you?" The boy indicated Sloane.

"Uh, yes. Yes, he's with me." She smiled at the boy. He did not reciprocate. She looked away and twirled her ring.

"He asked me if you were with me," she told Sloane. "He hasn't seemed to notice anyone else." She scanned the audience. No one spoke.

"He's not the new gardener, then?" the boy asked.

"The what?"

"Dammit, you heard me, woman! The gardener," he snapped.

"No. Uh, no he's not."

"Why are you so wet?"

"I got caught in the rain."

"I warn you, do not mock me! You came from the river, is that it? Your boat capsized in the wind."

"Huh?"

The boy scowled.

Marina whirled around and faced Sloane. "Do you know what he just asked me? Whether you were the new gardener and if my boat sank. What's happening? I don't understand what's going on."

Sloane seemed lost in thought. "So what did you answer?"

"What does it matter what I answered? None of this makes any sense."

"I command you to face me!"

Marina turned to see the boy's face livid with anger. Humor him, she decided. She quickly apologized. "Sorry. That was rude of me. I was just trying to talk to my friend here and—"

"What's wrong with that man anyway? Doesn't he speak anything but gibberish?"

"Wrong?" Marina was confused. "Oh, his speech you mean. Nothing's wrong. He just doesn't know the language."

In the background she heard Sloane tell his TA—his teaching assistant—to get a tape recorder.

"Just keep talking to him." Sloane touched her shoulder. "About anything. Ask him some questions if you can."

"Uh, Dmitri—"

The boy interrupted her. "He's sane, then?"

"Yes," Marina nodded.

"What did he expect me to do with that?" He pointed to the chalk on the floor.

"The chalk? He wanted you to write your name with it."

"Why?"

"He learns things by looking at other people's handwriting."

"A gypsy!" The boy's stern countenance underwent an instant transformation. He clapped his hands with delight. "That explains it. I thought he was retarded. I've never come across his kind before. Of course, Uncle Mikhail's told me all about them." His eyes grew large and he pulled at Marina's sleeve. "He says they live in caves and never wash. But they're good fortune-tellers regardless."

Marina laughed. Their conversation was getting more and more absurd.

Sloane imitated her and asked under his breath, "What's going on?"

"He thought you were retarded, but now he just thinks you never wash yourself."

"Swell. No wonder the poor kid threw the chalk at me."

The TA returned with the tape recorder and placed the microphone downstage from the boy. Dmitri didn't bat an eyelid. Marina heard the faint buzzer that signaled two-fifteen, the end of the period. The students in the audience were hesitant to leave until Sloane officially dismissed them with a wave of his hand.

"You'll be here long?" the boy asked Marina. His hostility had somewhat subsided.

"For a while."

"Did Uncle Mikhail invite you here?"

"Yes." Marina decided that as long as she was going to fabricate replies she might as well sound confident about them. "As a matter of fact, he asked us to spend the whole day."

She was feeling more comfortable around the boy, if that was what he was. He certainly wasn't John. His expressions weren't John's. Neither were his gestures. His tone of voice, his stance, his walk—everything about him was different. He was someone else. A different entity. Whoever he was, this boy, he was so far removed from the man she loved that it was as though John were no longer in the same room with her. Even his features seemed to be altered.

She halted the boy's interrogation with a question of her own. "Dmitri. That's a very nice name. What's your last name?"

"Ivanovich." He puffed out his chest. "It is a proud name in this country."

Marina looked properly impressed. "Indeed, I should say so. And how old are you, Dmitri?"

"Nine."

They'd gotten that part right, at least. "Well, Dmitri Ivanovich, it's nice to meet you." She extended her hand. The boy did not follow suit. "Don't you want to be friends?"

"I've already got friends."

"I'm sure you do." She slowly withdrew her hand. "I wasn't trying to take the place of any of your school-mates."

"School? I have my own tutor."

"Then how do you meet other boys your age?"

"Many live here, of course. The *jiltsy*, sons of local families. They're here to keep me company. The others are brought in. The guards have their names and they let them through."

Marina thought for a moment that she'd mistranslated his last sentence. Guards? He had mentioned them before. Why would a nine-year-old boy need guards? She was about to pursue the subject when the boy spoke again. Her questions had galvanized his suspicions.

"So where are you from?"

"Me? Quite a ways from here. I don't think you'd know it." She could tell that her answer didn't satisfy him. She shrugged. "Joplin, Missouri."

The boy stumbled over the name. "Mis-sour-i." He repeated it a few times. "Where is this place?"

"My friend can explain it better. He's really the navigator of this expedition." Remembering the boy's quick temper, she backed away facing him. "I'll ask him."

She motioned furtively to Sloane.

"What's wrong?" he said.

"He wants to know how to get to Joplin, Missouri, from where he is."

"So where is he?"

"I haven't figured that out yet."

Sloane tugged on his mustache. "Tell him it's over the mountains. There are always mountains around."

"Oh, really? Been to Kansas lately?" But Marina could sense the boy's growing impatience, and having nothing better to answer, she took Sloane's advice. "It's over the mountains a ways."

To her relief the boy nodded. "Near Tver?"

"Yes, just this side of it." Right next to Wichita, she thought.

"I've always wanted to go there. To Tver. Vladimir speaks of it often."

"Who's Vladimir?"

"My godfather." The boy's face glowed. For the first time the expression on his face matched his childlike voice. As he talked of this Vladimir, a childish enthusiasm surfaced. His face became animated, no longer solemn and furrowed by lines of skepticism. He stirred with restless vitality.

"He comes to see me nearly every week. He used to live in Tver." The boy spoke excitedly. "Last time he came he brought me a new *tycha* board. He'd carved it himself. And the first time we played, I beat him." There was a triumphant ring to his voice. "See those lines?" He swept his hand across the floor. "I was remeasuring them when you came. I figure I can still beat him even at this distance."

"I'm sure you can." Marina saw no lines and didn't know what else to say. She had no younger brothers or sisters and was unaccustomed to dealing with children. Her last baby-sitting job had been in her sophomore year of high school when her charge, a little girl of seven, had scribbled her a note proclaiming: "I hayte youre guts." She'd deduced, shortly thereafter, that child care was not her calling.

Remembering the name the boy had called out earlier, she asked, "Is Vasilisa a friend of yours also?"

"Hardly." The boy's reply was testy. "She is merely my governess. A subordinate."

A governess? Marina wanted to ask more about Vasilisa but was put off by the haughty manner with which the woman had been dismissed from the conversation. It was better to stick to neutral subjects.

"Right. And you say you can beat Vladimir?"

"And my Uncle Mikhail." The boy stifled a yawn, and Marina noted that the tense muscles in his face and neck relaxed. "Actually, Vladimir comes to see both of us, my uncle and me. He and Uncle Mikhail knew each other before I was born."

"That's quite a long time."

"Very long. They met at my parents' wedding. That was . . ."

Dmitri blinked his eyes rapidly as if trying to dispel a sudden urge to sleep. Marina waited as he slowly counted the years on his fingers. He yawned and shook his head a number of times to aid his flagging concentration, then squinted up at the ceiling as though shielding his eyes from the glare of the sun. Finally, through heavily lidded eyes, he looked back at her.

". . . the year 7088." The boy's voice faded and he seemed to drift off to sleep.

Marina felt a warm sensation on her neck—as though touched by those distant sun rays. Without knowing it, she had advanced into the fourth dimension, time. Her destination: the year 7099. Her vehicle of transportation: a nine-year-old with a beguiling smile. Dmitri Ivanovich.

Chapter Three

Dmitri opened his eyes and they had gone. As stealthily, it seemed, as they had come.

His initial reaction was not one of fright, nor shock, nor even righteous anger, though he had experienced all three upon confronting the strangers in his courtyard, but one of increasing puzzlement. How could they have vanished so quickly? Surely he had not fallen asleep while conversing with them, dozing on his feet like a weary horse spent by a day's hard work. And yet he felt the tug of sleep on his eyes even now, the slow, foggy functioning of his mind. Were he to submit to its pull and close his heavy eyelids for just one second, he would return to time's dark void.

Dmitri yawned and his ears popped, and only then did he become conscious of the thrashing noise behind him, puncturing the silence of the courtyard. He pivoted, half-expecting to see the woman pinioned in the arms of one of the guards, but no one was there. The nearest guard, a comic figure struggling to retain his cap in the stiff wind, was over forty *sazheni* away.

The noise continued, erratically. Letting his ears guide him, the boy walked toward the seesaw and exercise bars

built at the behest of his mother for the amusement of her
visiting ladies. There he found the sound's source: a long
leather thong that tethered one end of the seesaw to the
ground. The strip had become slack, and though it kept
the board from bouncing, it was flapping frantically in the
wind, sounding much like the crack of a fast whip. He
flinched involuntarily as a particularly loud snap split the
air, and kneeling down, mindless of soiling his clothes in
the dirt, he retied the thong, securing the varnished plank
of wood to its anchor, a ring driven into the ground especially for that purpose. He rose and brushed off the hem of
his gown.

Swirls of dust, fomented by the strong wind, made it
difficult for the boy to hold his head upright as he surveyed
the fringes of the courtyard. He blinked rapidly and finally
resorted to pressing his chin low to his chest and cupping a
hand over his brow. Still, no sign of the two foreigners.
The palms of his hands began to sweat. It occurred to him
that a higher vantage point might aid his search, but not
wishing to tackle the spiraling steps of the Naugolnaia-
Florovskaia tower, a climb that more often than not left
him dizzy, he veered toward the exercise bars and began
his ascent.

The structure, beautifully crafted with wood from
Yaroslavl, was an open framework of intersecting vertical
and horizontal rods, a gymnastic device to climb that was
well worn. Its bars had been carefully sanded and oiled,
both to reduce the likelihood of splinters in the ladies'
hands and to preserve the structure from the rapacious
effects of the inclement weather, cold enough in winter to
freeze spit and hot enough in summer to roast a man's
flesh. The boy dried his hands on his gown and grabbed
the first bar, moving easily from one rung to another,
swinging his small frame with the fluidity of a gibbon.
The bars were closely spaced, to suit the ladies, but even

so he had seen one or two lose their grip and plummet to the ground. There was no padding to break their fall, yet none of the women ever had been seriously injured. Their thick layers of clothes acted as a protective cushion of sorts.

The boy climbed higher and higher, pulling himself to the topmost rungs with the graceful agility of youth. When he could see the sky framed in the last box of bars, he hoisted himself to the small viewing plank at the apex.

He had forgotten how magnificent Uglich looked on a day such as this, swept clean and clear by the northern breeze, and he gaped with unabashed delight at the panorama. The river glistened and battered its banks with endless series of small waves, carrying with them broken branches and fallen leaves and other natural debris scattered by the wind. The fields over his left shoulder were ripe for reaping, and still farther out stood the woods, rustling with squirrel and hare and white fox. On the main thoroughfare, gusts buffeted walkers about like rag dolls, colliding with one another on their way to market.

The land spread flat before him, but he knew this was a green-textured illusion of spring. In winter the landscape was marked with hilly slopes and inclines: terrain that when covered with snow made for fine skiing. His *nartyn*— so precious to him in those winter months—now stood in his closet, two seasons away from being used again. If ever. For it was time that he got new skis, longer ones, better proportioned to his growing body. And he was growing, every day. Two fingerbreadths already this year.

He breathed deeply of the crisp wind, and his mind cleared of the fog that had earlier engulfed it. For a moment he forgot his reason for climbing the structure; then his puzzlement returned. How had they disappeared? Magic? Holding on to one of the rails, he peered across the courtyard for a trace of his two visitors. Again, nothing.

Discouraged but nonetheless refreshed by the spectacular view of the land that was his, he left his perch and nimbly swung himself, hand by hand, to the ground.

Had the peculiarly garbed and slow-witted pair been apparitions? Phantoms doomed to that twilight between the living and the dead? They had seemed so real to him, but as the Finn had often said, spirits so excelled in their imitation of the living that it took a trained seer—as the Finn was—to discern the truth. On many occasions Dmitri had listened to the Finn's long tales of his encounters with beings from the other side. Tales of evil, some of them, but mostly tales of good spirits who warned the Finn in time of danger and guided him in time of confusion. One simply had to stare into a spirit's face, the Finn explained, and ask the spirit for what purpose it traveled the earth. If the spirit replied that it came for evil measures of revenge, then one had to spit at it thrice, invoking the name of the Lord, and retreat from the ghostly creature, never once glancing back, lest one be enticed to do its pernicious bidding.

Spirits. Dmitri was not frightened by the idea. The two visitors had not cajoled him into any heinous acts; they had come for some other purpose. But what? He recalled the buzzing in his ears that had preceded the man's sudden intrusion into the courtyard and how it had taken several seconds for it to fade. A sign of the supernatural, no doubt.

Spirits. He was disappointed that he had not suspected the truth sooner, while they were standing before him. He should have known. The woman was unlike any he had ever met. Clearly not of his world. Even her speech was odd, her grammar . . . strange.

She must be a good spirit, he thought. Her eyes, clear and blue as the river that cleft his land, conveyed an immediate trust. Her voice rang sweet. An angel, that's what she was! An angel of beauty, the one he'd prayed his whole life to meet, who would enter his wretched life, this prison

of paradise, and grant him one wish, the missing piece of
his life that had tormented him since birth. He was incom-
plete; she would make him whole.

An angel, think of it! He'd be free. It would be his
turn on top, he'd be the one dispensing orders. He twirled
himself around and broke into laughter. Ah, blessed day!
He made plans to speak with the Finn. Surely he would
know how to call her back.

And then he noticed them. The footprints under the
layer of new dust. Footprints of his "ghosts." A surge of
bile rose in his throat and he struggled to contain it. These
strangers were flesh and blood. They'd left marks of their
physical presence in the ground, next to the *tycha* markings
he'd made, so deep that not even the fierce wind had erased
them. They were real.

Worst of all, they'd been just a few feet from him.

Close enough to kill.

The boy sank to the ground and ripped the pearl-studded
necklet from his throat. His breathing was labored and he
shivered as a clammy aura of fear enveloped him, rendering
him immobile. A man and a woman, aliens both, had invaded his private sanctuary, and he, instead of alerting
the guards, had betrayed every teaching drummed into
his head for the past five years. He had spoken with them.
He was lucky they were not the assassins his family feared.
Or perhaps they were. Perhaps he had only narrowly
escaped death's clutches.

What would his Uncle Mikhail say about his foolish
behavior? Panic-stricken, the boy tried to collect his
thoughts and form a rational explanation to present to the
large man. He bit his knuckles and concentrated, his fright
at having perhaps brushed death overshadowed by his
great fear of his uncle's wrath.

He considered pretending that nothing had happened
but discarded the idea. What if one of the guards had

seen him talking with the strangers and already reported it? Dmitri shuddered at the thought of the consequences should his uncle catch him in a lie of such enormity.

No, better the truth. Better to admit that he'd mistaken the man for Bruschek, the newly hired gardener. That the man was a halfwit—as the visitor in the courtyard surely was—had not seemed odd to Dmitri. His uncle, more paranoid with each passing day about the security of his family, had recently suggested recruiting servants with mental infirmities. They asked no questions, had few complaints, and were loyal to the household. "As a child is loyal to the parents," Uncle Mikhail had said. Dmitri remembered the statement because it had seemed so funny. Loyalty was unknown to his family. They were bound by mutual hatreds.

Yes, Dmitri could say he'd thought the man was the new gardener. But what about the woman? How could he explain not being alarmed by her presence, especially after he'd learned the man was not the gardener? He should have shouted for the guards. He should have run. Yet he had done neither. He had ignored his training, his uncle's caveats to be constantly on his guard, to be suspicious of anyone and anything out of the ordinary. In short, to act first and reflect later.

Moreover, he should have been offended by the woman's lack of respect for someone of his station, and by her audacity in carrying on a conversation with him instead of confining her remarks to answering his questions. He should have coldly and callously rebuked her instead of encouraging the familiarity. Yet he had not.

Put to the test, he had failed. There lay the crux of the dilemma he now faced. The hard knot in his stomach, the tightly wound coil inside of him that threatened to spring at any moment, the shaking of his hands, the weakness in his legs—all this an aftermath of the one question he was hard-pressed to answer: Why had he talked with the woman?

How could he tell his uncle it was because he hated this place? Because he hated him. Because his life crept by so slowly and with such unmitigated monotony that once, a few months ago, he'd deliberately slashed his arm, drawing blood, just to prove he was alive. His governess, Vasilisa, had been horrified. She suspected he'd botched a suicide attempt. How little she understood him. Drudgery was his enemy, and the enemy was winning. Until this woman appeared.

It was pointless to even try to explain. His Uncle Mikhail would understand no better than his governess. The boy rose and collected his *tycha* knives. A few *sazheni* from the entrance to the great house, a woman in gray approached him. She spoke with no inflection to her voice.

"I was just about to call you. It's time for dinner." The woman used only one side of her mouth when she spoke. The yellow teeth that showed were broken and decayed. Dmitri wondered if she consciously froze the other half of her mouth to hide gaps where teeth had rotted. If so, she'd never slipped and revealed those toothless gums. It wasn't hard. She never smiled.

"All right, Vasilisa. I'll wash in just a minute. Where is my uncle?"

"Are you all right? You don't look well." The concern in her voice was deceptive. Should the boy become ill while under her care, she would be severely admonished. It was her own state of health that was foremost in her mind.

"Where is my Uncle Mikhail?"

"He has just this moment arrived. In the hallway with your Uncle Grigory."

Dmitri mounted the steps to the entrance but paused for a moment at the threshold. From a pocket that he'd specially requested to be sewn into the lining of his gown, he retrieved the pearl necklet, and fingering the large opal sewn into its cloth, his good-luck stone, he refastened the collar about his neck. It would not do to be seen in his uncles' presence unadorned. He stepped up and over the bottom part of the doorway—a block of wood that stood a hand's breadth high and insulated the house in winter— and walked into the foyer. His uncles did not see him enter.

"Damn it all, Grigory. That son of a whore has the gall to talk to me that way. I do believe he wants to see me beg for that money. Well, he won't have it. I'll kill him first. I will, you know. One of these days."

"Calm down. Please. Here, have another drink. He isn't worth it. Face it, the cur isn't worth it."

"Do you know what he said to me? Do you know what that son of a bitch Bitiagovsky said?" The large man placed a gold goblet on a nearby table, and some of the honeyed liquid slopped over the side. "That I should kindly—mind you, kindly—remember who I was talking to, and that if he were me, in future he would start trying to act like a human being instead of a horse's ass. Said it to me! Straight to my face. Can you believe it?"

"And what did you reply?" A sardonic smile that crept on the smaller man's face went unnoticed by the other.

"Told him to go fuck his mother." The large man wiped the spittle from the corner of his mouth onto his beard. "Like every other man in town. Ha! And then I refrained from knocking his head off. Damn his eyes! I swear, I'm waiting for the day I can slit his throat. And I will, you know."

"That type of talk is dangerous."

"And who's going to repeat what I say? Eh, little brother?" The large man grabbed hold of the other's cloak and pulled him close. "You maybe? Spying for the old boy, eh? A little pocket money?" He roughly pushed him away and picked up his goblet. "Go away, you make me sick."

"I only meant that if you slit his throat, you slit all of our throats. Including the boy's." The smaller man fastidiously rearranged his cloak.

Dmitri did not move from his position by the hall staircase. He studied the two men, so alike in their appearance, so unalike in every other respect. Except one. Greed. Both dressed in dark clothes, their long beards bushy and in want of trim, their hair closely cropped, nearly shaved to their scalps. Brothers, obviously, from the similarity of their faces—yet their temperaments bordered on either extreme. Mikhail, possessing a temper that could and did flare up at the slightest provocation, a man who wielded an ugly personality that became uglier when he indulged in drink, which, as now, he did often. Grigory, a passive, sluggish man, a querulous fop who pouted when things didn't go his way, and who, if threatened with physical violence of any kind, would sell his wife rather than fight. These two were brothers, his uncles. Both quite despicable.

And inextricably a part of his life.

He questioned whether it was wise to interrupt their conversation. This did not seem the time to confront his Uncle Mikhail with more bad news. He started to back his way out of the room when he was spotted.

"Hey, boy! What are you doing lurking about in the shadows? You should enter a room as if all eyes are on you. Haven't I told you that time and time again?" Mikhail let loose a belch that rumbled in the hallway.

"Yes, sir. . . ."

"Ho, Dmitri. And how's my nephew?" Grigory smiled and added softly to Mikhail, "Our little bread and butter."

"Well, sir."

"What's that you say?" mocked Mikhail. "Well? You'd hardly know it, boy. You look as pale as moonlight."

Dmitri cast a quick glance at himself in the mammoth

hallway looking glass. The image verified his uncle's opinion. His skin had a ghostly pallor, and his lips, trembling slightly and flushed with blood because he'd been biting them, provided a sickly contrast.

"I had a bit of a fright."

"Eh?" Mikhail drained his glass and wiped his mouth on his sleeve.

The boy forced the words out of his mouth. "I met a strange woman in the courtyard." By omitting mention of the woman's companion he hoped to temper his uncle's impending outburst. The omission would also tell him what the guards had already divulged.

"What woman?"

"I don't know. She said she was a gypsy. She said you had invited her here. For Mother."

"So? What did Timorev say? Who was she?"

"I didn't call him. . . ." Dmitri's tongue moved heavily in his mouth, garbling his words.

"You what? You didn't notify the master of guards?" The eruption had started.

"I didn't . . . didn't. . . ." His voice trembled.

"Grigory, get Timorev in here! Now!"

Dmitri wrapped his arms around one of the poles supporting the staircase bannister and avoided his uncle's reproving glare. His cheeks burned as the silence between them extended to one minute and then two. Mikhail paced the floor, his buskins scuffing against the polished wood, barely containing his rage. It seemed to be taking Grigory an inordinately long time to fetch Timorev, thought Dmitri. At last, his uncle appeared in the doorway. Two men accompanied him. They had barely time to compose themselves before Mikhail launched into a tirade.

"All right, Timorev, how the hell did this happen?" The large man grabbed the master of guards tightly around the bicep.

"I don't know, sir. I was on the southern gate. I saw no one enter or leave, sir."

"Are you saying my nephew lied?"

"No, sir."

"Speak up man. I can't hear you!"

"NO, SIR! Merely saying the boy was nowhere in my sight, SIR!"

"Who was on the western gate?"

"I was, sir." The other man stepped forward, sweat coating his upper lip.

"And?" Mikhail put his face smack up against the guard's.

"I didn't see anyone," he stammered.

"You're sure?"

"Y-yes, sir."

"You don't sound very sure, Ishchenko. Did you see my nephew?"

"Yes, sir."

"Turn around. What color shirt is he wearing?"

"Sir?"

"My nephew. His shirt. What color shirt does he have on?"

"I . . . I can't remember, sir."

"And yet you were watching him all the time?"

"Well, I was f-facing—"

"Facing what?"

"I couldn't face the boy all the time, sir," the man said. "The wind, you see. It was getting in my eyes. I had to look south, you understand. But I could see the boy in the corner of my eye, I swear. I checked on him time and again—I did."

"GOD ABOVE I SHOULD STRIKE YOU DEAD!" Mikhail swung his huge fist and it flew above the head of the guard, who had thrown himself at his feet.

"No, sir! Please, sir! I swear to Almighty God, there

was no one who could have got by me!" The guard's body shook in terror. "No one, I swear."

"Swear you shall." Mikhail tore open the guard's shirt, revealing a heavy silver cross suspended on a chain about his neck. Mikhail tugged hard and the chain broke. Ugly red welts formed on the guard's neck where the chain snapped, and a small amount of blood oozed out and trickled down to the man's shoulders.

"Swear! Swear before Almighty God in the name of the Lord, Jesus Christ!" shouted Mikhail.

The guard rose to his knees, like a dog begging for a scrap of meat, and pressed the crucifix to his dry lips. "I swear! I swear before Almighty God that I saw no one. That no one passed by my gates. I wouldn't let any harm befall this family. I swear by Christ—*po Khristu.*" The man collapsed, sobbing. "Believe me . . . won't you believe me? I swear, *po Khristu.* By Christ."

Mikhail threw the crucifix to the ground, walked to the hall table, and poured himself another drink. "All right, you miserable creature. Get up. You have sworn."

"And you believe me? You believe me?"

"You have sworn."

"God bless you, sir. Th-thank you. You'll never have cause to doubt me again. Nev—"

Mikhail waved to the other guard. "Get him out of here."

The crying man pulled himself from the floor, retrieved his necklace, and retreated quickly to the door. The master of guards followed but was stopped by a strong grip on his shoulder.

"Break both of his legs and then toss him on the road. Understand?" Mikhail spoke in a low voice.

The master of guards' expression did not change.

"And if I hear of this happening again, it'll be you who'll pay. Now leave us."

Mikhail downed the contents of the goblet and moved to

where the boy had wrapped himself around the pole. "Look at me." The boy did not turn his head. "Look at me, dammit!"

Dmitri jerked his head up, barely able to hold his chin level without shaking.

"Have you no wits about you, boy? Do you not realize what could have happened?"

"Yes, Uncle, I do. . . ."

"Did you tell her anything?"

"What?"

"This woman—what does she know about you, about your schedule?"

"Nothing."

"You spent the whole time talking about nothing?"

"Well, I . . . I mentioned—"

"Were you so stupid as to jeopardize everything we've done for you? For your safety?" His uncle's face was florid with rage and drink. "I have raised you as best I could, Dmitri. I've taught you as your own father would have done if he were still alive. And yet you do this!" He was bellowing now. "I could—I could throttle you. I could—" He raised his fist and Dmitri watched it, big and hairy, the knuckles white and deformed from arthritis. He stopped looking, waiting for the blow to follow.

"For God's sake, Mikhail! NO! Do you forget yourself? Your oath?" Grigory grabbed his brother's arm with both hands. He whispered hoarsely, "Do you forget who he is?"

The terrible rage in Mikhail's face suddenly drained away, and as reason returned, he was confronted with the irrationality of his uncontrollable temper. His eyes bleared and the vein in his right temple throbbed, distended with fast-flowing blood. He flung himself at the boy's feet.

"Oh God, oh God, forgive me." The large man's eyes shut tight as if he were in tremendous pain. "Forgive me, forgive me . . . I lost my head. My love for you and concern for your safety made me lose my head. Please, forgive me"—he opened his eyes and gazed up into the eyes of the cringing boy— "Your Highness."

"Your Highness," the other brother echoed, bowing low to the ground.

Chapter Four

They assembled onstage—Sloane and Zugelder; the TA, Perry Larimore; and Marina and John—huddled around John's chair as though by being near the locus of the phenomenon they could rationalize what had just transpired.

"How many times do I have to tell you? I don't know how to speak Russian," said John.

"But you heard the tape," began Perry.

"Sure didn't sound like me."

"We were all here to witness it, John," said Sloane. "It's your voice."

"Couldn't we discuss this at another time? I'm supposed to be taking a math test right now. Marina, tell these people I don't know what they're talking about."

"The name Dmitri means nothing to you?" asked Sloane.

"No. For crying out loud, no. What do you think? I'm lying to you?"

"Look, John. I know this sounds crazy, but we need to go over a few more details. I'm sorry about keeping you late, but if you can wait a couple of minutes we'll solidify our plans for tomorrow."

"Tomorrow?"

"Yes. You see—"

"Uh, Professor Sloane, could I talk with him for just a moment?" asked Marina.

"Certainly."

She took John's arm and led him to the other side of the stage. "Quit acting like such an asshole," she whispered, "and cooperate with them."

"Cooperate? Fine. Can't I do it some other time?"

"You didn't see what we saw. You didn't see what happened to you. You were a different person."

"Come off of it, Marina. I don't believe any of this."

"You scared me." She tugged on his arm to get his attention. "I was frightened. And you should be, too. Don't you want to find out what's going on? Isn't that worth showing up late for your damn math class?"

"That math class is one of my breadth requirements, and if I don't pass it I don't graduate in June."

"You can always explain to Professor Sumner why you missed the midterm."

"Oh, really? Sure, I'll tell her I missed it because I was in a trance. One which my psych prof wouldn't bring me out of because I'd just told him I live in the seventy-first century. What's more, I was claiming to be nine years old and was talking in a language that I have absolutely no knowledge of." He paused. "You think she's going to buy that? I might as well tell her God was lonely and felt like chatting."

"You're making this whole thing so much more complicated than it is. Professor Sloane can always send her a note on your behalf."

John grumbled, but sat down once more on the stage.

"Well, then"—Sloane rubbed his hands together—"I think the only thing to do is meet again tomorrow and have another go at it. Ms. Kuryev, would you mind putting in another day as our interpreter?"

"No. Not at all."

"How about the rest of you?" Sloane looked at the others for consensus.

"Not that I don't want to appear a dedicated scholar, but this class doesn't meet tomorrow," objected John. "But I do. I mean I've got another class to go to on Tuesdays at this time period."

"Your enthusiasm for this project is simply bowling me over, John." Sloane smiled. "Look, you heard the tape. You know why we're so interested in your case. Do me a favor and stick it out for a few days."

"And having five units of A-plus won't hurt, will it?" Perry added from a corner of the stage.

Sloane laughed and gestured to John. "I can't promise you that, but I can put you down as a member of my research team and you'll get paid for those extra hours. We'll try to switch our meeting time to some other period. Deal?"

The prospect of monetary gain brightened John's outlook considerably. "All right. It's a deal." He eased his arms into the sleeves of his parka. "I don't suppose you'd care to enlighten me about what it is I'm supposedly suffering from?"

"I wish I could. Problem is we won't know until further study." Sloane faced the others. "Okay, how about tomorrow morning at ten? Sound good?"

The five agreed. John rushed from the room and Marina gathered her rain gear from the auditorium floor. She overheard Sloane tell Perry to get a videotape machine for the next day. The TA wrote himself a note and departed.

"So what do you think, Dus?" Zugelder thrust his hands into his coat pockets.

"I don't know. I've got a friend back East who's had some experience with cases like this. I thought I might give him a call. Could be some sort of split-personality manifestation."

"But what about the date he tossed out?"

Sloane chuckled, dimples creeping into his cheeks. "Maybe we've got a Slavic Buck Rogers on our hands."

The two men walked toward the door.

"You know," said Zugelder, "if this case develops into anything major, we won't be able to pursue it."

Sloane stopped dead in his tracks. "What do you mean?"

"Hell, Dustin—we've got our compliance study to think about. That publisher isn't going to wait forever."

"I'm well aware of that. But does it mean we've got to spend every minute of the day interpreting compliance data?"

"I didn't say that. Don't put words in my mouth. I'm just concerned. The tenure committee is breathing down our backs and I don't want to dally around."

"Nor do I." Sloane brushed a piece of lint from his sweater. "I didn't spend ten years breaking my ass to get a teaching position here just to lose it because of a bunch of old men."

"You know the saying—we publish or perish."

"Yeah. I know it. What a rat race. We sweat blood for a handful of prestige." He started walking again.

"Where do you suppose John picked up all that Russian?" asked Zugelder.

"Beats me. I asked Perry to stop by John's dorm to take a quick family history. He might turn up something. If not, we can go to the parents directly."

Zugelder scowled.

"All right, Cy. Let me amend that. We'll farm it out to somebody else who can go see his parents. Okay?"

"You really expect something to come out of this, don't you?"

"You don't?" Sloane raised an eyebrow.

"I guess I'm a little more jaded. No, I think it'll turn out to have some very logical and very dull explanation."

"Well," Sloane smiled, "we'll have to wait and see, won't we?"

Sloane held the door open for Zugelder. He reached for the light switch and spied Marina exiting out the side door. He yelled to her.

"Ms. Kuryev . . . uh, what did you say your first name was?"

"It's Marina."

"Marina. You sure you can handle the translation?"

"Positive. I neglected to mention that I took three full years of Russian as an undergrad. I'm rusty but I think I can handle it." She stepped through the doorway.

"Marina? One last thing."

"Yeah?"

"Stay out of bikepaths. Okay?"

"Oh," she replied lamely. "Uh, yeah."

"See you tomorrow."

The lights went off and she closed the door behind her. When she looked about her she was dismayed to find it raining so hard. She'd forgotten all about the rain while John was under hypnosis. The stage in 130–B had been lambent—almost as if gilded with a layer of bright sunlight. Almost.

John ran down the corridor to the math building. Sure, he could convince Sumner to give him a make-up test, but he'd have no time to study for it. Better to take his chances now while the material was fresh in his mind.

He rushed in the auditorium and looked at the clock. It wasn't as late as he'd thought, and the class had probably wasted the first five minutes signing the honor code. Good. He was only a few minutes behind.

He grabbed a test-and-answer book and headed for the rear of the room. As he made his way down the aisle, he could imagine the thoughts of those around him: "Poor schmuck—probably thought the test was tomorrow," or better yet, "Thank God for that moron—he'll lower the grading curve."

John was determined to prove them wrong. As he slid into his seat, a TA entered the room and wrote down the remaining minutes on the chalkboard.

John found the first two pages relatively easy. The third was a bitch. He skimmed the last two pages for easier problems, and ten minutes later returned to the third page. Damn, what was that equation? The TA wrote "ten minutes left" on the board.

John tried to quell his rising panic. He did as much of the third page as he could without the missing equation. Five minutes. He checked the work he had completed. Three minutes. He guessed on the problems he was uncertain about. He checked to make sure his name was at the top of each page.

One minute. Of course—the formula flashed before him. He sorted through his scratch paper for the right figures. The TA called time. John glanced around him. It would take the one hundred students in the room a few more minutes to work their way to the front. He kept sorting. Finally, he found the numbers and scribbled hurriedly as more students filed out of the auditorium. The TA called time again. No papers were to be accepted after this call. The rows cleared and a few stragglers rushed to the front desk. John finished his work and also went up to the desk. He met with a rude shock.

"Sorry. No late papers."

John was stunned. Profs always gave students a few minutes' grace after exams. But apparently not this TA. Goddamn martinet.

The TA spoke slowly and with studied officiousness to John and the other students. "The three of you worked practically five minutes overtime. You had fair warning. I announced at the beginning of the test that I wouldn't tolerate late work."

John saw tears well in the eyes of the young woman beside him.

"This is ridiculous," she protested.

"I'm sorry. Since Professor Sumner isn't here, what I say goes. You can save your paper and present your case to her during her office hours if you want." The TA turned his back and grouped the disordered pile of workbooks into neat stacks.

John tapped him on the back. "Hey, you."

The TA pivoted, as if steeling himself for verbal abuse.

"You're making one hell of a mistake." John moved closer to the front desk. "Do you happen to know who I am?"

The TA smirked. "No, I guess I don't."

"Good." In one swift move, John picked up a handful of workbooks and shoved his deep into the middle. He fled the room.

Perry cautiously approached the outskirts of Pratt Cluster, seven dormitories arranged in a tight circle that vaguely resembled a gigantic wagon train under Indian attack. He wondered which house was Miremonte, in whose lounge he had agreed to meet with John Greene. They all looked alike, these homes away from home. White stucco, interior courtyards, arched windows, red tile roofs. Splashes of Spanish Mediterranean on California plaster.

The story was that the wife of the university's founder had decreed that all of the university structures be roofed with red tile. That way, after her death, she'd be able to spot the campus from heaven. Perry didn't doubt the validity of the story. The woman had been, it goes without saying, a bit eccentric in her declining years, and in fact had so alarmed the trustees with her behavior that they dispatched her to a convalescent home, where she spent the remainder of her days talking to a walnut named Veblen (" 'Veblen isn't just any ordinary walnut, are you, dear?' she asked the putrefied walnut shell before she stored it in its secret hiding place"—unauthorized *Campus Daily* interview at the Happy Dale Nursing Home).

Despite the mandatory red tiles, many of the campus buildings were attractive. The origins of some were legendary.

Astin Hall, for instance. Named after the spinster who willed the university two million dollars, it had originally housed only females—as was a condition of Ms. Astin's grant—much to the chagrin of the male population, which remained in the older dormitories. Under pressure, the trustees found a loophole in Ms. Astin's bequest:

> The dormitories shall be equipped with one bathtub per floor, ironing rooms, a storage closet, and whatever else the girls might need to ensure their happiness.

What better way, asked the trustees, to ensure their happiness than by supplying them with boys? The following year, the dorms were coed.

Pratt Cluster, that monolithic eyesore on whose fringes Perry stood, was infamous for its sunroofs. A luxury in late spring, the roofs were hellish in winter, collecting pools of rain that threatened to collapse them. Until recently, mosquitoes had bred in the stagnant water, biting students and faculty alike, but they were exterminated as part of a project for Bio 138: "Biology of Natural Populations."

Perry wandered around the complex for fifteen minutes

before he spotted the doorway leading into Miremonte. He sidestepped a skateboard, entered the lounge, and found John lying on the lounge couch. "Thanks for letting me come by," he said.

"That's okay."

"I had a little trouble finding this place."

"The way the university constructed it, it's no wonder. Its head engineer must have had something against doors. I've lived here two quarters now and I've yet to find the entrances to four of the seven houses in this cluster."

Perry cringed at the brightly colored pink-and-orange walls. "Lovely color combination."

"Yeah, isn't it?" John smiled. "The resident associate picked out the colors. He calls them 'happy tones.' " John moved his feet so that Perry could sit. "We all have our own theories on what he did before he came here as a grad student. Personally I think he was a PSA steward who just couldn't hack not working in a pink-and-orange environment." He watched Perry thrash about in his backpack. "Need something?"

"Nah, it's in here somewhere. . . . Got it. All right, this questionnaire Sloane wants you to fill out is pretty basic." He gave his clipboard to John and got out his pen. "He just wants to dig into some of your background. See where you could have been exposed to Russian."

"It isn't going to help. I never learned the language. Sure, I've seen all the James Bond movies with SMERSH running around trying to blow up the world. But if that's where I picked up Russian, my vocabulary should be limited to 'Igor, kill Bond.' It's a little difficult to stretch that into a twenty-minute conversation."

"Right," Perry laughed. "But what are your alternatives? Would you rather believe that you're a mouthpiece for radio waves from the seventy-first century?"

"It would be about as likely. Hey, you can level with

me." John put his feet on the table. "This is all part of a psych experiment, isn't it?"

"What?"

"Don't get me wrong. I'm not accusing you of being unethical or anything, but you guys *are* using me as a guinea pig, aren't you? I mean, hell, you wake me up from this trance all groggy so that I'm late for my class and that puts me in a stress situation, right? And we all know how much you psychologists love studying people under pressure. Then you lay out this bogus story about me talking Russian and calling myself—what was it?—Sigmund?"

"Dmitri."

"Right. Dmitri. Anyway, you play me this tape which had this kid speaking Russian on it in a totally different voice than my own and then you watch to see my reactions." John swiveled his body to a sitting position. "That's it, isn't it? Just like you read in the psych books. Dumb, uninitiated college student falls for trick experiment. And boy, did I fall for it. You had me pretty fooled." He put his arms behind his head and sank into the couch cushions. "How many other suckers did you get with this one?"

Perry looked surprised. "No one."

"You expect me to believe that?" John stopped smirking.

"Really, John, it's no joke." Perry replaced the cap on his pen. "I don't figure you're familiar with the Bridey Murphy case?"

"Nope. Did she get taken on this experiment, too?"

Perry let the flip reply pass. "Bridey Murphy was an American housewife who was hypnotized at a party and suddenly started speaking with a rich Irish brogue. Her real name was Virginia Tigne, but she told people she was Bridey Murphy, a young Irish girl. As Bridey, she seemed to know everything there was to know about this obscure Irish village around the turn of the century, but

she swore, as Virginia, that she'd never been to Ireland
nor met anyone who could have told her about the town."

"So?"

"It later turned out that when Virginia was a little girl,
her mother had employed an Irish maid. A woman whom
the adult Virginia had forgotten, but who had made an
indelible impression on the child Virginia's subconscious.
The maid's name was Bridey Murphy." Perry paused to
catch his breath. "Do you see what I'm driving at?"

"Yeah," John said. "That I'm assuming the role of some
Russian I met. But you forgot one thing. I'm in the seventy-
first century. There aren't many Russians roaming the
countryside who can claim that."

"That's most likely your imagination at play. Could
be the person from whom you acquired your knowledge of
Russian didn't happen to talk about any specific locales
or events. So your mind just fabricated details. And
rather creatively, I might add, which isn't too surprising.
People who are highly susceptible to hypnotic suggestions
are often very creative. The correlation of the two factors
is practically point five."

"Still sounds pretty weird to me."

"It's rare, all right. But I assure you, none of us think
you're purposely hiding information from us," said the TA.

"Thanks a lot for the trust," answered John, his voice
tinged with sarcasm.

"Look, I've got better things to do with my time than
sit here with you." Perry rose from the couch. "Just fill out
the questionnaire and bring it with you tomorrow."

"Okay." John, also rising, rolled the paper into a tube.
"I'm sorry. I didn't mean to get nasty about this. But don't
worry. For the money Sloane's paying me I'll do whatever
you say. I want to make it clear, though. . . ."

John suddenly stopped speaking, as though the motor
controlling his voice had been shut off. His face froze in
mid-sentence, the mouth still drooping open, the eyes fixed

in an unnatural stare. He was that way for no more than two or three seconds, just long enough for Perry to become concerned.

"John? You okay?" Perry took a few steps toward the mute figure.

". . . . don't expect any miracle. It's probably just a fluke."

The young man's speech returned to him in a gush. He continued talking, displaying no apparent awareness of his momentary paralysis. Perry was about to comment on it when John cut short their conversation.

"God, I've got such a headache all of a sudden. Look, we're done here, aren't we? You won't mind if I go lie down?"

"No. I'm sorry you're not feeling well."

"Thanks for bringing by the questionnaire," John said. He walked toward the stairs leading to the living quarters.

"Uh, John?"

"Yeah?"

"Nothing." Perry decided not to mention the lapse of time. It probably wasn't as long as it seemed. John might just have been fumbling for the right word. "Wasn't important. See you tomorrow."

"Right."

"One more thing," Perry called to him as he disappeared around the corner. "I might as well warn you—Sloane's going to want to contact your parents. Obviously they'll remember more of your childhood than you."

"Don't count on it." John's disembodied voice curved around the staircase.

"Why not?"

"I was adopted when I was seven." His heavy footsteps pounded on the carpeted steps, growing fainter until there was nothing there at all.

Except silence.

The faculty "ghetto" where Sloane and his family lived was on the outskirts of campus. Rather than bother with the car, Sloane rode his bicycle to work every morning. He was now on his third. The first two had been ten-speeds. Each had been equipped with lights, pedal clasps, and expensive locks. Each had been stolen within six months of purchase.

So now Sloane knew better. His current model was a ten-year-old three-speed that had rusted into a one-speed. It had a light but no generator to run it, and its front fender was suspended by the grace of one of his son's tinker toys. The pedals were no longer cushioned in rubber. But he had owned it for over two years.

He walked the bike into his garage and inspected the front wheel. Chalk up another battle scar. He contemplated his wife's advice, following the last accident, that he stick little decals of people on the bike's frame each time he hit a pedestrian. It might discourage them from running out in front of him. Then again, they might think him strange. The Psychotic Psychologist. He thought better of the idea. The department faculty would never understand.

On the kitchen table was a note ripped from his wife's yellow legal pad, a holdover from her law school days. She was staying late at the Legal Aid Society, so the note read, and the two boys were out with friends.

Sloane opened the door to the freezer and inspected its shelves. Since both he and Blake worked, it was their habit to cook on the weekends and freeze the results for weekday dinners. He pulled out a large plastic container whose label had fallen off. The contents looked red and meaty. Probably spaghetti. He rummaged around for a while longer before settling on the red concoction. After sliding it out of the wrapper into a pan, and also leaving a pot of water on the stove to boil, Sloane picked up his briefcase and tramped to the rear of the house.

His den was, as usual, in disarray. Cluttered with pages of unfinished manuscript and lengthy sheets of paper crammed with experimental data, it had considerable charm. Near-empty cigarette packs lay stashed in every conceivable niche, and the venetian blinds, long since inoperable, sloped at thirty-five degree angles. Books lined the walls, slovenly arranged with that kind of picturesque carelessness that borders on the anarchic. Sloane reveled in the setting.

He sat down at his desk and began proofreading the papers before him, fragments from the study on compliance that he and Cyrus Zugelder were conducting. They hoped to answer the questions of why people comply, what situations they're most likely to comply in, and what personality traits appear in individuals who tend to overcomply. A year ago the two men had set a deadline for the study's completion. That deadline was fast approaching.

Sloane worried about the study. He needed to make a big impression with the chairman of the psych department; otherwise, he felt sure, he would be let go by the university. Already the department had more than its share of assistant professors. The members of the tenure committee, in an effort to weed out the less qualified among the staff, had sent Professor Adam Quigley to evaluate Sloane's classes. Though the unannounced visits unnerved Sloane, he knew that lecturing was his forte. As a teacher he was popular with the students and greatly respected. He strove to make his lectures both informative and entertaining and he generally succeeded.

But as a researcher? He felt inadequate. It wasn't that he was incompetent or jumped to hasty conclusions. On the contrary, he paid meticulous attention to detail. But his treatment of the data was prosaic; it lacked flair. Perhaps this was because his results lacked flair, especially his latest conclusions in the compliance study. After all his work, he'd discovered nothing new about the human psyche that hadn't been known since men were living in caves. All men seemed to comply at one time or another for the same reasons, most notably in the face of an authority figure.

He winced as he recalled the weeks he'd spent sequestered behind one-way mirrors taping students as they transferred liquid mercury to Coke bottles, drop by drop, using wooden ice-cream spoons. And why had he done it? To confirm that perfectly sane people will perform inane acts indefinitely if told to do so by someone "official." Nothing like seeing tomorrow's neurosurgeons happily balancing liquid mercury to assure one that all men are created equal. At least in terms of imbecility.

Sloane shoved the papers to one side and pulled a book on hypnosis from the shelf. The incident with John had been on his mind all day. Oddly enough, it reminded him of a case he'd heard about a long time ago. Years ago. The details eluded him, and the more he concentrated the dimmer the recollection became. The book, he realized, couldn't help him. Only one man could. He picked up the telephone receiver and dialed a string of numbers. Buzzing and then a click sounded at the other end.

"Hi, Karen? . . . It's Dustin. . . . Yeah. From California. Is Andrew around?"

Andrew Carter. The man who had done so much for Sloane in the past. Helped him establish himself in the department. Supported his curriculum proposals. Listened to Sloane's jokes and improved Sloane's tennis game. When Carter had moved to New Jersey, lured by Princeton's offer to coordinate a new psychology program, the void he'd left in Sloane's life was immeasurable.

And now Sloane was turning to Carter again. He felt

foolish. Sloane, the perennial student, and Carter, his mentor. He lighted a cigarette, watched the smoke zigzag in the air, and decided he was being too hard on himself. His decision to consult Carter about the incident this morning was a professional one, not personal. Andrew Carter was one of the foremost psychologists in the nation. It was his expertise Sloane sought, not his support.

". . . Andrew's not in? That's too bad. . . . No, I won't be back there for a while. Probably not until the next conference comes your way. How are you and the kids? . . . That's good. Look, do me a favor, will you, Karen? Tell him to give me a call sometime tomorrow. I'll be in my office from around three to five. Six to eight your time. . . . Uh-huh. . . . Oh, they're fine. Scott's discovered a new passion. Volleyball. . . . Yeah, it's coming along. . . . No, no, it's not about that. I wanted to talk to him about this new case we ran across. . . . . Yeah. . . . Okay, Karen. Nice talking to you. Bye-bye."

As Sloane hung up he heard Blake slam the kitchen door. "Anyone home?"

"Yeah. In the den. I'll be right out."

Sloane walked into the living room. "Hi, honey." He kissed Blake and watched her sink to the sofa, kicking off her shoes.

"God, it's been an absolute bitch of a day. How was yours?"

"Not bad. Mowed down one more human being in my crusade to reduce world population. Wrote a page for the study that Cy edited to one sentence. Also had a weird thing happen in class."

"Really? What?" She wiggled her toes.

"One of the students we hypnotized started talking in Russian. Swears he's never heard it though."

"You're kidding! He must have learned it somewhere."

"I know. But it's more than that. This kid has a really

lively imagination. Told us that his name is Dmitri and that he was speaking to us from the seventy-first century."

"Seems a bit unlikely, doesn't it? He should have made it the thirty-first. That's much more credible."

"I'll tell him when I next see him."

"Who is he?"

"Greene. John Greene."

"Greene." Blake ran the name through her mind. "He isn't the one that you age-regressed into the dentist's chair and he bit you?"

"No. That was Arnold."

"Ah, yes. Arnold. How could I forget dear, sweet, insecure Arnold?"

"Arnold wasn't actually all that bad. And besides, he taught me an important lesson. Now whenever I age-regress someone I always tell him to regress to a *pleasant* day in his life. I don't want to have to collect my disability pay before I'm forty."

"So what are your plans with this Russian?"

"Greene? We're all meeting again tomorrow."

"You have the time? I mean, I thought you had to count your gallons of liquid mercury." Blake flashed him a wry smile.

"Very funny. No, Cy and I are meeting later in the day."

She yawned. "I'm exhausted. What's for dinner?"

"A surprise."

Blake sniffed the air. "Smells good, whatever it is. I must have made it." She gave Sloane a playful hug and padded across the hardwood floor to the kitchen. Sloane turned on the evening news. Over his shoulder he could see Blake lift the lid off the pan on the stove, give its contents a stir, and then dip in a teaspoon.

"Good?"

"Yeah. Real good." She dabbed at her mouth with a paper towel.

Sloane rearranged the pillows behind his back.

"Dus?"

"Yeah?" He kept his eyes focused on John Chancellor.

"Why are you boiling water?"

"For the spaghetti."

The television picture wavered. One hundred and sixty-two people had died in a plane crash in Jamaica. The president had met with the prime minister of Great Britain. Fighting had broken out on the Sino-Soviet front. And Masha, one of the Moscow zoo's pandas, had given birth to a bouncing baby panda.

"Dus?"

"Yeah?"

"Why do we want spaghetti with our chili?"

Sloane walked to the kitchen and sampled the steaming batch of chili. "I thought it might be a nice change of pace."

"Sure you did." She smiled and poured the water into the sink. "Some other time."

Sloane walked back to the living room and settled his large frame in front of the television.

The Soviets had finally agreed on a name for the new panda. Dmitri.

Chapter Five

Marina's apartment was freezing. The heat was on full blast, but it dissipated about three inches from the vent. She contemplated plugging in the cheap portable heater she'd gotten from her grandfather, but the cord was frayed. Instead she put on a sweatshirt.

She tested the casserole in the oven. Not done yet. She looked at her watch. John was due at six-thirty. It was six-twenty.

She turned on the television for company and sat down to read the day's newspaper. Most of it had been soaked through. Those damn carriers never seemed to get their weather right. There had been perfectly sunny days when Marina found the paper tightly encased, like a mummy, in clear plastic. Today hadn't been one of them.

A news blurb on the television caught her interest. The Moscow zoo had named its panda Dmitri. Something to do with the historical significance of the name. The newscaster didn't elaborate.

The doorbell rang.

"Dressed to the hilt for me, didn't you?" John leaned

against the door, admiring her rumpled blue sweatshirt and thick wool socks.

"You know how I get carried away with these girlish, frilly clothes." She closed the door after him. "Dinner will be ready soon. You want some wine? I was just about to pour some for myself."

"Yeah, thanks."

"How did the test go?" she called over her shoulder. "Did you rearrange it?"

"No, I took it."

"You took it? Why?"

"I didn't want to have to restudy for it. Easier this way."

"You had time to finish?"

"Sort of."

"What does that mean?" She walked into the living room with the wine.

"I'll tell you about it later. You got any aspirin? My head is killing me."

"Sure. You know where it is. Medicine cabinet. Right-hand side." As he washed down the aspirin, she said, "Pretty weird today, huh?"

"Yeah. Seems I missed a lot of excitement. Wish I'd been there to see it." He sat down on the couch.

"You really don't remember any of it?"

"Nope. Man, that recording sounded really tinny. If that was my voice, the tape recorder must have distorted it."

"No, that's what you sounded like. I could barely believe it when you first started talking. At first I thought you were joking."

"When did you decide I wasn't?"

"When you started giving me the creeps." She frowned. "You were so nasty and you . . . you didn't even recognize me. You just kept ordering me about."

"God, I didn't realize it upset you that much. Look,

why don't you tell Sloane to get someone else to do the translation tomorrow?"

"No, I don't feel that way anymore. It was just at the beginning. When I still thought I was talking to you. That's when I was scared."

"What do you mean?"

"I mean, it's not like I'm talking with you at all. It's a whole other person."

For the first time, John seemed a little taken aback. "But the words are coming out of my mouth," he said.

"I know. But it's not the same. I . . . I can't explain. It's like you're not even there anymore. You don't even look like yourself." He said nothing. "What do you suppose it is?" she asked.

"I don't know," he said, staring at his hands. "I really don't know."

"Well, I didn't mean to ruin both our appetites. Come on, dinner's done. Let's eat."

He didn't move.

"John?"

"Oh, right. Dinner."

They left the television on.

"Look, there's that story about the Russian panda," Marina said near the end of the meal.

"What story?"

"I saw it on the local news.. Seems the Soviets have one-upped us. They had a panda born in captivity before we did. Came from the two pandas that China gave them last year."

"Don't tell me. They named the newborn 'Friendship,' right?"

"Wrong. Unfortunately the baby panda came a day late. China and the Soviet Union had a border clash yesterday. Its name is Dmitri."

An uncomfortable lull in the conversation ensued until

John spoke again. "How silly of me not to have guessed." He crunched on an apple. "Why Dmitri?"

"Why 'Ling' or 'Sing' or whatever we named ours? Guess the panda liked it."

"I hear pandas aren't an extremely fussy lot."

As Marina headed into the kitchen, John turned up the volume on the television and started adjusting the other knobs.

"John, bring me over the dirty dish, will you please?" She dumped the remains of the casserole into a container.

John was busy trying to achieve the perfect balance of contrast and brightness.

"John?" She got his attention. "The dish?"

"Oh, right."

"And don't strain yourself carrying it over here. Make two trips if you have to."

John dropped the dish into the sudsy water and started washing the things in the sink. Marina sponged off the table.

"Anyway, it's a coincidence that you used the same name. Dmitri." She scraped a fingernail against the dried particles of casserole that had fused to a plate before handing the plate to John.

"I knew you were going to bring that up again."

"I can't really ignore it. Aren't you curious to find out about this Dmitri?"

"Of course I am. After they figure out what he is and stick him in someone else's body."

"John, you don't have to worry. I know there isn't anything wrong with you. This . . . this boy isn't a part of you. It's like he invaded your system."

"You have a funny way of comforting a person."

"You know what I mean."

"So you think I've got a little person from the ninety-first century broadcasting through my mouth?"

"Seventy-first. As in fifty-one centuries away."

"Or thirteen." John placed the last dish in the dishrack and rinsed his hands.

"Huh?"

"Depending on how you look at it."

"I don't get it."

"According to the Jewish calendar which is hanging in one of my history classrooms, we are in the fifty-eighth century." When Marina did not respond, he added, "Get it? Seventy-one minus fifty-eight equals thirteen."

"John, that's it!"

"What's it?"

"Dmitri's date. The year he told me: 7088. It must be referring to a different calendar."

"You think so?"

"If only we knew which one. What we need to do is look up 'calendar' in the encyclopedia. That'll give us a starting point."

"You don't own an encyclopedia."

"I know. But the library does."

"Oh, no. No, you don't." John backed away from her. "I'm not going to the library at this time of night to look up 'calendar,' for Christ's sake."

"Oh, come on. This could give us our first clue."

"No way. It happens to be raining."

"All right. I'll go by myself. Just thought you'd be interested, since, after all, it does concern you."

"All right. I don't want a martyr on my hands. Tell you what: If you'll proofread my history essay while I'm gone, I'll go xerox the section on calendars. Sound reasonable?"

"You got yourself a deal."

"What did you find?"

"That there are a hell of a lot of calendars in the world. You were right. They all run on different scales. Here—

see for yourself." He handed her the xeroxed pages, per-
meated with the unmistakable odor of the photocopier.

"See? It starts with the Egyptians and then goes
through the Greeks and Romans. Explains Julius Caesar's
and Augustus' modifications." John moved his finger down
the page. "And here is where the pope instituted the Gregorian calendar." He flipped the page and continued.

"This is the stuff I was talking about. The Hebrew
calendar operates on the belief that the world was created
in 3760 B.C., and it runs on a cycle of nineteen years. Really
quite fascinating. You should read this part." He skipped
to the bottom of the page. "The Mayan calendar we Cali-
fornians all know and love from our fourth-grade class
on our Mexican heritage. See what you missed by growing
up in Missouri? All you got was Lewis and Clark's diary
on dysentery. We learned all the gory details about human
sacrifice. Let's see . . . the Mohammedan calendar has July
16, A.D. 622, as its starting point. And the Chinese calendar . . . nah . . . the late 4300s." He scanned the pages. "As
clear as I can tell, none of these calendars goes as high as
the 7000s."

"Damn it." Marina frowned. "Disregard the numbers.
What about a Russian calendar? That's the logical thing
to look for."

"I did look for one, you ingrate." He shrugged his shoulders. "Nothing."

"Nothing? That's just not possible. I know it's there.
It's got to be there."

"Marina, don't get so upset. We just started looking.
The only reference I even see to Russia is this." He pointed
to the page.

" 'In 1918 the USSR adopted the Gregorian calendar.'
So what did they use before?"

"I don't know. All I remember is that they had to add
on or subtract about eight days to make the switch."

"I should have told you to look up 'Russia' while you

were there. Guess I'll just have to go tomor—" John handed her a stack of papers. "What's this?"

"Farsighted, aren't I? *Bartrell Encyclopedia*'s very own rendition of Russian history."

"I knew you were good for some things. It's long, isn't it? Well, shall we start? Which half do you want?" she asked.

"You really think this is worth plowing through?"

"I know it is. There's got to be a mention of that old calendar. And a reason why Dmitri's using it instead of the modern calendar."

They read in silence for some time. Then Marina shook John's arm. "Look! Read this!"

Peter the Great's reign was notable for its attempt to "Europeanize" Russia. Among Peter's many reforms was the adoption at the turn of the eighteenth century of a calendar based on the birth of Christ. Prior to that, years were dated from the supposed creation of the earth, over five thousand years B.C.

The transition to the new calendar was complicated by confusion over which month marked the beginning of a new year. Peter, emulating his Western counterparts, ordered that January be declared the lead month, not September as had been the case with the old calendar.

Marina quickly analyzed the chart accompanying the article. The year 1 B.C. on the new calendar was the same as 5509–10 on the old calendar. Something clicked in her mind. Dmitri's parents were married in 7088. Translated: A.D. 1579–80. That explained why Dmitri's language was so formal, so . . . archaic. She'd been wrong: It wasn't the future she'd been unraveling—it was the past. And Dmitri, this nine-year-old boy with the icy stare that could bore through steel, was her ticket through the turnstiles of history. A ticket to a past so besotted with evil and malice, so rank with a festered malfeasance of power, that the journey would haunt her for the rest of her life.

TUESDAY, MAY 11

Chapter Six

※ ※ ※

"It's you again."

"I'm glad you recognize me."

"How could I forget? I saw you only yesterday. You lied to me." The boy spoke caustically, his upper lip curling unattractively. "My uncle never asked you to come. He told me that if I ever saw you again I should run and get the guards. If you don't explain why you're here, I'll scream and they'll come and they'll kill you. They don't ask questions."

Marina couldn't believe what she was hearing. A threat from a nine-year-old. A nine-year-old. Already she was convinced that John, the adult, was no longer in command of the body onstage. But who was this kid? A spoiled brat, to be sure. She glanced surreptitiously at the list of questions Sloane had handed her, then crumpled it in her pocket. This kid was too clever to be pumped for information right away. She'd have to come up with some answers of her own first. It seemed best to begin by appeasing him.

"I'm giving you five seconds and then I'll scream!" he warned.

"I'm sorry. I did lie to you, but it was only because I

thought you'd throw me off the grounds." She racked her brains for a plausible story general enough to fit the scanty details she had learned about Dmitri. "You see, I don't have any money."

"What happened to your friend? Doesn't he have any?" The boy paced the stage. He was jumpy and seemed ready to bolt at any moment. He kept his distance from her.

"My friend?"

"Yes, you know. The tall, stupid one." Dmitri glanced around nervously. "He isn't here, is he?"

"No." Sloane had retreated to the auditorium floor immediately after hypnotizing John. "He's in the city trying to earn us some." She lowered her head in mock bashfulness. "We thought if we could tell the town people that your uncle had hired us for, uh, psychic consultations then maybe they would want to hire us, too." Sounded reasonable. Marina congratulated herself.

"My uncle will be relieved to hear that. He thought you might be here as. . . ." Dmitri's voice trailed off.

"As what?"

"Nothing. I'll go tell him the real reason. You stay here. He'll want to see you."

The face before her changed instantaneously. All life seemed to flow out of it, draining it of its youthful glow. Those brilliant eyes, like prisms refracting a hot blue flame, dimmed until only a flicker of light remained. The boy's eyelids slowly closed, just as they had done the day before. Sloane motioned her to keep him talking.

"No, wait," she said.

The boy's eyes opened and the pallor disappeared. Marina felt a shiver travel down her spine.

"What? You've got five seconds. Speak quickly."

"Uh, couldn't you wait for me to leave? I'm too ashamed to have to meet him face to face."

"I suppose so. After all, you're only a girl," Dmitri said

haughtily. "You couldn't have done anything to me by yourself. I doubt that he would want to punish you."

"How considerate of him," she murmured.

"Besides," he said as the superior look on his face melted into one of curiosity, "you still haven't explained how you've managed to get by the guards."

"I didn't see any guards."

"Surely you must be joking."

"No, no joke."

The tremor in Dmitri's voice triggered a stream of questions in Marina's mind. What was so important about this boy that warranted private bodyguards? And was his life in so much danger that their absence would terrorize him?

"I'm calling the guards!" he said frantically. "You're lying! I shouldn't talk to you."

"No, please. Don't do that. I'll tell you how I got in. Stay." She moved toward him but he backed away.

"How?" Again, the distrust in his voice.

"Magic. I'm a gypsy, remember?"

"I don't believe you. I'm leaving."

"Wait. I'll prove it to you."

"Prove it? How?"

How, indeed? thought Marina. Damn, why couldn't she have said she sneaked in with a delivery. Then an idea came to her.

"Just stay there. I won't get any closer to you." She walked backward across the stage, retreating to where the moveable blackboard and chair stood. "I'm going to do an old gypsy trick. It's called, uh, dematerialization."

"What does it mean?"

"It means being able to make yourself invisible."

"You can't do that," Dmitri said.

"Yes, I can. I'll make a deal with you. If I can do it, you won't leave. Okay?"

"Go ahead. Make yourself invisible." He crossed his arms over his chest.

"All right. You ready?" I'm going to feel really stupid if this doesn't work, she thought. "One, two . . . three!" She dashed behind the blackboard and hopped on the chair so that her legs would not show. She heard the boy gasp.

"You did it! You did it!"

A wave of relief passed over Marina. She'd guessed correctly; the boy saw and heard nothing but her. To him, the stage and everything on it were nonexistent. He didn't see the chalkboard that blocked his sight. Nor the chair that supported Marina's weight.

"You promise we can carry on a civil conversation now?" She stepped out from behind the chalkboard.

"Oh, yes," breathed Dmitri. His miasma of fright had lifted. "My uncle will be even more pleased to know how you got on the estate. He thought one of our guards had been derelict in his duty. Or bribed."

Marina realized that this was the time for her to take the initiative. "You don't have to tell your uncle everything, you know. If you don't tell him how I got in, I could come and visit you every day." She added, "I could teach you some magic."

"I don't know."

"What, you don't trust me?" She drew closer to him. "Or is it that you're afraid of me?"

She knew her remark would goad his boyish chauvinism.

"Not in the least."

"I'll teach you how to read palms."

The boy still held back. Marina had almost reached her breaking point. The kid was a royal pain in the ass.

"Is it a deal?"

"Okay," he replied. "But we'll have to move over here so

none of the guards will see us. My uncle will be furious if
he finds out."

"Where are the guards?"

"At the house—there." He pointed off in the distance.
"And at the Spasskie gates. See?"

"Got it," said Marina, although all she saw in front of
her was rows of seats.

Dmitri circled her, assessing her trustworthiness for a
final time. After a few seconds, he planted himself in front
of her. "Go ahead. Teach me how to disappear."

"Later. That takes time." This child certainly has a
will of his own, thought Marina. "First, I want to get to
know you. Know a little about you."

"Like what?"

"Like, for instance, who lives here besides you and
your uncle?" Finally she had touched Sloane's list of questions.

"My mother and her other brother. A couple of other
relatives. The *jiltsy*. The servants."

"Vasilisa?"

"Yes, her too." He started to walk to the end of the
stage. Marina panicked for a moment, afraid he would
topple off the edge. She ran to head him off and stumbled
over the videotape cord, which stretched across the right
section of the stage.

"Oops. Stubbed my toe." She walked him back in the
other direction. "Vasilisa. Is she the one who teaches you?"

"She's taught me some things. I've had a tutor for my
major studies."

"What's your favorite subject?"

"Writing."

"Really? So's mine."

"You? A gypsy woman, write? You make me laugh."

"I'll prove it to you." Marina turned her back to him,
and without his knowledge lifted a piece of chalk from the

blackboard runner. Pretending to take it from her pocket, she knelt on the floor.

"Ready? My name, Marina. M-A-R-I-N-A. See if you can do any better."

The boy rose to the challenge immediately. Taking the chalk from her hand, he scrawled out "Dmitri" in Cyrillic, the Slavic alphabet.

"That's probably the only thing you know how to write. Spell out the date for me and I'll concede you the victory." Marina folded her arms across her chest and waited.

The boy labored painstakingly over each word. When he'd finished, Marina examined his work. It was neatly written: "Dmitri. Tuesday, May 11, 7099." She was stunned. He'd written the day and date of the current month. Only the year separated her era from his.

"That's beautiful, Dmitri." She couldn't tear her eyes away from the date. "Your writing is much nicer than mine."

"Vladimir's been helping me with it," he boasted.

"Vladimir. Your godfather?"

"Yes. He was a friend of my mother's once."

"What do you mean 'once'?"

"She doesn't see people much anymore."

"Why not?"

"She gets ill easily. Too much company tires her out."

"I'm sorry to hear that."

"Yes. So now when Vladimir visits he only sees me and my Uncle Mikhail."

"You're very fond of him, aren't you? Vladimir, I mean."

"I want to be like him when I grow up. His estate is one of the best managed. He has influence. And he is popular with the townspeople. Probably because they are all a little afraid of him. He is so tall and dark. He's also the only one who ever listens to me, who likes talking to me. Whenever the attacks come—"

"What attacks?"

The boy hesitated, as if he thought he'd divulged too much to this stranger already.

"I'm not sure what they are. Every once in a while I get sick. I black out. But almost always, when I wake, there's Vladimir. He stays by my side until I feel better. And he always tells me stories of the places he's been and the people he's seen. Lithuania. Poland." The boy seemed lost in a daydream. "Do you know that if you go down the Volga for five days you will reach Yaroslavl? That's a place I've always wanted to see. Vladimir makes it sound so exciting, not like Uglich. I hate it here."

"How long have you lived in Uglich?"

"Ever since I can remember. My mother says we moved here when I was almost two. My father died and we moved."

"Where did you move from?"

"From Moscow. I was born there. But when my father died, my brother moved my mother and me here. He didn't want us around." The boy spoke with a bitterness and maturity rarely found in children.

Marina was distracted by a noise from the auditorium floor. Sloane was tinkering with the videotape machine, and it had started to emit a slight whir. Dmitri did not hear it.

"I never see my brother." The boy was working himself into a rage. "I can never go to Moscow and he never comes here. Occasionally he remembers to send a messenger. On my name day he sent my mother some furs and Chinese silks. I ripped them to pieces. Just as I'd do to him if I saw him. He makes our lives so miserable."

Marina stood mute as the boy vented his anger, vocalizing a hatred that had been smoldering in his heart for years.

"It's ironic, you know. I hear stories of his spending

lavish sums in Moscow. Yet he can't send us the amount which we need in order to live as we're entitled. My Uncle Mikhail—he fights with Bitiagovsky, my brother's agent for Uglich, almost daily. My brother wants me to be humiliated. I know. I hear my uncles talk. That warlock Godunov has him under his spell. He wants to deny me my rightful inheritance to the throne if my sickly brother dies childless." Dmitri nearly choked on the words.

"Your brother is a king?" Marina said with astonishment.

The boy stared at her in disbelief. "My brother is the ruler of all Rus: Tsar Feodor, unworthy successor to the glorious monarch who made this country what it is—my father, Tsar Ivan IV."

Marina's mouth dropped open. Dmitri was a prince? His brother the sovereign of a great nation?

And Ivan IV. He was perhaps the best known of the Russian tsars. Now, what was the nickname he'd gone by? Ivan the Great? No, that was Ivan III. Suddenly she remembered.

Ivan the Terrible. The ruler whose bloodthirsty reign had catapulted him into the annals of infamy. And she was talking with his son.

Chapter Seven

"Is there any way we can move that videotape cord so that I don't trip over it again?" Marina asked.

"No. The machine has got to rest on the auditorium floor, and the only plug is there"—Sloane pointed—"against the backstage wall. It has to stretch across. Just remember to step over it."

"Why are you even bothering with the cord?" asked Zugelder. "Surely you're not planning on continuing this study. Don't you think you're all getting a bit carried away?" Zugelder paced the length of the small conference room adjoining 130–B. Marina watched his reflection in the highly polished floor-length mirror on the wall opposite the door. "Obviously John is just a very creative individual who was exposed to the Russian language and culture sometime in his childhood and can't remember it. Good Lord, we don't even know if this Dmitri character existed." He swung his lanky body over a chair. "It's my guess that he's purely fictitious."

"What if he isn't?" Sloane blew on the cup of coffee in his hand.

"So what? All it proves is that John had a very good primer in Russian history."

"But that's not true," Marina interjected. "John swears he hasn't ever learned Russian history. Why won't you believe him?"

"Marina, what people learn and what they remember learning are two separate things. It's not a question of my choosing not to believe John. It's a question of what he's forgotten. A kind of amnesia."

"It's not that. I know it isn't." Marina resented the short shrift Zugelder was giving the case. "You know that date Dmitri gave us?"

Zugelder interrupted her. "Precisely my point. John— or rather, this Dmitri fellow, if we must call him that— gave us a date that corresponds exactly to today's date. Except for that crazy year he keeps attaching. Don't you see? John's mind is controlling all of this. He subconsciously gave us today's date." Zugelder leaned across the table to Sloane. "I'm surprised I even have to tell you any of this, Dustin."

"As I was saying"—Marina was determined to be heard—"John and I did a little research yesterday. The year Dmitri gave isn't as arbitrary as you think, Professor Zugelder."

"What do you mean?" Sloane swirled his coffee around in the Styrofoam cup.

"I looked up some stuff in the encyclopedia last night and this is what I found." She slid the xeroxed pages to Sloane. The relevant parts were circled in red. Perry, the TA, scraped his chair across the floor to peer over Sloane's shoulder. Zugelder merely loosed a large sigh and tapped his pencil impatiently on the table.

"It wasn't until the 1918 revolution," she said after the two men had finished reading, "that the Gregorian calendar was adopted by the Russians. Prior to that time the most recent modification was that change by Peter the Great, who was, if I remember correctly, a contemporary of England's William and Mary. So that means he was alive around 1700. I'm vague on Russian history, but I know that Ivan the Terrible was before Peter."

"So what's your point?" Dr. Zugelder balanced his pencil on its eraser.

Marina took a deep breath. "The calendar they used before Peter, hence in Ivan's time, was dated not from the birth of Christ but from the supposed creation of the earth, about 5500 B.C. So the date that Dmitri first gave us, 7088, translates to the period from September 1579 to August 1580." Marina paused to let the implications of what she'd said sink in. "And I'm willing to bet almost anything that Ivan IV married in 7088, just as Dmitri said. And, moreover, that Ivan had a son, Dmitri, who was nine years old in 7099, or 1591 on our calendar."

Zugelder threw his pencil exasperatedly in the air. "So John knows a little more history than we gave him credit for. As Perry told us earlier, John can't even account for the first seven years of his life. His parents were killed and he was immediately adopted. God knows what he learned in those early years. He's forgotten virtually everything about them."

Zugelder clasped his hands tightly, causing the knuckles to whiten. He continued, "And I'm sure you're aware that there have been many experiments proving that hypnosis can enhance memory under certain conditions. Why, police departments all over the country now use hypnosis to elicit detailed descriptions of crimes by witnesses. I happen to know that the Los Angeles police have had great success with it.

"By rattling off these facts John is no more proving that he is this Dmitri Ivanovich than I can prove that I'm Napoleon Bonaparte. He's simply a living example of 'hypermnesia'—enhanced memory under hypnosis."

Zugelder sat back in his chair, smug with conviction.

He handled himself like a confident courtroom attorney. Only, in this "case," the defendant might well have been dead for nearly four hundred years.

"Yeah"—Perry spoke for the first time since they'd entered the conference room. "But even if John was exposed to Russian as a child, what kid in his right mind would bother to memorize something as picayune as the wedding date of Ivan IV? And even more puzzling, where did he learn to transpose the calendar dates like that?"

"Assuming, of course, that the dates are accurate," said Zugelder.

"Yes. Assuming that his story checks out." Perry drew out his words lazily, the faint hint of a southern accent in his voice. His speech, like his actions, was unrushed. He tilted back his chair. "It seems a little hard to believe that he's just regurgitating all these facts and weaving them into a story."

"It's been known to happen before." Zugelder unlocked his hands. "Of course, there's only one way to find out for certain. Thoroughly investigate John's background for any trace of contact with Russian-speaking people. However, with these new adoption laws concerning privacy of files, I'm sure that will be rather difficult. Damn near impossible, as a matter of fact."

"Somebody who knew John as a boy has got to be around," interjected Marina. "He wasn't a baby when he was orphaned."

Sloane had been leaning back in his chair all this time, stirring his coffee. "There's another way," he said. "Cy, you haven't disproved the notion that John, very possibly, might never have encountered Russian history. This could be a facet of extrasensory perception. That's been known to happen before, too."

"What are you suggesting? That we run him through a battery of ESP tests?" Zugelder asked.

"Perhaps. That's one of the avenues we could explore," answered Sloane. "At any rate, it's an alternate explanation. I intend to get in touch with Grant Thorton at the Psychic Research Lab. I'd also like to start John on some personality tests. And voiceprints." The voiceprints Sloane wanted were two electronically recorded spectrograms: one of John's normal speaking voice and one of his voice while under hypnosis as Dmitri.

"Anything I can do?" asked Marina.

"You can find us another interpreter."

"Why? Am I doing something wrong?"

"No, not to replace you. I want someone who can give the three of us an instant translation of what's going on while you're talking with Dmitri. You know anyone who would do it without asking questions?"

"Yeah, this guy—"

"Fine, get him." He had not meant to sound so abrupt. He smiled at her so that she would not misconstrue his sharpness as a reflection on her.

"You know," Marina said hesitantly, "you're overlooking one other avenue."

Sloane anticipated what she was going to say. "The history books."

"Right. What if—" She caught Zugelder's look of disdain and qualified her statement. "This is purely theoretical now, but what if this Dmitri is for real? If somehow— I don't know how—his thoughts have wound up in John's body? The only way we'd be able to know is to compare what he says to what history has recorded. The date he gave us today, May 11, 1591. What was the real Dmitri doing then?"

"Assuming there is a Dmitiri," sighed Zugelder. "Come now, Marina. I think you've seen a few too many science-fiction movies. If we go off on these tangents we'll just be wasting our time."

Marina slouched in her seat. Sloane took a sip of coffee and flinched as the still-hot liquid burned his tongue.

"Granted, it is a little farfetched," he said, waving air into his coffee. But Marina saw a glimmer in his eye that made her think he felt otherwise. "Go ahead, Marina. See what you can dig up. But let me add one thing—and this is important: Under no circumstances are you to reveal anything you find to John. If this Dmitri turns out to be a real person in history, I don't want John to know about it."

"Why not?"

"Because we want to keep this a 'controlled' experiment. The more variables we can regulate, the better. If we're to discern whether Dmitri is the result of John's faulty memory, then we can't refresh that memory with new facts. It would be disastrous. You must promise to tell him nothing."

"All right, I promise."

"Good. That's settled." Then he added, in a voice audible to her alone, "I'll be interested to see what you find."

Chapter Eight

It was, without a doubt, the most exciting thing Dmitri had ever done, and the mere thought of it thrilled him to the quick. The best part was that it was secret. It was secret and it was exciting—and yes, dangerous, too. Dangerous not because she posed any threat to him (he understood that now), but because his uncle might find out about the pact. Dmitri really didn't worry about that possibility. The gypsy was far too clever to be spotted. Were she not so crafty could she have twice visited him without detection? No, Uncle Mikhail and the master of guards would assume that she was long gone. No one else, save the listless Grigory, knew she existed. That is how it would remain.

He washed his hands in the large ceramic bowl, carefully removing all particles of dirt from beneath his fingernails, and visualized the woman in his mind. He remembered her eyes. So large and blue and calm, flecked with white specks like the sky outside his windows on a lazy day.

He double-checked his appearance in the looking glass before heading downstairs for midday dinner. Uncle Mikhail had asked that he remain indoors all day, and he did not want to give his uncle reason to question him. Strange, he no longer really feared him, though if the large man were to discover his deception not even dull Grigory would be able to deflect the blow. Yet the tenor of their relationship had changed; the balance had shifted overnight. Their confrontation yesterday had filled Dmitri with greater confidence in himself. He was heir to the throne of Rus—not Mikhail Nagoy. He was a sovereign prince. Evidently his uncle had been reminded of that same fact, else his order that the boy remain inside would not have been couched in the polite guise of a request. Disobeying that order had given Dmitri a small glimmer of life as it should be for him, without others manipulating his moves as if he were a puppet. He was tsarevich of the realm, responsible to no one, and he intended to act like it. Today was a start.

Actually, he had not expected to see the gypsy again. He'd gone outside to practice *tycha*, and when she'd appeared he'd had every intention of calling the guards. But she'd proved to him that she meant no harm, and he viewed her now as a welcome relief to his insufferable ennui. Even better than the Finn. She was young and pretty and had openly displayed her magic. The Finn was old and decrepit and only talked about magic.

Perhaps she would teach him how she was able to appear and disappear at the drop of a pin. If only he had such power! He closed his eyes and imagined materializing in Feodor's court. The tsar's retinue would gape at him, and he would stride boldly up to the royal throne and demand the crown. In awe of him, the congregation would drop to its knees, and the tsar, his hands shaking, would present Dmitri with the seals of office. A new epoch would begin. The reign of Tsar Dmitri, the Good and Just.

Yes, thought the boy, continued visits by the gypsy

seemed more and more appealing, especially now that she wasn't accompanied by that halfwit. All that mattered was that he be discreet. Dmitri laughed to himself. Discretion, how his Uncle Mikhail prided himself on that! How he thought no one saw him bring the women to his quarters, there to lay with him—after removing their crucifixes and covering the icons like the pious zealots they weren't— then to return home to husbands who one day would expose their misconduct and banish them to nunneries, where they would take the holy oath and live out the rest of their lives dreaming of their lover. And in the heart of Mikhail Nagoy they would be replaced as easily as a lost button.

The boy descended the stairs, two leaping steps at a time, and found his food waiting for him on one of the smaller dining tables. Uncle Mikhail was nowhere in sight. He crossed himself, more a matter of habit than an indication of spiritual devotion, and nodded to the server. The man moved toward the table, his manner the epitome of servility, and uncovered each silver dish with a flourish. Dmitri glanced perfunctorily at the contents and waved to the taster, who briskly traversed the room, and with the utmost delicacy scooped a small sample of each food on his finger and ate it. The man had large pockmarks on his face, and Dmitri hated him as much as he did the routine. It was such a bore having to wait as the taster chewed and swallowed each sample, constantly scrutinizing the man to make sure he wasn't palming food and substituting it for the food on the table. Dmitri drummed his fingers impatiently on the arm of his chair.

The taster chewed with exaggeration, moving the entire lower half of his jaw in the manner of a cow. He'd assumed this affectation, no doubt, to assure his master that he was indeed eating the food and not lodging it between his cheek and teeth, as some tasters were wont to do. Dmitri wondered how the man was able to consume the food with such apparent calmness. Though he faced death with every bite he took, the taster's face showed no sign of trepidation. He refused to let the morbid possibility of death detract from the enjoyment.

Dmitri supposed that only a man like this—one who'd already faced death and spat in its face, as attested to by his pockmarks—could be so nonchalant. The boy knew he would never be able to face death as fearlessly, and he hated the man for it. Secretly, he hoped that today's food actually was poisoned so that he'd no longer have to tolerate that contented smirk. He stared expectantly at the taster's face, looking for signs of shortness of breath or bulging eyes or cramping in the stomach. None were to be had. Tired of waiting, Dmitri waved the taster to sip from his goblet.

Finally, when the man had not dropped dead of asphyxiation and Dmitri could no longer bear the sight of his cratered face, he waved both servants away and greedily devoured his meal. After consuming the last of the cream pastries, he licked his fingers and noticed a dark form standing in the doorway.

"Good afternoon, my son."

His mother stepped across the threshold and into the room, her figure suddenly illuminated by sunlight secreted from the narrow windows. She had, so he decided, heard nothing of the incident yesterday afternoon or she would have been bedridden by her nerves. Even so, she moved like a high-strung mare, the disquieting air of taut wire about her.

"You look well, Dmy. Vasilisa informed me that you've been upstairs practicing your writing since early morning."

"Yes, Mother," he lied. "I wanted to get it done before going out with Uncle Grigory."

"That is good. Handwriting reflects the kind of man you are, and yours must be perfect."

He rose to kiss her cheek, but his lips did not actually touch her flesh. He left her thick layer of makeup unscathed, kissing the air next to her ear instead. She did not seem to notice, or if she did, it did not bother her. He pulled back from his mother and thought for a moment that she might be ill, because her cheeks were such a bright red, but he realized that this, too, was paint and represented no evil flame within her. She took his head in her hands, and her greasy lips lightly brushed his forehead.

"Ah, my little Dmy. You are growing up, aren't you? Look at those sleeves. Why, they're far too short for you. You must have a new batch of clothes made."

"Yes, Mother."

"You're beginning to look so much like your father. His lips, his nose. . . ."

He could see the hint of tears well in the blacks of her eyes where the white had once been, threatening to spill onto those brilliant red cheeks. Like the other fashionable ladies of the day, she had dyed the whites of her eyes black through a process with which Dmitri was unfamiliar. Here, in the poorly lighted dining room—her pupils flared to many times their size outside, virtually obscuring their brown irises and bleeding into a spread of black—her eyes looked like two large jet-black orbs set within the frame of her face. They recalled the sunken hollows of a skull. As if maggots, deprived of corpses over the long winter months, had found his mother and feasted there in the gel of her eyes. Eyes so black that Dmitri could not tell what she was looking at; indeed, if he had not known better, he would have thought her sightless. The oneness of the black dye and the black pupils reminded him of the white film over the eyes of the blind beggars in the streets of Uglich. Wretched beings who held out their caps and called to anyone who passed, "Give me and cut me, give me and kill me," and who were spat upon and kicked by drunkards. And this is what he thought of when he gazed into the blackness of his mother's eyes.

Her teeth were black as well; she had varnished them to suit the prevailing style. Dmitri wondered if the trend had originated to hide rotting teeth like Vasilisa's or if it was merely a grotesque cosmetic match for the black eyes. Either way, she appeared toothless.

The lines around his mother's nostrils were deep. Dmitri assumed they'd come with age. He did not realize they were a byproduct of the years she'd spent worrying about their safety. She had, to be sure, little else to do with her time but worry. Such was the bane of being a woman of her rank. Her day consisted of applying the thick make-up on her face and neck and arms, of embroidering dainty table covers that would never be used, of praying many times a day, of sleeping, and occasionally, of venturing outside the palace walls in her carriage, her face veiled in a *fata*, peering through the bladder-skin windows that obscured her from the view of lesser passersby.

She did not eat with the males of the family. The see-saw and exercise bars built for her visitors had not been used in some time. She rarely saw anyone, in fact, not belonging to her personal staff, only appearing publicly at banquets of great importance that dictated her presence. Yet her exile was not self-imposed. She was a pawn of social custom.

Most of her time was spent in the *krestovaia konata*, the prayer room, surrounded by her icons and her candles, on her knees praying to a God that had turned a deaf ear to her. She conferred often with the Finn, and had adopted his animistic overtones to her religious practices, believing there was a soul in every rock or tree. Dmitri overheard her talking to a squirrel once, soliciting its view on the unity of nature. The squirrel had scampered off and left her in shambles, sobbing that even the gentlest of God's creatures had forsaken her. She cried often and for no reason, and would sometimes call Dmitri by different names, many that he did not recognize.

In short, she was slowly losing her mind.

She clutched her rosary beads even now, twirling the strands between her fingers. The beads made clacking noises as they hit against one another. Dmitri could not tell whether she fondled them as a tribute to God or to ease the pangs of her cursed nervous disposition.

He wondered what color his mother's hair was now, under her cap; whether the few strands of silver that he had seen a year ago had broadened into streaks. He tried to conjure up a picture of what she had looked like as a young woman, when her hair had flowed free and her eyes had been clear and her face had not been marred with lines of quiet desperation. His Uncle Mikhail had said that she'd been quite pretty. He'd said that she was carefree and that only after her marriage did she fray like a worn rug. Once, many years ago while still tsarina, around the time that the divorce rumors began surfacing at court, she had stopped talking and eating altogether. She'd never gained back the weight she'd lost, and to this day was far too thin. To create the illusion of the ideal plump figure, she wore her many-layered clothes even in the midst of the summer heat.

But there was nothing she could do about her gaunt face with its deep lines and its sharp nose and its black eyes. Except slather it in makeup. And this she did, religiously, every day of her life.

For all intents and purposes, Marie Nagoy was a mother to Dmitri in name only. She had borne him but not raised him. She'd nurtured him as an infant but not reared him; he'd been reared by a horde of nurses, each one as stoic as the last. Ending with Vasilisa. He'd been raised by them and by no one. He had no mother. His father was a portrait on the wall.

Ironically, Marie's life was one that other women

dreamed about. She was a widow with a male heir and thus entitled to at least a semblance of equality with men. Without Dmitri, she would have faced a bitter old age. Perhaps in a convent. With him, or rather because of him, she wore the finest of clothes: silks and gold cloth edged in fur and set with pearls and stones, so fine and with so many layers that Dmitri often had to assist her in rising from her chair.

The aspect of her life that was most envied by other women, however, was that she was not beaten. It was a Russian tenet that a husband must beat a wife regularly to keep her in line. Were she not beaten, a woman would believe her husband had lost his fondness for her. At least, this is what the men thought would happen, and so the women of Rus sported bruises and cuts as a sign of their men's love.

Dmitri supposed his mother still had the whip she'd received from his father on their wedding day—one of three traditional gifts from the groom to his bride, the others being fruit, to assure her that nothing good would be withdrawn from her as long as she was good, and a sewing box filled with needles and thread, so that she would apply herself diligently. The boy did not know how often his father had used the whip on his mother. That he used it on their weding night—when it was customary for the husband to touch his bride with it before coupling—of this the boy was certain. But after that? Surely Ivan would not have been able to beat someone with his mother's face. The face that reminded him so much of his first wife, the ethereal Anastasia, the woman he'd worshipped, whose untimely death had driven him into a steep decline from which he'd never fully recovered. It was said that Ivan hoped to pattern his life with Marie after his life with Anastasia, going so far as to give to Dmitri, his son by Marie, the name he'd given his first son by Anastasia.

There was a second reason that made Dmitri believe

his father had not beaten his mother. Ivan had killed another son—his namesake, Ivan Ivanovich—in such a manner. In a blind fury one day, he had raised his staff and split open the skull of his heir. Alone in the room, after others had run for help, Ivan had watched his son's face turn into a mask of blood. How could he ever trust his strength after that?

But that was all in the past. People Dmitri had never known. Places he'd never seen. His father was dead. His mother remained. Part of her, at any rate. He spoke to the once-angelic face before him.

"Have you eaten?"

"Yes. The whitefish was quite good. Did you have some?"

"Yes. I liked it. Is Uncle Mikhail home?"

"Upstairs resting, I believe." She licked her lips, making an effort to keep the conversation going. "I understand you and Uncle Grigory are taking the gerfalcon out this afternoon."

"Yes. Uncle Grigory says it is much more powerful than the goshawk. He wants to see how its training is going."

"That's splendid. Your father had a great interest in predatory birds, you know. He had many of them. He used to say you could learn much about the foibles of human nature by watching them. Someday you will want to own your own birds." She paused and added, with a sudden fanatic gleam in her eyes, "Yes, when you are tsar and live in Moscow."

He did not want to be around her any longer. Nor was it imperative that he stay. Whenever she mentioned Moscow, her speech became rambling and incoherent. The past that she had lived became fused with his future, and he never knew whether she was talking about him or his father. For her, demarcations of time were meaningless.

The past and future were both here, contained in the present, to be shaped and molded in her brain just as easily as she might mold a lump of clay. Neither were beyond the grasp of change.

So ran the clock of a madwoman.

As he left the room he heard her tell someone, belonging to either period of time, perhaps not yet born or long dead, to hurry and adjust the hem of her dress or she would be late for the coronation. He plugged his ears, climbed the stairs and threw himself down, face first, on his feather-bed. He closed his mind to everything around him, a technique he'd taught himself long ago, and in a few minutes he was asleep. He and most of the inhabitants of Rus, their shops closed, their voices hushed. Except for the *krestanin*. The plows of those *kholops* in the fields, those slaves to the land, were never still.

It was next to one of those fields of grain that Dmitri and his Uncle Grigory, after their midday rest, along with assorted friends, menservants, and the trainer, took the recently acquired gerfalcon. The boy stood a distance from the great bird and watched the creature dart its small head from side to side, flashing a beak that could easily crunch through a man's finger. The trainer raised his leather-sheathed arm and gave the falcon a command, the call to kill, and the mighty creature spread its vast wings, soaring up and up in the air, a hellish vision, and plucked sparrow after gentle sparrow from the sky. It dropped the corpses at Grigory's feet.

The pile of sparrows grew and the green blades of grass became matted with blood. Still, his uncle called for more, more. The bird rose and killed several more sparrows before digging its bloodied talons into the leather arm of the trainer for the last time. Grigory cooed at the bird, a sick grin plastered on his face, and remarked on its exquisite form.

Dmitri gazed at his uncle and realized that he despised the man, perhaps even more than he hated the brother in Moscow he did not know. Hated this man who would never be able to kill but who delighted in the killings by others, be they human or nonhuman; hated the lurid spectator who ached to see blood drawn but who couldn't hold a sword in his hand lest he fall and impale himself. Grigory's golden rule: The more violent the kill, the better.

Dmitri had seen his uncle in countless arenas. The last one had a pit stained brown with dried blood; they'd come to see a man fight a bear. The contest had barely begun when the beast reared itself to attack and the man responded, thrusting his wooden fork deep and hard into the animal's sternum. The bear roared with pain and fell down, but not before taking the man's arm, severed just at the shoulder, with him.

Dmitri's uncle had been pushed to something beyond a mere observer's excitement, beyond a lust for gore and a vicarious enjoyment of the kill. He'd gasped with unnatural pleasure, his body twitching, and bits of foam collected in the corners of his mouth. The two combatants died in each other's blood, one a man and one an animal. But their blood was the same. Red and thick and warm. And the spilling of it had touched the raw core of his uncle's soul.

Here again, in more pleasant surroundings, Dmitri had a window into his uncle. The depravity of the man shone like a beacon. Grigory announced that he was satisfied, that the bird would be a great champion, and the party walked back to the house. They passed a field where barley was being reaped, and Dmitri lagged behind to watch the *krestanin* bless the grain. One of the peasants looked up and caught the tsarevich's eye. Dmitri blushed and averted his face. The man had looked at him with the same distaste Dmitri felt for his uncle. He realized how foolish he was being, intimidated by a mere peasant, and he raised his head, but the *krestanin* had returned to work. Dmitri considered having the man struck down but thought better of it. Nothing could change the expression on that man's face. He walked away, leaving the peasant to spill his life into the furrows of the field, just as the man in the arena had spilled his.

The men followed a side road to the hothouse, and there they stripped naked and heated the *palati*, the ovens. The hothouse was large and could hold many people. Dmitri had been here on many occasions, often two or three times a week, to sweat the evil venoms from his body and to keep his constitution strong.

There were public bathhouses as well, scattered over the face of Muscovy and much frequented, but Dmitri had never been to one. He'd heard stories about them, though. Particularly from foreign tongues. The English could not understand the great store the Russians put in the steam-baths and likened those who used them to hot pigs on a spit. Even the Germans, who valued the hothouses in their own land, were shocked by the risqué, even de-bauched behavior of the Russians in the public hothouses, cavorting as they did in the nude, disregarding the separate compartments assigned the sexes.

Dmitri loved sitting in the hothouse and absorbing the cleansing sensation given by the fiery air. His flesh grew warm and his eyes smarted. Inside his body he could feel the warmth as well, flushing out his system and carrying any seeds of illness to the surface in streams of sweat. It was a process of purification. His body would be pure and so would his mind. In here, he could hold no ill will to-ward that man in Moscow who was of his blood and of his flesh. He could not hate the uncles who lived off his name or the mother who did not know him. Nor could he pray for the death of Godunov. All that was impossible in the hothouse. He was pure, and with that purity he was transported to another time and place, one where assassination did not lurk around every corner, one where movement was not restricted, one where life did not mean another's death.

The men left the bathhouse and Dmitri was alone. He lay back against the wood wall, conscious of the sweat running down his body, and enjoyed the solitude. He thought about many things. Especially about the woman in the courtyard.

The heat grew unbearable and Dmitri's lungs were scarcely able to pump air, so intense was the steam, its pressure not unlike a pile of rocks on his chest. He rose and dashed outside to the Volga, where he joined the others by leaping into the water. The drastic change of temperature took away his breath and he surfaced gasping for air, as if he'd been held under the water for a long time. His skin tingled and he paddled lazily in the water, calling to the others and laughing with them. Then he reversed his course and dove into the river, into the depths of the Volga. Once he was down as far as he could go, he relaxed his muscles and let himself be carried by the current, floating in the comfort of the cold water, carried by a liquid plane of blue that was the color of her eyes.

When they pulled him from the water, no one seriously believed he had been trying to kill himself.

Chapter Nine

ЯР ЯР ЯР

"No way." Zugelder slammed his fist on the top of his office desk. "I say we hand this case over to someone else in the department or drop it."

"You're not being reasonable. You can't tell me those dates didn't intrigue you."

"Dustin, we don't have time to fool around with this kid. Sure, it's fascinating the way his mind is taking over the role of this Dmitri. But that's all it is. A role."

"Will you listen to me? I just looked up Dmitri in the goddamn encyclopedia. He existed! He was real—'son of Ivan IV of Russia.' "

"Doesn't change a thing. We still don't have the time."

"Cy, just go along with me for a couple of weeks. A lousy couple of weeks."

"We don't have those weeks to spare. We've got to finish that compliance study. Remember? That minor consideration called tenure?"

"We take off a few weeks and what will anyone care?"

"We'll lose two or three weeks to compile data, that's what. And we'll look like damn fools in the eyes of the tenure committee. Running around talking to ghosts." Zugelder rolled his eyes.

"Nothing's going to improve that study of ours, Cy. Two weeks won't matter to it. But we've got something in our hands that might make every university in the nation want us. That's the potential."

"What if we spend a bunch of time talking with John and we discover he learned Russian as a child?"

"Then we fall back on our compliance study," answered Sloane.

"But what have we gained? Nothing. Just made our chances for tenure that much slimmer."

"You're wrong. We gain money." Sloane's eyes lit up.

"Money? Are you crazy? From whom? Who's going to give us money, Dus?"

"Use your head. Psychology is a popular market these days. It brings in big money. My God, we could easily write a book on this kid. Think of it. Ivan the Terrible's son. Even if it doesn't pan out, if this is just a case of hypermnesia, we can still write about it. Hell, do you realize all the money those people made off of the Bridey Murphy case?"

"You've got it all figured out, haven't you?"

"Yeah."

"And even if I don't agree to the study you'll go ahead with it anyway."

"You're probably right." Sloane stroked his beard. "Cy, if Philip Zimbardo of Stanford can go around selling books on shyness and Herbert Benson of Harvard can make big bucks telling people how to relax using the mantra 'one,' why shouldn't we cash in on hypnosis?"

"Don't beat around the bush, do you? All right. I'll give you one week. One week. And if I still think it's a waste of time after that, we pull out. Understand?"

"Sure."

"I'm not doing this for the money, either."

Sloane smiled. "That's what they all say."

"I'm agreeing to this so that you can get it out of your

system and return to the compliance study." Zugelder smiled also. "God, I should have listened to my wife when she warned me about participating in joint projects."

"You won't regret it."

"Oh, yes I will. One week. And I'm warning you. I'm going to do everything I can to convince you that this is hypermnesia."

"Fine with me. Always like a spirit of competition."

"You're incorrigible."

"I'll see you tomorrow, okay?" asked Sloane.

"Yeah."

Sloane left, and Zugelder shuffled a few papers on his desk. Near the letter opener he came across a folder marked: "Compliance—The Authority Syndrome. Cyrus Zugelder/Dustin Sloane." He sighed and filed it away in his drawer.

Marina climbed the steps to the Milton Graduate Library. The building had been constructed during that decade when long flights of marble-white stairs were in vogue. It boasted authentic Ionic columns, renowned chiefly for the pigeons that roosted in their crevices, and the only vending machine on compus that sold Zig-zag cigarette papers. A grotesque combination of neo-Palladian architecture, ornate friezes, and Plexiglas, the library capped the only hill on campus. There was no ignoring its presence. The students called it MITMA, short for "man's inhumanity to man."

Marina disregarded the information desk and went straight to the card catalogue. She searched the DIL–DOM index. Pulling out a card labeled "Dmitri," she assumed she'd latched on to a book about the young prince. The subheading, however, said "The False Pretender." She read the one-line description on the card. No, this book wasn't about Dmitri Ivanovich but about someone pretending to be him. Even so, it confirmed her suspicion that Dmitri had existed and she felt exhilarated. But how odd, she thought, that a book had been written about a man who had impersonated Dmitri and not about the boy himself. She made a note about "False Dmitri" in her binder.

The legs of a fat man in his forties blocked her access to the FAB–FIN file. Normally she would have politely informed him that she needed to get to it, but Marina was fed up with people who with selfish obstinacy obstructed the files as they flipped through the cards.

She pulled open the file, ramming it into the man's shin. "Oops, excuse me. I'm really sorry. Can't seem to get this file out."

He glared at her and moved to one side.

"Feodor. See Theodore," the card read.

She returned the file to its cubbyhole. Under Theodore, the anglicized distortion of Feodor, she found six listings but no mention of Dmitri. Instead she noticed numerous cross-references to a Boris Godunov. Godunov. Where had she heard that name? Oh, yes. Dmitri had mentioned it. "That warlock Godunov," he'd said. Wonder who the guy was? After checking the overflowing Ivan IV index, she stepped to the left, found the Godunov cards, and dutifully copied down more call numbers.

Fumbling in her backpack, Marina freed her student identification from her wallet, waved it at the attendant, and passed through the turnstiles to the Stacks, that enormous collecion of library books spiraling upward for eight floors.

The books she needed were six floors up, somewhere in the 940s. She arched her neck and peered up the twisting treads. It unnerved her a bit, this wrought-iron staircase. She always imagined she'd wrench an ankle on it or slip through the gaping steps, landing amid texts on the mili-

tary-industrial complex and the welfare state, not to be
found until days later by a frazzled poly-sci student.

She reached the sixth floor and turned down a dimly
lighted hall. The rows were marked by cards so sinuously
calligraphic that she decided someone had deliberately designed them to promote eyestrain. Probably an artistic
optometrist-to-be. An advocate of energy conservation,
Marina made matters worse for herself by ignoring the
light switches. She squinted in the dark and slammed into
a pile of books on Catherine the Great left by a negligent
scholar. Gradually, she worked her way down to the books
on Ivan's reign.

Here were the records of all of Russian history. Hundreds of years of toil and sweat encompassed in assorted
publications, each one stashed away in a deserted corner of
a schizophrenically constructed library. It seemed, so she
suddenly thought, the United States had gone a little over-
board in celebrating its Bicentennial back in 1976. Two
hundred years old. Barely a drop in the proverbial bucket.

Succumbing to the need for light, she flipped a switch.
Matching the call numbers inscribed in her binder with
those on the books, she pulled a load of texts off the
shelves and placed them on one of the desks stationed
along the side wall. The desks were carefully spaced out,
with dividers attached to the front of each. Carrels, really.
The dividers did not keep out sound. Nor did they mask
the unmistakable stench of a peanut butter and jelly sandwich clandestinely consumed by a student behind a volume
of Rousseau's *Confessions*. They did, however, create the
illusion of snug privacy. And their varnished plywood was
a gallery for graffiti connoisseurs.

The library also provided brick-red vinyl stools equipped
with wheels. Marina had never seen anyone sit on one.
The clatter they made on the metal floors discouraged
their use, as did their proclivity for tipping over without

warning. They'd been pushed to one end of the room and remained there, like red-capped bellboys waiting for tips.

Marina carried a last pile of books to the desk and sat down. She divided them into stacks dealing with Ivan, Feodor, Boris Godunov, and Russian history in general. Taking one from the latter stack and flipping to its index, she found, in addition to a listing for False Dmitri, not one but two Tsarevich Dmitris. The second entry was followed by "prince of Uglich" in italics. She knew she'd found her boy.

The index listed two sections about Dmitri, prince of Uglich. The first was brief but informative. It substantiated all that the boy had said. As she read she discovered:

Dmitri had been born to the seventh wife of Ivan the Terrible, a woman named Marie Nagoy, whose marriage to Ivan was not formally recognized by the Church, since under canon law only three wives were allowed. When Ivan died, his son Feodor succeeded him. Although Feodor's succession was uncontested, many court attachés were disgruntled. Those who opposed the new tsar naturally turned to the infant Dmitri, then two years old, as a possible rival to the throne. The Nagoy family, an ambitious clan, especially Marie's brother Mikhail, was receptive to the idea. But before any action was taken, Feodor banished Dmitri and the Nagoys to Uglich.

Marina stopped reading. How could John have accumulated enough knowledge about this obscure historical figure to assume his role? The answer eluded her. She turned to the second section listed in the index and found the heading "Boris' Tragedy." Somehow Boris Godunov and Dmitri were linked. She skimmed the page and halted at a passage, transfixed:

It has never been determined whether Boris Godunov was responsible for the young tsarevich's death. It is no secret that he wished to rule Rus *de jure* just as he was already ruling Rus *de facto* as Feodor's regent. Should Feodor die without an heir, Dmitri would be an obstacle to Boris' rise.

The passage gave no date for the death of Tsarevich Dmitri. Marina flipped hurriedly through the pages. The paragraph stated that Dmitri had been young when he died. Her mind raced. How young? Within seconds, she found her answer:

On the fifteenth of May, 1591, the quiet of the Saturday afternoon was interrupted by the knell of the tocsin. Dmitri Ivanovich, the nine-year-old prince of Uglich, was dead.

She looked again at the date: May 15, 1591, a Saturday. Today's date, she reminded herself, was Tuesday, May 11. Saturday would be May 15. Just as it would be for the boy speaking from John's lips. She shuddered. If, by some miracle, this boy was more than just a vivid image in John's mind, an image now personified with startling accuracy, then there was but one inescapable conclusion: Dmitri had four days to live.

Chapter Ten

꽃꽃꽃

When Sloane called Grant Thorton to confirm the scheduling of John's ESP tests, the line was busy. He wrote himself a note to call again. No sooner had he hung up the receiver than his secretary buzzed.

"Andrew Carter on line four."

He reached across the desk and collected a pack of matches from the depths of a brightly painted gourd, a gift from an anthropologist friend. He lighted a cigarette.

"Andy. Thanks for returning my call. How you doing?"

"Not bad for a man who is being subpoenaed by the United States House of Representatives," said Carter.

"What for?"

"Nothing I have to fret about. Seems they want to carry the banner against juvenile crime and they need some statistics on aggression. Should be interesting."

"When's this great oratorical display scheduled?"

"The twentieth. But you should be overjoyed to know that I'll be out your way before then. I'm attending that conference in San Francisco on the seventeenth."

"Great. Blake and I'll have you over for dinner."

"I'd like that. How's Blake doing?"

"Fine. She's doing fine. Kids are fine, too." Sloane

scavenged his desk drawer for a pad of paper. "Andy, what I called about yesterday—remember that hypnosis case you worked on in which a woman spoke ancient Egyptian?"

"Remember it? Sure. It's bothered me ever since. Why?"

"We've got a similar case here."

"How so?"

"A student I age-regressed has been speaking what seems to be an antiquated form of Russian."

"Can anyone understand it?"

"Yes. It isn't like your case in that respect." Sloane doodled on the pad. The hypnosis case in question, one Carter undertook while visiting Egypt, had been a puzzling one. After being age-regressed, the young subject, an American studying archeology, had conversed in a totally unknown language. Linguists guessed that it was a derivative of Egyptian. It wasn't until two years later that their suspicions were confirmed when Dr. Alja al-Mitu discovered a pharaoh's tomb from a late dynasty in the Valley of the Kings. Inside were tablets written in the same dialect of Egyptian that the woman had spoken. The tomb, to the best of al-Mitu's knowledge, had never been burglarized.

"This kid claims he's the son of Ivan the Terrible." Sloane doodled a crown on the pad. "Of course, out of hypnosis he says he has no knowledge of Russian."

"Have you checked out his background?"

"We're working on it." Sloane drew deeply on his cigarette. "He's spewed out an incredible assortment of names and places that we haven't checked out. None of it the sort of stuff a kid would be likely to memorize from a history book."

"Have you got someone working on that end? Comparing what he says with the books?"

"Yeah. In fact, an assistant of ours discovered that the dates he gave us make sense only according to a medieval Russian calendar used in Ivan the Terrible's time. If the kid's that meticulous about his details, I'm almost positive the rest of his story will check out. What I really wanted to know is this: When we put him under and age-regressed him, he stopped understanding English. Did that happen in the Egypt case?"

There was a brief silence on the other end of the phone. "Yes."

"Whatever happened to that woman?"

"Since none of us could understand her, we just taped her. After the fourth day we were forced to abandon the study."

"Why?"

"She regressed to her own self at age thirteen. Couldn't recall ever having spoken in Egyptian. It really was a funny scene now that I think back on it. All these linguists and psychologists and psychiatrists gathered around this woman, waiting anxiously for her first words after the induction, and she starts talking in English about her new braces and the cute basketball coach at her junior high. Shocked the hell out of us."

"Didn't you ever try again?"

"Oh, sure. Nothing ever came of it, and I learned more than I ever wanted to know about the workings of an adolescent girl's mind. Eventually I had to return to the States." Carter cleared his throat and asked, with a note of curiosity, "You think your case is more than hypermnesia?"

"I don't know yet. I wanted your advice before sending the kid over to Grant Thorton at the PRL."

"Keep with the historical end, by all means. Learn all you can about this son of Ivan," urged Carter. "How long are you going to keep testing him?"

"At least this week and next." With a little push to Cyrus Zugelder, Sloane thought.

"You know, Dusty, I could fly out a few days early to help look this kid over."

"I wouldn't want to put you to the trouble. It may turn out that he had a Russian baby-sitter when he was three. Problem is he was adopted when he was seven, so we may never know."

"No, really, it'd be no trouble at all." Carter's inflection changed. "I'd like to come out."

"Okay. We'd love to have you. You want me to pick you up at the airport?"

"That would be great. You sure it won't be putting you out?"

"No problem. Just come sometime in the late afternoon."

"How about Thursday?"

"Fine."

"I'll call you when I get the flight time."

"Good enough. Thursday it is. Bye-bye."

Sloane thought back, recollecting bits and pieces about his friend. Andrew Carter, a charming, articulate man whose pleasant disposition dissolved only when his projects did not run smoothly. It irked Carter to abandon a study or have it disintegrate in his hands. The Egyptian case had been such a study. Now, ten years later, it was clear that Carter wanted to pick up the threads of that inquiry. The cast of characters had changed, however. Instead of an Egyptian princess calling for her handmaiden, the lead role belonged to a Russian tsarevich. The lyrics—time, place, and nationality—had changed. But the melody stayed the same.

"Dmitri Ivanovich? There were two of them, actually. Both sons of Ivan the Terrible. Let's see, I'm a little shaky about the details of the first one."

Sloane wound his watch as Basil Tillard, a gaunt man of sixty-three, plucked a book from his walnut cabinet. Tillard, a world-renowned scholar of Russian history, had taught at the university for many years. So long, in fact, that members of the history department spoke of curriculum changes as "post-Tillard" or "pre-Tillard." Students flocked to his classes in droves, perhaps because he possessed that rare combination: a brilliant research mind coupled with an invigorating teaching style that stirred even the most lethargic. He had known Kerensky, had advised three presidents, and had been awarded innumerable honorary degrees. Yet Tillard's real love was medieval Russian history. One could tell by the exuberant lilt of his voice.

Tillard flipped a page and tapped his finger on a chart chronicling the royal families of Rus. "Yes. The first Dmitri was born in October of 1550 and died a little less than one year later. Seems he drowned when his nurse dropped him while boarding a ship. A tragic incident, just one of many in Ivan's life.

"The younger Dmitri—the one you're probably dealing with—was a product of Ivan's seventh marriage, to a woman named Marie Nagoy. Dmitri was Ivan's fourth son, Marie's first. Born more than thirty years after the first Dmitri, in October of 1582. Ivan died two years later, and Dmitri and his mother were shuffled off to a town about two hundred miles away." He sifted through the pages. "Uglich, that's right. The boy's older half-brother, Feodor, became tsar. Apparently his advisers thought it would be best to remove Dmitri and his mother's relatives, a power-hungry family, from the court scene. Of course, it all was handled very diplomatically. Dmitri was installed with a court of his own in a northern principality, or appanage, as it was called at the time. Adequately supplied with all the trappings befitting a state personage."

"I'm a bit confused," said Sloane. "You said that Ivan

had four sons. The oldest was the first Dmitri and he died as an infant. The youngest was Dmitri, prince of Uglich. Ivan's successor was Feodor. Who's the missing son?"

"That was Ivan's namesake. Ivan Ivanovich."

"He must have been between Feodor and the second Dmitri, right?"

"No. He was between the first Dmitri and Feodor."

"I don't understand. Why didn't he succeed Ivan the Terrible instead of Feodor? I assumed medieval Russians practiced primogeniture."

"You're quite correct. The eldest son did inherit the father's estate. But Ivan Ivanovich was already dead by the time his father died."

"How? What did he die of?"

"Ivan the Terrible murdered him. He pummeled his own son to death with a cane."

"But why?"

"Over a minor argument, really. Ivan the Terrible disagreed with his son about some issue involving Ivan Ivanovich's wife."

"How awful."

"Yes. Believe me, the murderous machinations of the Russian tsars are surpassed only by those of the Julio-Claudian emperors of Rome." Tillard wiped his glasses on his vest. "Take, for example, the boy you're investigating."

"What do you mean?"

"Dmitri, prince of Uglich. Perhaps the most notable victim of one of those power-play murders. Found in the courtyard one afternoon with his throat cut. He was nine or ten. You must understand, Dmitri was an epileptic; they called it the 'black illness' back then. The story goes that he was with some friends playing *tycha*, a game with knives something like our darts, and fell on one of the knives during a seizure. Recent scholars have supported this interpretation of his death despite evidence to the contrary."

"What evidence?"

"For one, the fact that Dmitri's carotid artery was neatly severed in two as if purposely cut."

Sloane was flabbergasted. Not only had Dmitri existed, but he was the focal point of a historical dispute. "Wasn't there any sort of investigation into his death?"

"Oh, indeed there was. But it was hardly what you'd call a fastidious effort. And it was handled by a man named Shuisky who served the unconcerned tsar—or rather, served the man who controlled the tsar: the regent, Boris Godunov."

A crumbling memory tried to piece itself together in Sloane's mind. All he was able to recreate of it was a faint stanza of music. An aria.

"The Pushkin opera?" he asked tentatively.

"Actually, it's Moussorgsky's opera. He based it on Pushkin's drama. The drama that marked Pushkin as the foremost advocate of the theory that Boris hired someone to kill Dmitri. Until the nineteenth century virtually every historian assumed that Boris had murdered Dmitri so that he could ascend the throne after Feodor. I can recommend some fine books on the topic if you'd like."

"That would be helpful. But clarify something for me, Dr. Tillard: What power did Boris wield in order to exert such control over Feodor?"

"He was one of the original Council of Five, an advisory group set up by Ivan IV. Feodor, you see, was feeble-minded. Probably a little retarded. Once on the throne, Feodor could be overthrown easily by any powerful boyar."

"Boyar?"

"A member of the aristocracy. So Ivan took measures to secure Feodor's crown—one of those measures was the establishment of the Council of Five." Tillard shuffled a stack of papers on his desk, moving a bronze paperweight to one side.

"What happened to the other members of the Council? Why didn't they have any influence over Feodor?"

"To begin with, Feodor was married to Boris' sister, Irina. Boris had shrewdly arranged that years before. In fact, there had been a double wedding. Ivan IV and Marie, the second Dmitri's mother, were married in the same ceremony. As for the other four councillors, two were accused of antigovernment conspiracies and either shipped north or forced to enter the order of St. Cyril. That was a common political punishment of the day: turning one's competitors into monks. One councillor died. And the fourth—the fourth was a very powerful boyar named Ivan Shuisky. His family was second only to that of the royal family in terms of prestige and wealth. But he, too, was accused of a crime against the state. Most of his family was arrested and exiled. He himself was executed, and Godunov became regent."

"Did any of the allegations against these Council members have substance or were they all just fabricated by Boris?"

"I believe one—the Shuisky conspiracy—actually was a plot against Boris."

"Shuisky. Isn't that the same name as the man who headed the investigation into Dmitri's death?"

"Yes. A relative. The man who served on the investigation committee was one of the second generation of Shuiskys who'd been pardoned and permitted to return to court." Tillard's heavily veined hands moved rapidly in the air as he talked. "Of course, there's always the theory that Dmitri killed himself. Committed suicide. I don't recall how the theory evolved. Guess there must have been rumors about previous attempts. Then there's also the theory that Dmitri didn't die. That he was whisked off somewhere for protection. You see, the boy's body was exhumed about a year after burial—so that he could be entombed in Moscow as a saint—and when the grave-diggers opened the coffin, they found a flower clutched in his hands that only blooms in the fall; yet Dmitri was buried in the spring. So people began to suspect that the body was not Dmitri's but that of another boy who'd died and was substituted sometime later in Dmitri's empty coffin.

"I don't personally subscribe to the theory, but it does pose some interesting considerations. Like who housed him. But as I said, I think the theory's unfounded. Probably just a byproduct of the material used to support the legitimacy of a pretender to the Russian throne who claimed he was Tsarevich Dmitri."

"A pretender?"

"Yes. A False Dmitri. By convincing the public that Dmitri had never died, this usurper was able to marshal a considerable force behind him. Eventually he became tsar."

"When was that?"

"I can't recall the exact date. It was 1605, I believe. Years after the real Dmitri had died."

"And when exactly did the real Dmitri die?"

"I can look it up for you." He handled the book with reverence. "Here it is . . . May 15, 1591. It was a Saturday, around early afternoon."

Tillard touched his temple, as if suddenly remembering a dissertation from years past.

"And do you want to know the oddest thing of all? Although the Uglich court employed a sizeable staff of maids, gardeners, and handymen, except for Dmitri's personal attendants there was not a single servant around at the time of his death. All were outside the gate walls.

It was almost as though they'd been propelled outside by a great force.

"Quite a mystery, wouldn't you say?"

Chapter Eleven

"Hello, Mr. Greene? This is Cyrus Zugelder. I understand your son has already called about me. . . . Great. . . . Actually, we were hoping we could drop by and see you in person. Both you and Mrs. Greene. . . . I guess John hasn't explained it to you. Let me see if I can capsulize it.

"Your son is in a class on hypnosis, and on a preliminary test of hypnotic susceptibility he scored extremely well. As in all cases in which a subject earns a high mark, we asked your son if he would volunteer to be a participant in our experiments. All of these experiments are harmless. Mostly we test things like memory enhancement or increments in strength, sight, or hearing. That sort of stuff."

Zugelder carefully avoided mentioning the tests on pain reduction. Although perfectly safe, the tests often frightened those who knew nothing about hypnosis. Especially the one that produced ischemia. This name alone evoked frightening connotations. And for good reason. The test involved placing a tourniquet-like cuff on the subject's arm. Gradually, over a period of about twenty minutes, the pain built. Every few minutes the subject was asked to rate the pain he felt on a one-to-ten basis. At ten, the cuff was removed. Then, after the subject had been hypnotized and had received a suggestion to feel no pain, the entire procedure was repeated. The intensity of pain recorded in both trials was compared in order to judge the efficacy of hypnosis in blocking pain.

Zugelder had always hated watching subjects endure the Ischemia Test. Tourniquets, he felt strongly, should be reserved for life-and-death matters. Ultimately, he'd been instrumental in persuading the department to switch to the Cold-Pressor Pain Test. His colleagues had agreed for less-humanitarian reasons. They simply didn't like waiting the twenty minutes. In the Cold-Pressor Test, pain built in the subject's arm—immersed in a tub of ice-cold circulating water—in a matter of seconds.

Zugelder listened intently to Mr. Green's response. "Yes, that's right. So we were using your son to demonstrate age regression to the class. That's where the subject receives a suggestion to go back into his past and relive a certain segment. As it turned out, John started speaking in Russian. . . . Yes, that's right. We were surprised by that, too. You can't recall where he might have learned it? . . . Hmm. . . . Yes, John told us. . . . Right. . . . I tell you what, Mr. Greene, would it be possible for Professor Sloane and myself to come by when both you and your wife are home? . . . Tomorrow would be fine. . . . No, I think I know the way. . . . Good-bye."

Sloane's eyes were beginning to glaze. His vision blurred as he read the clock on the wall. Twelve-thirty. He'd been at his desk since dinner and his fingers were cramping. How nice an electric typewriter would be, he thought. No pounding, just the soothing purr of the motor. He wished he and Blake hadn't been so enthralled with owning a food processor. But for the sake of "Easy French Country Pâté" his fingers would still be limber.

He viewed his progress with dismay. Not a damn thing that every other psychologist hadn't ascertained already. No one would be fooled by their revamping of the Milgram experiment. That portion of the study was a waste. And the BART study was just a reworking of scenarios used in earlier psychological analyses of the New York commuter. Sighing, he closed the folder and picked up one of Basil Tillard's books, spending the next hour totally engrossed in it. As he inserted a bookmark between two pages, he heard footsteps outside the door.

"Still working?" Blake's face was lined with wrinkles from her pillow.

"Yeah." Sloane rubbed his eyes. "You should see the fascinating stuff I'm learning. For instance, I bet you didn't know that Dmitri had blond hair, blue eyes, and a mole on his cheek. Scintillating, huh?"

"Don't you think you've done enough for one night?"

"Can't stop." He yawned and smiled at her. "I'm just getting to the good stuff."

She sat down in the armchair next to his desk. "You have class tomorrow," she reminded him.

"I know. But that isn't until afternoon."

"You still have to get up early for your meeting with the Russian."

"Yeah, yeah." He folded his arms on the desk and rested his head against them.

"I think you've spread yourself out too thin. Why don't you drop the hypnosis experiment?"

Sloane jerked up his head. "No way. It's the only interesting thing I'm doing these days." He covered one of her hands with his. "Honey, do you know how much money could be at stake here? If we can just squeeze a couple more days out of this kid, even if we never find out what caused him to speak Russian, we'll hit the jackpot. A book about Dmitri could really take off."

Blake lightly touched the circles under his eyes. "Dus, you're exhausting yourself needlessly. You should be expending your energy on the study with Cy and not on this. What matters now is your tenure, not any pipe dreams about money rolling in." She picked up one of Tillard's books. "This'll only throw you farther behind on your part of the compliance study, and frankly, I don't think you can afford to slough it off anymore." She brushed an eyelash from his cheek. "Got to keep your priorities straight."

"What priorities?" he snapped back irritably. "As far as I'm concerned, this compliance study can go to hell."

"Well, isn't that just dandy for you," Blake bristled resentfully. "Look, Dus, I needn't remind you what this study with Cy means to us. A publisher can get tired of waiting. If you don't complete the book there's no chance the tenure committee will consider you. Which means, of course, that we move. Now, that may be fine with you to pack up and find another job, but I like where I am. I like my job at the Legal Aid Society. I like the people I work with. It's not fair for you to expect me to give it all up."

"Who's talking about moving? Blake, let's talk about it tomorrow. It's late and I've got a ton—"

"And another thing. I don't want to move our boys again. They're settled now. Scott's getting too old to uproot again."

"Christ, Blake. Do we have to discuss this now? I'm perfectly aware of your sentiments on the subject. I'm not exactly looking forward to a rejection from the tenure committee, you know."

"It's just that I don't think too highly of your cavalier attitude. Your acceptance by this tenure committee would be the culmination of everything we've worked and sweated for these last twelve years. All those moves we made from city to city, from one university to another—they were all leading to this. To your position as a member of one of the best psychology departments in the nation. I kept my sanity during those early years only by reminding myself that once that goal was achieved we'd be able to settle down for good. Now that we're here I'm not willing to let it slip through our fingers. Dus, other people survive boredom. You're not the first."

"What a surprise."

"All right, if that's the way you're going to be about it, you're right. There is no point in talking. Good-night." And she stormed out of the room.

Marina pulled her bathrobe tighter around her waist and gulped her third can of diet soda, part of which had spilled when the typewriter carriage knocked it to the floor. One more paragraph to go, she told herself. One more paragraph and her paper, due tomorrow, would be done. She had no idea how well it read or what she would title it, but these were mere trifles at this late hour. Hell, the sun would be coming up before long.

She finished the last page, and crumpling the aluminum can, tossed it into a box with the other recyclable goods. She wanted to turn on the stereo to relax but knew it would wake John, who was sleeping in the bedroom. A hot shower would do as well, she supposed, and she headed for the bathroom.

The medicine cabinet was slightly ajar—John had taken aspirin for a headache earlier in the evening—and she closed it. She wiped the fingerprints off the mirror and studied her face. Almost symmetrical. A few blemishes here and there, but on the whole, a pretty good face. She noticed a few extra wisps of eyebrow and felt around in the cabinet for a pair of tweezers. As a baby Marina had looked like a little Neanderthal. The hair had grown across her brow without a break. She grabbed the stray hairs and yanked. Replacing the tweezers, she stepped into the shower.

The hot stream of water felt good against her skin. She worked the soap into a lather and lazily rubbed it over her body. She was washing her face when she heard a scream. Having lived in a dorm as an undergraduate, Marina was inured to screaming, especially the kind emitted when someone flushed the toilet while the shower was in use, scalding the poor occupant. But this was no ordinary scream. It was bloodcurdling. High-pitched. And it didn't let up.

She frantically tried to clean her face of the soap but opened her eyes too soon. A burning sensation quickly followed and her eyes teared. Blindly she threw aside the shower curtain and lunged for a towel. The scream was coming from her bedroom.

She wiped her eyes and quickly turned the shower off. With the towel wrapped around her midsection she dashed for the door, slipping on the wet linoleum. Someone was pounding on her front door.

"What is it?" a muffled voice asked. "Do you need help? Open up!"

Through her living room window, she saw lights go on in the other apartments in the complex. Dark forms peered out of them.

"Just a minute," she called to the person at the front door.

She ran down the hall to her bedroom, the wet ends of her hair whipping her face. In the background she heard renewed pounding. A second voice said they ought to get the manager and his master key.

The knob to her bedroom door slid in her wet hand, and grabbing it with the end of her towel, she flung open the door and rushed into the room.

John was sitting in a corner of the bed, his knees pressed to his chest. Screaming.

"John! What's the matter?" She shook him. "Babe, what's wrong?"

He continued to scream. His breathing was forced, erratic. She took his face in her hand and slapped him.

The pounding on her front door was stronger, reverberating down the hallway. She heard the lock jiggle.

"John, speak to me!"

She slapped him again, tears streaming down her face. Finally, he spoke, a torrent of words pouring forth. His face registered an unimaginable horror. He repeated the same phrase over and over.

"*Ja pogib. Ja pogib. Ja pogib. . . .*"

I am dead.

WEDNESDAY, MAY 12

Chapter Twelve

✙✙✙

"What do you mean you're quitting?" Sloane angrily stubbed out his cigarette.

"Just what it sounds like. I'm done with this study. Go get yourself someone else." John leaned against the first row of seats in 130–B.

"Oh, sure. I run into cases like yours all the time. When did all of this come about, this decision?"

"Last night."

"I wish you'd decided this before all of us started investing our time, rearranging our schedules. What made you change your mind?"

"Nothing in particular. It's just not right for me."

"John, people don't do one-hundred-and-eighty-degree turns for nothing. What happened?"

"I didn't sleep well."

"Surely there's more to it than that."

"Get off my back! I said I'm quitting!"

Sloane was surprised by the intensity of the young man's response.

"John, if something happened to you that concerns this experiment you've got to let us know. We can help."

John shook his head.

Sloane turned to Marina. "And you support him?
Why?"

She looked from Sloane to John and back again. "He had
a nightmare."

"For God's sake, Marina. I told you—" objected John.

"I know what you said. But this isn't something we
should keep to ourselves. They deserve to know."

"Know what?" asked Sloane.

"This nightmare," John said with a sharp intake
of air, "I had this nightmare about the kid last night . . .
Dmitri. Only, this time I was really him. I could see everything, feel everything. . . ."

Sloane waited a moment before speaking, afraid to push
too far. Then he said, "What happened?"

"I was being grabbed. This viselike grip across my
chest. And then, then there was a knife. Just suspended
there, hanging in the air. God, it looked so sharp. I even
could see the gleam on it from the sun. It started moving.
Like slow motion at first but then faster.

"It was plunging straight for my throat. I struggled to
get away but that grip held me. Constricted me. I couldn't
move. And I saw this woman. In a long dress. Her face was
buried in her hands. She wasn't trying to help me. That's
when I felt the knife. I could feel warmth spill over my
chest. I gagged, choked, I couldn't breathe. The next thing
I knew, Marina was on the bed, shaking me. My voice
was hoarse. She said I'd been screaming in Russian."

Sloane let out a low whistle. "What was he saying?"

"He just kept repeating 'I am dead, I am dead,' " Marina
answered hoarsely.

"Did you tell him anything about Dmitri?"

"No! I kept my promise. Is that all you're concerned
about? Whether I kept my promise or not?"

"It's important, Marina. You told him nothing about
Dmitri?"

"No."

The professor turned slowly to the young man. "John, this dream, it's just your mind's way of dealing with the apprehension you've been feeling about this study."

"I don't believe that. You knew this was going to happen, didn't you?"

"No, I most certainly did not."

"How come you weren't all that surprised, then?" His voice quivered. "That's how he died, isn't it? Our little Dmitri. Someone slit his throat."

Sloane hesitated to answer. Telling John what he had learned from Tillard might cause him to withdraw from the study. Yet hiding the truth entailed other risks. "Dmitri," this phenomenon that defied explanation, possessed a greater power than Sloane had imagined. Its entry into John's objective state of being—which meant that its appearance was no longer contingent on a subjective hypnotic state—indicated a formidable force. What would happen to John if it was unleashed at the wrong moment?

On the other hand, Sloane wanted the experiment to stay alive. He hadn't realized how desperately he wanted it until now. In less than one minute he had come to understand the insatiable longing that had plagued Andrew Carter for all those years. To know. To understand the infinite intricacies of the human brain. He agonized over his decision.

"I really don't know. There is the possibility that he was murdered, stabbed to death."

"Swell."

"Listen to me. The dream, it won't go away by your ignoring it. For your own sake you've got to continue."

"What do you mean 'for my own sake'? If I hadn't gotten involved in your demonstration, none of this would have happened in the first place."

"You don't know that. Don't be fooled into thinking Dmitri is just a product of hypnosis. Hypnosis is merely the tool that enables us to talk to him. He's the product of something else entirely."

"Of what?"

"That's what we're trying to figure out. That's why we need your help. You've got to let us get to the root of this."

"I d-don't know." John ran his hand through his hair.

"John, Dmitri isn't some nightmare you can try to forget. It's more serious than that. Give us the chance to find out what he is."

The young man stared at the ceiling and rubbed his neck with his right hand. The tension was not just in his neck, however, but throughout his body, inside of him, in places where he could not reach. Sloane might be right. His best shot at ridding himself of the boy might be a psychological exorcism. He moved his hand down and massaged a snarl of nervous tension in his shoulder.

"All right," he relented, "for a little while longer. But anytime I want out, that's it."

"Agreed."

"And I don't want anyone finding out about this. I don't want any stupid school reporters asking me questions."

"It'll go no farther than possible."

"Okay. Then let's get the damn show on the road."

They mounted the steps to the stage.

"I brought you a present."

"What is it?"

"Here, eat it."

"You eat part of it first."

"All right. If you insist." Marina chuckled at the boy's continuing suspicion and unpeeled the wrapper. Taking a bite, she handed it back to him.

"What is it?"

"It's called a chocolate bar. We eat them all the time where I'm from."

"Missouri?"

"Right, Missouri." She was surprised he'd remembered. Maybe he wasn't such a self-centered little bastard after all.

He licked his fingers and took larger bites from the candy. "Do you always wear those weird clothes?"

Marina looked down at her jeans and flannel shirt. "What's wrong with them?"

"I've just never seen a woman dress like a man before." He leaned back on the stage floor, propping himself up by his elbows.

"Oh, the pants. A new fashion. It, uh, hasn't spread here yet."

He stared at her head.

"What's wrong now?" she demanded.

"Doesn't anyone . . . well"—he stumbled over his words—"ever say anything about . . . I mean, don't you ever get embarrassed?"

She didn't have the faintest idea what he was talking about, but she was damned if she'd let him know.

"Never, why should I?" she said righteously.

A sparkle of pink appeared in his cheeks. "I guess gypsies have different customs. If my mother was caught outside with her head uncovered like that, no one would ever let her forget it."

She wasn't able to maintain the facade any longer. "My head? You're talking about my head?"

"Of course. What did you think I was talking about?"

"I don't know. Something a little more exotic than my head, though."

Dmitri folded his arms across his chest and lay flat on the floor. "You're stupid." He threw an arm under his head and used it as a pillow."

"No, I'm not. We went through that already. I'm just as smart as you."

"No. All you told me was that you could write. That doesn't prove. . . . His argument was cut short when he rolled to his side and noticed her feet, one an inch and a half longer than the other.

"What did you do to them?" he said.

"To what?" Marina surveyed the ground frantically. She saw nothing.

"Your feet! Ooh, they're all deformed." He touched one of her toes.

"You really know how to flatter a woman, don't you? I was born with them that way." She slid her feet out of her thongs. "Here, take a better look." He raised his head slightly to get a closer view. Before he was able to act, Marina had his nose firmly entrenched between two toes on her left foot. Her big toes were as apposable as her thumbs, and as a child she'd delighted in pinching people's ankles.

"Let me go!" Dmitri jabbed her foot until she laughed and separated her toes. "It's not funny. You squashed my nose."

"You deserved it. Honestly, to make me eat that chocolate bar first as if I'd poison you. I'd rather toe you to death."

He made a big show out of rubbing his nose, but Marina saw him smile.

"So why are your feet so peculiar?"

"There's really no reason. It's just like the people who can roll their tongues or the people who have two differently colored eyes. We're all just born that way."

"Like Vladimir," he said gleefully.

"What about Vladimir?"

"He can roll his tongue. Can touch it to his nose, too."

"Really? I've always wanted to see someone who could do that."

"I'll introduce you the next time he's up. You'll like him."

Marina regretted that she would never be able to meet Vladimir, the Russian who was so deeply embedded in Dmitri's heart. To have broken through the defenses of this boy, Vladimir must have been quite a man. Gentleness incarnate. And his physical attributes as Dmitri had described them—his height, his craggy good looks, his dark hair—sounded striking.

"So how's your Uncle Mikhail today?" She tucked her hair behind her ears.

"He's fine. He's talking to Bitiagovsky."

"Your brother's agent for this area?" Marina vaguely remembered the name. Dmitri had spoken of the arguments between his uncle and Bitiagovsky over Feodor's allotment of money to the Uglich palace.

"Yes. A *d'yak*." Seeing her puzzled expression he added, "A state secretary."

"Oh. What's he like, this Bitiagovsky?"

"Pleased with himself. He thinks he can control me."

"Can he?"

"No."

"But he controls your source of revenue."

"I don't need his money. I can get funds elsewhere."

"From whom?"

"People I know. People who recognize that I am the rightful heir to the throne. That I should be treated with greater respect."

"What about your half-brother? Won't he stop those people from giving you the money if he intends to designate a different heir?"

"My brother is a stupid ass. He'd never know about the money unless the *pravitel* found out."

Marina was disturbed by the boy's volatile nature. Discuss anything to do with Feodor and Dmitri's demeanor changed instantly.

"The *pravitel*?"

"Our name for the regent of the Empire."

"Boris Godunov?"

"Yes. Do you know him?" The boy seemed surprised that despite her ignorance of the customs of Rus, Marina had heard of the regent.

"I know of him."

"He is behind all of this, the plot to keep me here forever. He covets the crown. He chose Bitiagovsky as *d'yak* because Bitiagovsky has a son my age. They want to keep constant surveillance over me."

"What's his son's name?"

"Daniil. A stupid boy. I like to scare him. He frightens easily. I once threatened to hack him into a thousand pieces and he just stood there shaking, practically crying."

"Your mother, what is she like?"

"She worries about me a lot. A nervous woman. But she is a good woman. It is not true what they say about her."

"What's that?"

"That she displeased my father. That he was going to divorce her before he died. Feodor and Boris have spread this vicious rumor to try to discredit me."

"That's awful."

"Yes. But I will have my revenge." The boy's eyes fixed on hers and he grinned. "You will have to meet my mother—she'll have you read her palm." He nudged Marina's elbow. "She pays well. My Uncle Mikhail's brought many soothsayers to the house to predict her fortune and mine. The Finn, he is our resident astrologer."

"The Finn?"

"Yes. I'm not exactly sure how long he's been with us. Forever, it seems. I know my uncle paid a handsome price to acquire his services. The Finnish are the best psychics, and we couldn't be the only major house in Rus without one."

"Of course not. What sort of things does he predict?"

"He has prophesied that someday I shall rule all of Rus. I'm not supposed to know about it, but I hear talk among the servants. And I'll make his prediction come true."

"How do you plan to do that?"

"I have ideas." He laughed. "I could always poison Feodor's *pirogi*."

"*Pirogi*? What's that?"

"Meat pies. It is traditional to send them to the sovereign on one's name day. Too bad Feodor has someone taste all his food."

"When is your name day?"

"October. October 19. You see, my real name is not Dmitri. That's only my secular name. My baptismal name is Uar. I am named after the great martyr on whose day I was born."

"I see."

"Yes. Uar was a famous . . . a famous. . . ." The boy gasped and cradled his head between his hands.

"Dmitri, what's wrong?"

"It's happening again, so soon." His torso jerked and he fell to the floor.

Marina grabbed for him and screamed, "Oh, my God! Somebody do something!"

"What happened?" Perry ran to the stage.

"I don't know." She knelt by the boy helplessly, grimacing as his slim frame writhed spasmodically, racked with convulsions. "Help him, please, help him. John! John!"

Sloane rushed from the darkness of the auditorium. He scooped a ruler off the chalkboard and thrust it between the boy's teeth. Dmitri's face had blanched. His eyes were rolled back in their sockets and he gritted his teeth.

"It's an epileptic seizure. Here, I've got one wrist. Hold the other."

"What do you mean 'epilepsy'? John isn't an epileptic," Marina said, stupefied.

"Marina, get hold of yourself," Sloane retorted. "It's Dmitri—he's the epileptic."

The boy's free arm shot up and Marina screamed. Blood dribbled down her arm. The next thing she knew Dmitri had a lock on her wrist and was twisting it.

"Make him let go! He's breaking my arm!"

Perry tried to pry the boy's fingers apart, but they dug deeper into Marina's flesh.

"He's hurting me! Bend back his fingers!"

Perry ripped back the boy's little finger. The sound of tearing cartilage seemed to rouse Dmitri and he released Marina's arm. She cried softly to herself.

Dmitri's spasms subsided, but his face remained contorted. Sloane released his hold, and Perry, who'd pinned the boy's right arm under his knees, followed suit. Zugelder checked the unconscious boy's pulse.

"We should get him to a doctor," Zugelder said. "Dus? Do you hear me?"

"Yes." Sloane's voice sounded as if it were traveling from a far distance. "It's epilepsy—the 'black illness.'" He could barely believe the scene before him. The exact picture of Dmitri that Basil Tillard had painted. An epileptic. A bitter, pampered young prince. How could John have known these details? The attack Sloane had just witnessed could not be simply a product of hypermnesia. It could not.

"I don't know where you got your sudden medical expertise, Dus, but this boy needs a doctor." Zugelder ran out of the room.

A murmur arose from the stage. Dmitri was slowly regaining consciousness. He tossed his head from side to side.

"Marina?" he whispered.

"Yes. I'm still here." She wiped the tears from her face and slid closer to him.

"I feel weak. I guess I blacked out."

"Don't talk. Just lie there."

"No, I'll be all right." He blinked his eyes rapidly and waved a hand at her. "See? Recovering already." His arm fell back to place with a thud. He turned his head and saw her nursing her arm. "I hurt you, didn't I?"

He began to cry. She pulled him to her and cradled him in her arms. "It'll be all right. Just wait. Everything will turn out fine." She rocked him back and forth, stroking his hair. "You don't have to worry about anything. I'm here. There's nothing to worry about."

Her words reverberated in the empty auditorium, echoes rebounding on the ceiling. The boy slipped back into unconsciousness.

Chapter Thirteen

He woke with the smell of stale tobacco and sweet mead
in his nostrils. Without moving a muscle, he felt the
wracking ache in his body and he knew that he'd been
stricken again. His limbs were like heavy weights, so heavy
that even if he exerted himself and tried to lift them they
would only quiver, unable to respond to his brain's command. The familiar weakness that settled over him was
that of a man who had run one tortuous race after another.
But he had run no race. The marathon was in his mind.

He opened his eyes, and gradually the room came into
focus. His room. There, by the side of the bed, stood his
Uncle Mikhail, his face half in the shadows and half in the
soft light of the lantern, a chiaroscuro figure. For a moment
Dmitri thought it was night. Then his uncle moved, and
the boy saw that the small windows in the wall were cast-
ing sunlight on the floor. He did not know if an hour had
passed or two or an entire day. With the black illness he
never really knew. He merely rejoiced that he was still alive
to see the light. The *svaya* bolts, playthings which he'd
carried to the courtyard in case one of the guards asked
him why he was outside, had been carefully stored next
to his table.

His uncle's mouth was open and he was breathing heavily on the boy. Dmitri did not find the combination of odors unpleasant but wished there was a bit more distance between him and the large man. He tried to ask for a drink of water, but his lips were numb and he gurgled instead. His uncle moved closer and propped up the boy's head, afraid his nephew might be choking.

Mikhail's face was set with worry. And why not, thought the listless boy. If I die, where will he be? I am a kite and he is my tail. Wherever I rise—to wealth, to fame, to power—so will he. But if I do not rise, if my ascent is cut short, either by natural or unnatural means, he will go nowhere. Even if I am destroyed, he will be unable to sever the string that binds us. Society has a long memory. So worry, Uncle. You are a parasite who lives off me, and if I go to an early grave you will go hungry. Or worse yet, you will accompany me to my tomb.

His uncle's concern was better than none, supposed Dmitri. Had he been a young *krestanin*, struck down without warning in the field, no one would have paid him the slightest attention. They would have shoved him out of the work area and left him to swallow his tongue or choke on his own vomit. Or would they? Dmitri had never known any of the *krestanin*. From afar, they seemed simple folk with simple tastes. They seemed to lack the guile and duplicity and avarice of the upper strata of society. What's more, they seemed truly fond of one another, and when the overseer split families to work on different farms they were genuinely bereaved. Perhaps these people would not let one of their own die so easily.

Dmitri turned his head and gazed directly into the lantern's light. The lantern, a symbol of his station in life. Had he been any other boyar in Uglich but heir to the throne of Rus, his room would have been lighted by wax candles. Or had he been one of the poor, he would have depended on light from *mushiki*, birch bark dried in ovens and cut into long shivers. *Mushiki* burned rapidly, and once a family's supply was exhausted it was left in darkness. In winter, the darkness drove many mad.

But no, he was prince of Uglich. Next to his small form sat a lantern that had required hundreds of man-hours to come into existence. Hours to mine the soft mica, called *slivda*, which was cut and torn into thin flakes of glass. Hours to melt and process the iron ore. Hours to hunt and kill and skin the seals of the north for their precious train oil. All this work because he was a prince.

But this disease, this black illness, did not care that he was a prince. It was not impressed by his fancy clothes or intimidated by his education. It struck when it chose, to sap him of his strength like a leech sucking blood. Sometimes it drained his mind as well, stealing it for a day, and he could not remember the date or where he was or what had transpired just minutes before. And sometimes he could remember everything. Every second of that agony, enduring, enduring.

"Dmy! Can you speak? Are you all right?"

He moved his head and his mother came into view. Her cap was askew and it added a comical touch to her garishly painted face, almost as though she were a jester. She smelled distinctly of rosewater. He avoided her black eyes and concentrated instead on her eyebrows, slashed so thickly across her high forehead that her face seemed nearly bisected.

"He'll be all right, woman. Soltzen!" His uncle beckoned the servant standing in a corner, and the man approached, balancing a chalice and a pitcher on his salver. Mikhail accidentally bumped against the tray and the chalice wobbled. Some of its contents sloshed onto his shoes, and as the horrified servant knelt to clean the mess, Marie Nagoy, taking advantage of the distraction, moved to her son's side.

"Sit up, Dmy. Can you sit up? That's right. Here, eat a little of this. Please, Dmy. Just a little."

He recognized the mushy mixture on the spoon almost immediately. A piece of bread soaked in wine, both of which had been consecrated. He did not want to take it.

"Please, Dmy. Open your mouth," she whispered. "It will make you healthy. The Spirit of the Holy Ghost. Come, let yourself be healed. Let Jesus Christ help you."

He parted his lips slightly and she pressed the mixture into his mouth. It fell to pieces and glided easily down his throat. His mother beamed and replaced the spoon and mixing vial back into her sleeve. He knew she had taken a risk in slipping it to him while his uncle's back was turned.

"All right, Dmitri. Be a good boy. Hold your chin up." His uncle loomed before him, pewter chalice in hand.

Dmitri did not have to see the contents of the cup to know what was in store for him. He had drunk this medicinal draft many times. It was just a few weeks ago, at Easter, that he'd last been given it. Just a few weeks. Was it his imagination or were the attacks occurring with greater frequency? The boy shuddered. He did not want to die, not this way. Shaking to death. He was a prince. A prince should die a glorious death, his body pierced by an enemy's lance. Not a body rattled and pulled apart at the seams.

The smell of the draft was overwhelming, a concoction of "strong water"—this time brandy—garlic, and pepper, with a slice of onion for good measure. His uncle was a firm believer in its curative properties. It had a foul taste and Dmitri always gagged when it was administered to him. He did not know if it helped him or not. Though he inevitably felt better the next day, he attributed his recovery more to bedrest than to the purgative elements of the mixture. Clearly both were preferable to his mother's proposed remedy of dousing him in holy water and leaving him overnight at the church altar. "In God's care," she called it. Yes, God would watch over him, all right. He'd watch Dmitri get chilled in the drafty pulpit, then He'd watch him die, and lastly He'd guide Dmitri's spirit to heaven. The boy preferred to take his chances with his uncle's vile tonic, in the comfort of his warm bed.

He raised his head as far as it would go, and his lips touched the cold rim of the chalice.

"Good," said Mikhail. "Drink it all. Slowly now. It will make you feel better."

It did not make him feel better. It seared his throat and he coughed, spitting up part of the odious liquid into his mouth. He forced himself to swallow it again, knowing his uncle would brew another batch if he didn't. The pepper irritated his nose and soon he was sneezing and coughing all at once, holding his sides to keep from retching, and struggling to keep his spinning head from pitching back into unconsciousness. Overhead, he heard the joyous shouts of his mother. With each sneeze he took, she praised the Lord that her son was expelling the evil within him. Hallelujah. Amen. With each cough, she fingered her crucifix and said a wordless prayer.

The back of his neck was wet with perspiration and he sank into his bed, the feather pillow conforming instantly to the contours of his head. He closed his eyes and wished they would leave him alone. Leave him to get well, or die, or sleep forever—whatever fate had in mind. His little finger ached horribly—he didn't know why—and his stomach churned. He turned over onto his side. The door to his room opened and closed, and he heard footsteps going down the hall and the low murmur of conversation. He was breathing easily now, and as he rearranged the coverlet a cool hand brushed the wet hair from his forehead. Without opening his eyes, he saw the gypsy woman

before him, anointing him with sweet perfume and applying a damp cloth to his face. He fell asleep, dreaming of a
cool, exotic garden, completely undisturbed by the black-
eyed woman who sat on the edge of his bed, humming
softly to her son.

When he woke again, it seemed as if hours had passed,
he was so refreshed, but he could tell by the level of the
lantern's oil and the lingering taste of garlic in his mouth
that he had not slept very long. He had dreamed of being
in Moscow, of a visit arranged by his brother in response
to a note Dmitri had written him. The note was real, one
Dmitri had written a few months ago. But the only response the boy had received was in dreams such as this one.
Pulling himself out of bed, he saw that he was alone in the
room, but he guessed that either Vasilisa or Irina, his
nurse, were within earshot. He crept to the window and
looked outside. The sun had moved only a fraction in the
sky.

He moved to the door and opened it slowly. In the hallway sat Irina, her head resting drowsily on her chest. He
was relieved that it was she who was stationed outside his
door and not the humorless Vasilisa. The governess never
would have fallen asleep while on duty. But Irina was a
different story. The girl could fall asleep anywhere. In a
chair, in church, and once, in Dmitri's winter sledge,
crouched at the bottom of his feet on their way home from
town. What's more, she slept like the dead, her body never
moving, never stirring. It would take a shrill trumpet
placed next to her ear to wake her from slumber. He
slipped past her and stepped quickly down the stairs, halting midway at the bend when he heard laughter coming
from the dining room.

He'd forgotten all about the banquet. No wonder his

uncle had looked so pained by his bedside. God forbid his nephew should die and spoil all his preparations for this feast. Especially considering its purpose—to boost support for Dmitri's claim to the throne. When reports about Tsar Feodor's deteriorating condition had begun circulating, Mikhail Nagoy had embarked on a campaign to garner powerful friends on Dmitri's side, in anticipation of a dispute with Boris Godunov over the succession. He'd visited the homes of numerous boyars, cultivating them as allies and wooing them with promises of a better shake under the next tsar. There was nothing treasonous about it, Mikhail told the men he solicited: Dmitri was the tsar's brother. This groundwork, he said, was merely to make the transfer of power less complicated, so that the country— meaning him and the particular boyar he was conversing with at the time—would not suffer.

Of course, Mikhail never mentioned the small obstacles to Dmitri's candidacy. Trivial matters such as the boy's questionable legitimacy; many believed the courts would rule him a bastard. If a boyar alluded to such rumors, Mikhail adroitly switched topics to the "unusual and dangerous" amount of influence the *pravitel*, Boris Godunov, held over the tsar, and the probability, should this man reach the throne, that he would rule as a despot. Mikhail emphasized that Boris would view the boyars as rivals and would devote his reign to destroying their power and prestige.

By this time in the conversation, the boyar would be shaking his head in agreement and Mikhail would deliver the clincher. "I have heard rumors," he would say, "that the tsar's illness is not attributable to natural causes. His doctors fear . . . poison."

That would usually do it. The boyar would pat Mikhail on the back and affirm his support for the tsarevich's succession. The son of Ivan, who was the son of Vasilly, who was the son of. . . . Hurray for the glorious dynastic tradition of Rus! May the line never be broken.

And now Mikhail Nagoy was bringing all these men together, to swear allegiance to the young, noble Dmitri Ivanovich.

The boy edged down the staircase, resisting the urge to slide down the bannister, and tiptoed into the long hallway. Guests were still arriving. He heard a commotion at the entrance and hid as one of the most magnificently dressed men he'd ever seen entered the foyer. The man wore a caftan of gold cloth, studded with precious gems and held closed by great gold buttons that reflected the servants around him. The caftan was girt to him by a large Persian girdle, embroidered in detail, from which he hung his knives and spoon. Dmitri gazed admiringly at one of the knives, a brightly polished and sharply honed blade set in a half of exquisitely carved *rybii zub*, walrus tooth. The man's cape hung smartly from his right shoulder, fastened to his blouse by an ornate brooch; he removed his cap as he walked into the dining room.

The man's head was closely shaved, according to social dictum for one of his standing, and he moved with long strides to Mikhail Nagoy's table. Once there, he crossed himself thrice and bowed low to the icon mounted behind Mikhail's chair, his arms extended, his right hand touching the ground. He then rose, and as the guests before him had done, took hold of his host's hands, kissed them, and said, "I wish you good health." Mikhail returned the man's salutation and the two of them bowed to each other. Each man eyed the other's distance from the ground in an effort to be lower and thus more polite. The two men jockeyed for position until their heads nearly touched the ground. When neither could bow any lower, they rose and promptly slapped each other on the back.

The ritual was not over yet. Good dinner behavior dictated that the guest quibble over his placement at the table. It was bad form to acquiesce to assigned seating without first asking to sit near the host. This man, so elegantly attired, would be no tyro at such affairs, thought Dmitri. He would make a big fuss.

The man did not disappoint the boy. He complained that he was too far at one end and must be moved to the middle of the table where he could hear better. His request was honored.

Dmitri pulled a cushion from one of the chairs in the hallway and sat down in a dark niche that gave him a clear view of the proceedings. The last of the guests arrived, and when all were seated they were poured a *charka*, a small cup, of Rus wine, which they downed in one gulp. It was all they would drink until the end of the meal, when they would begin the innumerable toasts, drinking voluminous amounts of alcoholic beverages. The session would not end until each and every diner was drunk. It was, so Dmitri knew even now at his young age, an impropriety for the host to allow any guest to return home unless clearly intoxicated. Sobriety was an unpardonable sin. A man who, at the end of a banquet, was not staggering under the influence of alcohol was a man who either had not been properly attended by his host or who held himself in ill repute.

Muscovite society revolved around drink. Only those belonging to the upper classes had access to it; the poor either went without or, more often, drank *kvass*, a weak fermented beer they made themselves. Though the government owned all the taverns, called *kabaks*, and considered private distillation illegal, bootlegging flourished.

Alcohol was the mainstay of all festive occasions. Sometimes it was also the ruin of those occasions. It put a damper on a party, for example, to discover that some of the revelers had wandered outside in a drunken stupor and frozen to death. Even weddings went awry. If the groom's father, posted outside the bridal chamber awaiting news of the marriage's consummation, received an unfavorable report from his son concerning the bride's performance, he would hand the bride's father a goblet. An unusual goblet. One with minute holes drilled in it, plugged by the man's fingers, that would dribble wine once the goblet was passed to the bride's father. Not the pleasantest way to celebrate nuptial vows.

Dmitri saw no need to worry about the group his uncle was entertaining. The men would do themselves proud with their toasts. But until that moment, the only sips of strong water they would take would be from their *charka*s and from the goblet of his mother. It was one of the few times that Dmitri had seen his mother at a gathering of this size. Obviously Uncle Mikhail considered it prudent to have the former tsarina grace the company. She made a grand entrance, precisely the impression Mikhail wanted, descending the staircase in a scarlet gown of silk, her hair pinned underneath her *shapka zemskaia*, edged with sable and set with all kinds of precious stones except pearls. Lately the wives of mere *d'yak*s and merchants had begun embroidering their caps with pearls; it was not fitting that she continue a style adopted by the common rabble.

She carried a golden goblet in her hand, and as she was introduced to each man she pressed the goblet to her lips, smiling with her black teeth, and passed it to the man. He sipped from the cup and returned it to her. Dmitri, from his position in the darkness of the hallway, wondered how the last few men she approached could abide the ritual. By the time their turn came, the wine consisted mainly of backwashed saliva. Each managed, somehow, with a smile to match Marie's own.

After his mother had made her rounds, the feast began in earnest, a spread of truly obscene proportions. The boy's stomach grumbled. He was hungry but remained at his listening post, knowing that he could always sneak food to his room after everyone had gone.

The parade of courses began. First the *zakuska*, or appetizers. Iced *ikra*, caviar collected from the very river that ran through Uglich, and pickled herring served with black bread and sweet butter. After these delicacies had whetted the men's appetites, a dazzling array of meats, fish, and fowl was presented. Among them: pike's head dressed with garlic; hare's kidneys stewed in milk and ginger; woodcock with lingonberry sauce; and sturgeon with saffron cream. Followed by platters of *pirogi*, flaky pies filled with meat and cheese. The vegetables accompanying the entrees were all highly seasoned and cooked with garlic and onion, which were Rus staples. One dish was new to the household: *pelmeni*, the Muscovite version of Italian ravioli, the latter introduced to Rus by the Italian architects imported under Ivan IV. Tureens of soup appeared next on the tables, and after the last drop of each was consumed the servants brought in the elaborate puddings and fruit purees.

There seemed no end to the amount of food these men could pack away. They ate with abandon, as if starved at home, grabbing this and that with their fingers. The plates that each man shared with his neighbor, and on which he deposited his uneaten remains and bones, were overflowing. Servants prowled the room, exchanging empty plates for full ones.

The room, which had poor ventilation and was normally stuffy, positively reeked by the time dessert was set before the assemblage. The constant belching and farting that went on, both unrestrained and uncensured, resulted in a most-unpleasant stench, and great wafts of the foul-smelling emanations hung in the air.

Round after round of enormous explosions sounded throughout the dining room, particularly after a dish heavily garnished with onion had been served. The men paid not a modicum of attention to the great bursts, both fore and aft, with which they punctuated their speech. They were as routine to a meal as licking one's fingers.

Ladies, on the other hand, did not fare as well. When present at a banquet, though seated at separate tables from the men, they appeared rather disturbed by the free letting of gas, particularly if they were highly intoxicated. In such cases, surrounded by effluviums, it was quite common for one of the female guests to abruptly keel over in a dead faint. Eventually, a friend would take notice of the woman's rather hasty departure from the table and have her shuffled off in her carriage. The woman's note to the host the next day usually copied a standard form: "I was so merry yesterday that I do not know how I got home!" Mikhail Nagoy prided himself on the notes he received and on the inebriated lurchings of the women's husbands.

Dmitri watched with waning interest as the men devoured their desserts. Their conversation, what little there was of it between all the eating and belching and farting, was mundane. Obviously his uncle's strategy was to let one of his guests broach the subject of the tsarevich's succession. That way, Mikhail would appear less a kingmaker and more a simple catalyst for the movement. When it came time to discuss nominations for the young tsar's regent, he would be waiting for them. Humble, unaffected Mikhail Nagoy. The perfect choice. The man who wanted nothing more than fair treatment for his beloved nephew. As the spider wanted fair treatment for the fly.

At last the samovars, two large brass urns that dispensed tea, were carried in by the servants. They were beautifully crafted vessels, beaten and rubbed to a high sheen, and they bore the stamp of one of the finest metalworkers in all Rus. Dmitri's spirits lifted at the sight of them. Their appearance signaled a renewal of conversation.

"I heard the tsarevich had a spell this afternoon, sir,"

began a portly man who was picking his teeth with a ragged fingernail. "I do hope he's well."

"Oh, quite so," replied Mikhail, his facial muscles perfectly under control. "He has them infrequently and they pass quickly without any lasting effect."

"When do we see the boy?"

"Didn't I mention that before? His Uncle Grigory, my brother, took the lad out boating. He's a bit young to fully comprehend the meaning of this meeting. I'm sure he'll be back in time to visit before you leave."

Dmitri squashed the impulse to stagger into the dining room, looking sickly and frail, and collapse at the speaker's feet. Though it would humiliate his uncle, it would also dash his hopes for the succession .

"Up and around, yes? That's good to hear. Enfeebled tsars, as we all know, are the very stuff that allow inferiors to usurp their power."

It was the first reference to Boris Godunov, however veiled, that Dmitri had overheard that evening.

"I assure you, good Dnietorin, the tsarevich will make a strong and able ruler. And remember, I will be by his side. Always . . . as his loving uncle, of course."

"And . . . with due respect to you, sir . . . what assurance do we have that we will have greater access to Tsar Dmitri than we have now to Tsar Feodor?" The man blew his nose on his fingers.

"SIR!" His uncle leapt from his chair, his face flushed and the vein in his right temple bulging. Instantly he rethought his course of action, and smiling that unctuous smile, he said calmly, "Your assurance, gentle sir, is the close alignment of our interests. And, as I will constantly remind His Majesty, Tsar Dmitri, we would not want the alliance that helped him to power to gravitate toward someone else merely because we could not come to agreement over some minor . . . compensations? You . . . and you, good gentlemen"—Mikhail swept his hand across the room—"will always have the ear of Tsar Dmitri."

"Excellent," chortled the fat man, his double chins folding on top of each other. "You must pardon the poverty of my intelligence. When the sorrowful time comes that a new tsar ascends, we will understand one another."

The man with the walrus-tooth sword rose and proposed a toast. "To Tsarevich Dmitri!"

Choruses of "Hear! Hear!" accompanied the clink of glasses, and the bacchanalian merrymaking commenced. Dmitri stood up and stretched in the darkness, kneading a cramp in his calf. A shadow wavered beside him in the looking glass. He turned and stared into the blackness of his mother's eyes.

"You should be in bed," she said.

"I feel better. Uncle Mikhail is right. The illness passes quickly."

"Nevertheless, you should be resting. In your weak—in your state, you should be in bed."

"But I like listening to the men."

"You will have all the time in the world to listen to such men when you are older."

"And if I don't get older?"

"Don't say such things!" She grabbed his shoulders with surprising strength. "Never say such things! Not to me!"

"I want to hear these men. They are talking about me. About my future. About the power I will have."

"Power." She spat out the word derisively. "That elusive power that all men are driven to possess. They steal for it, lie for it. Kill for it. And for what? Power cannot heal the sick. It cannot mend a heart. It can only feed off itself, twisting the lives of those it touches until they snap. Do you know something, Dmy? You are a prince, that is true. But I am still your mother, and I am older and have seen more of this world than you. And I tell you this power of yours can wait. It can wait! You are just a boy!" She fingered her rosary. "Would that I could keep you from it forever."

"You cannot talk to me like that! It is treasonous! I will be tsar."

His mother did not seem to hear him. She spoke rapidly, her pupils dilated. "Power that evades restraint. That destroys more easily than it creates."

"Mother—"

"And when men achieve that power, they gloat and imagine they will blaze a new path to glory, earn a place for themselves in history. But they are duped. Slowly, little by little, they are eaten away by that power, eaten away until one day they are nothing but a shell that breaks when the next man who lusts for power comes along."

"I think you should go upstairs."

"If only I could have taken you away from this place. Hidden you away before anyone realized you were missing. Yes, then it would have been perfect. Then we could have lived in peace—"

"Irina, Irina!" Dmitri called to the nurse at the top of the stairs.

"There is still time. I know there is. To get you away from those men. They mustn't see you. Because if they do, if they see how small and vulnerable you are, they will get ideas. Even Mikhail. Even my own flesh and blood."

The young servant scurried down the stairs and into the hallway.

"My mother needs to be put to bed. She is exhausted."

"Yes, Your Highness." Irina took his mother's arm.

"I know what we can do, Dmy. We can fake your death. No one will know. Then I will have you to myself." His mother broke free from Irina's hold and threw her arms around Dmitri. "Oh, Dmy. My little Dmy. Don't leave me. Please don't leave me. . . ."

Tears smeared her makeup and he saw spots of gray skin, so gray that it brought images of cadavers to his mind. Her mouth, so perfectly painted when she'd entered the hall, resembled a gash, and the blood red of her rouge dripped down the sides of her face. She was a macabre spectacle, a grotesque caricature of a woman. He wriggled free from her.

"You!" She turned and pointed at the portrait of his father on the wall. "You are doing this! You are taking him away from me! You are killing him! You are killing us all!" She opened her mouth to scream, but Dmitri muffled her cry with his hand. Pain shot through his swollen little finger.

"Go upstairs, Mother. Everything will be all right. Let Irina take your hand."

She was crying softly as Irina led her away. "They won't get you. It will be easy. We'll get a boy your size and with your color of hair. . . ."

He heard a roar of laughter from the dining room.

"A toast!" said a man with a ruby necklet who stood unsteadily on his chair. "To the Tsarevich Dmitri. May as much blood remain in the veins of his enemies as in this cup!" The man raised the goblet to his lips, draining its contents, and turned it upside down on his head to much applause.

To the side of the main table where his uncle sat, the servers cleared away a space and improvised a stage. As Dmitri returned to his niche, a group of jesters and jugglers filed into the room and began displaying their talents, mostly ribald singing and joking. The men rearranged their chairs so all could watch.

One of the tables was overturned, and four jesters moved behind it to prepare for a skit. Two of them stood, only their upper torsos showing, and placed their hands in shoes, a red pair for the jester playing the male role and a yellow pair with pearls for the jester playing the female role. When the two jesters' bodies were then covered by shirts, their hands made very respectable feet. The two jesters hidden below the table reached up their arms, and sliding them through the empty sleeves of their comrades' shirts, completed the illusion of two very small people sitting on the edge of the table. Each little person wore a crown, and the little female was laden with jewelry.

"But my queen, my angel," complained the first jester, "must we have your brother over for supper again?"

"Yes, dear. You know how much Boris loves my pudding."

"But sugarcakes, I haven't once objected these past few years, have I? And each night when Boris dines with us I've never suggested that he make his visits more infrequent."

"No, you haven't." The queen pursed her grossly exaggerated lips. "You've been very good."

"Don't you suppose that we might try spending tonight differently? Alone?"

"Whatever are you suggesting?"

"Don't be shy with me, Irina. Remember, I'm the man you married."

The queen sighed. "I try to forget."

"Playing hard to get, eh?" The king drew closer to the queen and rubbed his distorted trunk along hers, giving the audience a lascivious wink.

"No!" The queen plopped down on one side of the table.

"But sugarcakes, what could be wrong? I've got wealth, I've got fame . . . I've got power!"

The queen sidled over to him and looked down at his groin. "That much power you don't have."

The men in the audience roared with drunken laughter and spilled beer over one another in their struggle to keep from falling off their chairs. Dmitri, alone in his corner, was not laughing. He was not thinking about Irina's much publicized barrenness and its probable cause. He was thinking of the reason these men had gathered here and the gleam in his uncle's eye. He gazed with disinterest at the skit before him. His ears heard only the one word: power.

Chapter Fourteen

"We want to thank you for taking the time out to see us, Mr. and Mrs. Greene."

"Don't be silly. We're happy to have you. Won't you come in, gentlemen?" Mrs. Greene held open the screen door.

"Nice to meet you." Mr. Greene shook Zugelder's and Sloane's hands.

"Would either of you care for anything to drink? We've got coffee, tea, orange juice, soft drinks," said Mrs. Greene.

"Coffee will be fine, thank you."

"Same here."

"Coming up," she said, and disappeared into the kitchen.

The three men made small talk until she returned. She put the milk and sugar on the table and poured four cups. A large picture book lay to one side of a marble ashtray.

"John hasn't told us much about this experiment." She handed a cup to Sloane. "It must be very important to have two professors so interested."

"Yes, Mrs. Greene, it is," Sloane answered.

"Actually, from what little he has said I must admit that I'm having trouble believing it all."

"That's not unusual. A lot of things about hypnosis are difficult to envision unless you've already witnessed them." Zugelder reached for the creamer. "The first time I saw someone operated on with hypnosis as the only anesthetic I almost passed out. But believe me, the story about your son is true. He's been speaking fluent Russian for three solid days now."

"Seems rather incredible, doesn't it?" Mr. Greene drew on his pipe. "Oh, I hope you don't mind if I smoke. My girls are always getting on my back for it."

"No sir, not at all."

Greene repeated his comment. "Yep—pretty incredible. You know, Anne and I would like to help you, but quite frankly we're as baffled as you."

"Your son didn't speak Russian when you first adopted him?" asked Sloane.

"Not a word."

"And his natural parents, they weren't Russian?"

"No, not to our knowledge."

"Did you know either of them?"

"No."

"How about brothers or sisters? Did John have any?"

"No. His younger sister, Natalie, died as an infant."

"How did you adopt your son? Through an agency?"

"No. Our church arranged it, and then we went through the courts. Our pastor knew that Anne and I had filed our adoption papers, and he heard about a seven-year-old boy who'd been orphaned in a nearby town. He persuaded us to take John in as a temporary foster child. And, well, though we were planning on adopting a younger child, we just couldn't part with John."

"What town was John from?"

"San Mateo."

"Did your pastor know your son's parents?"

"No, I don't believe he did."

"Then how was the adoption arranged?"

"Through another pastor. The minister who officiated over John's parents' church."

"Why wasn't the boy taken in by a relative?"

"Apparently he had no close living kin."

"Do you have the name of the San Mateo minister?"

"I've forgotten it, but our pastor would probably remember."

"What's your pastor's name?"

"Martin Evans. He's with the Unitarian church on Grove Street."

"Your son—he never mentioned anyone who spoke Russian?"

"No. Not that I remember."

"No, never," concurred Mrs. Greene. "A few of his parents' friends kept tabs on him for a while. None of them were Russian."

"How did his parents die?"

"In a fire. Faulty electrical wiring or something. John was sleeping over at a friend's house. The fire ravaged the structure. Little was salvaged."

"What did John do about clothes, personal belongings?"

"Naturally, we replaced them as quickly as we could. We also got hold of a few things that hadn't been destroyed in the fire and put them in our house. We hoped they might make John's transition easier."

"What sort of objects?"

"Oh, this and that. A few vases. A copper chest. A couple of things we really didn't know what to do with." She put her coffee cup down on a coaster. "There was really only one valuable piece. It's supposed to be an antique. I packed it away somewhere. . . . Let me think a minute where it might be. . . . Oh, I think I know—if you don't mind waiting, I'll be right back."

She returned shortly with a large box and tore off the

top. Peeling away layers of tissue paper she pulled out a large metallic object.

"Kind of pretty, isn't it?"

As Sloane leaned forward to get a better look, Zugelder picked it up and passed his hand over the smooth bronze surface, slightly darkened with tarnish.

The samovar gleamed dully back at him.

Marina moved next to the window and rearranged the books on her desk into neat stacks. Dozens of paper markers protruded from between their pages, and she removed one and reread a passage. Though Dmitri had denied it, Ivan IV had, in fact, almost divorced Marie Nagoy in order to wed an Englishwoman, Mary Hastings. The tsar formulated the plan in 1582 because he was anxious to build an alliance with England. He dropped the idea when it became apparent that diplomatic relations with England were developing of their own accord as a byproduct of trade. Elizabeth I, the English queen, had even sent her personal emissary, Giles Fletcher, to accompany one of the later trade expeditions.

The revelation caused Marina to wonder how much of what the boy said was accurate. Could it be that Feodor really held no enmity toward Dmitri except in the boy's mind?

She turned the page. Two illustrations had been carefully pasted into the book. One was a reproduction of an icon painting of the dying Tsarevich Dmitri. Dressed in the finest silks, his face slightly to one side—emphasizing the sharpness of his nose, the dark mole on his cheek, and his full lips—he was slumped to the ground in his uncle's arms. The other plate was a floor map of the Nagov palace.

Marina flopped on her bean-bag chair and sipped a glass

of wine. She didn't know a damn thing about wine, but this one was white and not too expensive, cold and not too vile, so she drank it contentedly. Most importantly, it steadied her nerves. The events of the afternoon had left her jittery. It had taken her a quarter of an hour to stop crying after John had been brought out of hypnosis. Though he recalled nothing of the epileptic attack, he was understandably distressed when he learned of it. On the drive home, he had once again talked of quitting the study.

Marina was uncertain whether or not that was the course of action to take. On the one hand, she saw a pattern in what was happening to John. Things were getting progressively worse. First the headache, then that horrible nightmare, and now today's seizure. And as each incident unfolded, John grew more sullen, more silent. In the car, his lips had been pulled tight over his teeth and he'd taken deep, quick breaths as though he wasn't able to get enough air.

On the other hand, she was afraid to discontinue the study. Professor Sloane's logic was sound. It might be more dangerous to terminate the hypnosis sessions than to continue. It was clear now that Dmitri was no passing quirk. Without the sessions as an outlet for Dmitri, what might happen to John?

And there was another reason why she favored continuing the study. One she could not tell John. He would not understand her growing attachment to Dmitri. The boy had wormed his way into her heart and she could not abandon him.

Damn, she thought to herself, I'll make a lousy psychologist. Probably fall in love with every patient I have.

John joined her in the living room. Nestling down in the armchair with his sandwich, he seemed to revive a little.

"Don't cripples eat?" He offered her half of his sandwich.

"Not hungry." She adjusted the sling around her neck. "How are you feeling?"

"The same as I was ten minutes ago. Fine. I feel fine. You don't have to keep checking on me."

"I'm sorry. It's just that you—"

"I wasn't there to see myself. I know. But believe me, I feel fine. No aftereffects. Except my little finger hurts like hell. Perry must have given it a good pull."

"That's all that's bothering you? Really?"

"Yes. Now quit worrying about me. You're the one who's been hurt."

"I'm okay. I still think you should have gone to the hospital with the medic."

"And tell him what? That I felt fine? No, thanks. It's Dmitri who had the attack. Not me." He paused. "God, did you hear that? I said it was Dmitri who had the attack. I'm starting to talk about him as if he really exists."

"He does, John. That's why you've got to continue the study."

"Why? Just this morning you supported my decision to quit one hundred percent."

"But that was this morning."

"What changed your mind?"

"Talking to Dmitri. John, he's so real. I swear, he exists. He was with me today."

"How can you be so sure?"

"I don't know. Maybe all the coincidences. It's just something I feel."

"What coincidences?"

"I'm not supposed to tell you."

"What do you mean?"

"Sloane told me not to tell you anything further about Dmitri."

"My God, Marina. This is hardly the time to keep anything from me. Either tell me or I'm quitting."

"All right. Just this once." She walked to her desk and picked up the copy of *Boris Godunov* by Platanov. "Look at this paragraph. Sloane was right: Dmitri was an epileptic. See? He got a seizure on Easter of that year. Practically chewed off his second cousin's hand. He suffered from epileptic psychosis, a fancy term for rage."

She picked up another book. "Okay, this is the amazing part. He had an attack on May 12. It was a Wednesday just like today. And the same time of day. That is, on the morning of Wednesday, May 12, 1591, Dmitri Ivanovich had an epileptic seizure. And today, Wednesday, May 12, at exactly ten o'clock, our Dmitri had a similar attack."

She flipped a page. "Let me read you this part:

'The young Dmitri often suffered from bouts with the "black illness," or epilepsy. Many scholars have suggested that this disease accounted for the rumors of Dmitri's violent temperament. Giles Fletcher, the English envoy who visited Rus, was only one of the many foreigners who remarked that the Tsarevich displayed signs of his father's irascibility.

'Fletcher described an incident in which Dmitri, early one morning, constructed figures in the snow. Labeling each with the name of a follower of his brother, he then hacked the sculptures to pieces. Later he was quoted as saying, "That is how it will be for them when I reign."

'Dmitri's mother may very well have turned to the soothsayers in order to deal with her son's inexplicable rages. After his death, she testified that she had heard him talking to the spirits on the Wednesday prior to his demise. That May 12 fit was, in fact, one of Dmitri's more violent outbursts. During it, he cut Marie Nagoy with a *svaya*. . . .'"

Marina paused, a perplexed expression taking form on her face, and then read the next lines hurriedly:

'A *svaya*, a kind of sharp-edged bolt used in a game similar to *tycha*, the popular target game played with knives. She had run to his aid after hearing of the attack. . . .'

Marina closed the book as if in a daze.

"What's wrong?" asked John.

"There's been a break in time. A warp of some sort. Dmitri is real. He is. . . ." She sounded dreamlike.

John shook his head. "Marina, it's just a big—"

"You don't believe me? Then explain this." She removed the sling from her arm and unwrapped the bandage. "All Dmitri did was hit me and twist my arm, right? Then tell me what this is."

She thrust her forearm in front of John's face. Before him was a six-sided cut about an inch and a half around. A hexagon. Exactly the type of wound that would be left if one were hit by a swinging bolt.

John's sweat suit was soaked with perspiration by the time he finished jogging. The run had released some of his tension and allowed him to mull over everything that had happened today. Waking in the morning with the memory of that nightmare so clear. Coming out of hypnosis with the medic standing over him, and wondering, as he frantically examined himself for stab wounds, if his nightmare had come true. And just a little while ago, seeing that cut on Marina's arm. It all seemed so unreal.

Was he losing his mind? Had he once learned about Dmitri and was it now resurfacing in this bizarre manner? Had he unconsciously injured Marina in a way to match the outlines of a four-hundred-year-old toy? He could not believe it. Sloane and Zugelder were psychologists. Surely they would tell him, try to help him, if he were going insane.

If he wasn't crazy yet, John felt he was in danger of becoming so. To accept Dmitri as part of himself, to acknowledge the voice coming out of his mouth as real, would be the action of a madman. He had to hang on to the few shreds of reality around him. He needed to go someplace for a while. To get away and unwind. Especially to decide whether to continue the study.

He stopped by the dorm kitchen on the way to his room. Another resident of the house, Sheila Adams, was raiding the icebox.

"You going on the raft trip tomorrow, John?"

"I thought that was next week."

"Nope. There's a reminder on the bulletin board."

"What time are people leaving?"

"Six in the morning. What a drag, huh? But by the time we drive up there half the morning will be shot." She stuck a piece of cheese in her mouth. "Didn't you already pay? I thought I saw your name on the board."

"Yeah, I did. Only problem is I'm supposed to be participating in an experiment tomorrow."

"Can't you skip it?"

"Well, I. . . ." He poured himself a glass of water and thought about it. The trip wasn't exactly the peaceful, solitary excursion he'd had in mind, but it would get him miles away from campus. He couldn't be sure that another opportunity like this one would present itself. As for Dmitri, John felt safe from his encroachments. So far he'd only appeared while he was asleep or in trance. "I guess it really wouldn't hurt if I took a day off as long as I tell the people in the study. Sure, I'll go."

"Great. I'll see you tomorrow, then. Early."

"Right." John climbed the stairs to his room, called Sloane's secretary to cancel the next day's session, and dressed quickly for his next class, "Politics in China."

The class was a popular one and received high marks in the *Class Evaluation Record*. Its prof was as witty as he was easygoing, but he spoke fast, making notetaking a chore. John's hand usually cramped after the first thirty minutes of a lecture. So it was with mixed emotions that he observed there was a guest lecturer, a visiting professor known for his dull, uninformative talks. Notetaking would be a breeze, John realized, as long as his mind didn't wander.

He doodled as he listened to the visiting prof. A TA turned out the lights, and the visitor showed slides of a trip he'd made to Peking. Occasionally John interrupted his doodling to jot down a few key names or facts in his notebook. In the dark he really couldn't see what he wrote and just guessed where the lines of the paper were.

He dozed sporadically as the professor named every shred of food he'd consumed during the three-week trip. John sensed, however, that his hand seemed to be following the lecture. Taking notes without a conscious effort on his part. Almost automatically. He was jarred from his near-reverie by the young woman to his left.

"What did he say the name of that village was?"

"What village?"

"The one that set up that experimental commune."

"Wait a sec. I wrote it down." John squinted in the darkness. "I can't see anything. Wait till the lights come back on."

About twenty more slides flashed on the screen. A smiling picture of a woman outside the "Forbidden City." An equally smiling portrait of Deng Xiaoping. A photo of workers on bicycles.

The slide show ended and the lights came back on. John

laid down his pen and put his elbows on the desk. The student next to him poked his arm.

"Oh, yeah. The commune. Lemme check."

The page was covered with script. Each line was filled with neatly inscribed letters. But the handwriting was as unfamiliar as the alphabet. He broke into a cold sweat.

Before him, a Cyrillic message bearing an elaborate signature that he recognized from the book Marina had showed him:

"Dmitri, prince of Uglich."

Chapter Fifteen

Zugelder straightened the picture frame on the wall and sighed. He and Sloane had been discussing John's apparent seizure for over twenty minutes and had not yet agreed on the probable cause of the attack. Their tempers were wearing thin.

"Dus, John has a record of allergic attacks. You heard his parents. He must have eaten something earlier in the day that disagreed with him."

"That violent an attack and recover that fast? Without a trace of ever having been stricken."

"It's been known to happen."

"Christ, Cy." Sloane felt himself grow progressively more agitated. "You're willing to toss this whole case out the window on the grounds of one little samovar? One lousy Russian teapot, salvaged from the ruins of a house that John Greene once lived in, is your proof that he was introduced to Russian language, culture, and history as a child. Don't you think that's a little presumptuous?"

"Of course I do. The samovar merely indicates that we should keep investigating John's background. That was my only point. I was just trying to show you the importance of not getting trapped into thinking that this Dmitri is a supernatural phenomenon. You have no monopoly over what theories can or cannot be proffered to explain his appearance, you know."

Sloane held his head in his hands. "I know."

"I'm not saying I want to abort the study, Dustin." Zugelder took a pen from the desk on which he sat and rolled it between his fingers. "But I think we could postpone it. At least until we've turned in the compliance study to the publishers."

"No. No postponing."

"Why not? What's so awful about it? We can take the results of the personality, PRL, and voice tests, put them to one side, and contact that minister later. There's no rush about it."

"You gave me one week, Cy. Today's only Wednesday."

"Damn it. Don't be so unreasonable."

"One week."

"You're being so shortsighted about this. Don't you think I—" He stopped short as Sloane waved a small white card with printing on it.

"Recognize this?"

Zugelder reached for it. "So?"

"Something tells me Dean Peters' little dinner party on Saturday has thrown a scare into you."

"I admit it. It has. I tell you, Professor Sloane, I'm going to feel like a fool when he asks how we're doing with the Everhill stats and I tell him we haven't even looked at them yet."

"Cy, you're letting them get to you."

"You're goddamn right I'm letting them get to me." Zugelder jumped off the desk and leaned with both hands on the windowsill, looking out on the courtyard below. "All right," he said, striving to be calm. "One week. I owe you that. But you and I are meeting first thing Sunday to go over those statistics."

"Fine. I'll agree to that."

Zugelder grabbed his coat and left without saying good-bye.

As John paced the apartment, Marina painstakingly translated the Cyrillic message in his notebook. She hoped that the note would shed some light on how Dmitri was able to crisscross time. Gradually, she realized it was merely a reproduction of a letter sent by Dmitri to his brother in the spring of 1591:

My Dear Brother and Most Exalted Tsar,

How good it was to hear, through our intermediary, Andrei Nagoy, greetings to Myself and My Mother from Your Royal Majesty. I am pleased to report that We, at the Uglich Court, are all well and that the Appanage as a whole is in splendid order, as our Late Father, Tsar Ivan IV, *Gosudar*, would have wanted.

I am growing, spiritually and physically, every day and continue to receive the education and training befitting one of Our Issue and Station. It is my dearest hope, Beloved Brother, that I may someday be called by Your Majesty to assist You at Court. Until that joyous reunion, My thoughts are with You and Your Magnificent Queen, the Tsarina Irina. I pray for Your good health in this glorious vernal season.

Ever Your Servant, Your Loving Brother,
Dmitri, Prince of Uglich

How Dmitri must have loathed writing such a note, Marina thought. Yet how desperately he longed to leave Uglich and journey to the city of Moscow, which he imagined he would someday rule.

"Done," she said, and handed the translation to John.

He quickly read the note. "Jesus. I can't believe I wrote this. My hand made the marks but his mind was controlling it. Like I was his puppet. Or . . . or a trained animal."

Marina watched helplessly as John shook with anger and fright. The note did not have the same impact on her as it did on him. She'd already become convinced that Dmitri, through some kind of time warp, was here in their time period. But for John, who had refused to acknowledge Dmitri's presence all along, the note signaled the shattering of his disbelief. He was forced to recognize the boy's existence, forced to recognize that he was being used, that Dmitri was expropriating a part of his life. And for reasons that escaped them all.

John crumpled the note into a ball and threw it into a corner of the room.

"John? Are you okay?"

"Just give me a second. This whole thing's just too impossible to believe."

"What should we do about the note? Do you want to call Professor Sloane?"

"No. I don't feel like talking to him right now. Give it to him tomorrow."

"So you're going to continue with the study?"

"Yeah." He sat down on the couch, his face white and sweaty. "It's no longer just up to me. There seem to be two of us involved."

She picked up the translation from the floor and smoothed it out as best she could. "I'll staple the translation to the original note and stick it back in your notebook."

"No. You'll have to give it to Sloane. I'm not going tomorrow."

"But I thought you were continuing the study."

"I'm going on a river trip tomorrow. With some of the people from my house."

"Can't you pull out of it?"

"I already paid."

"John, that's no reason to go. Just forfeit the goddamn money."

"No. Marina, I swear I'm going to bust if I stay around here one more day. I just want some time off. It won't hurt the study. Sloane said I could take a rest whenever I felt like it. Well, I feel like it."

"Do you think it's wise? I mean, what if something happens while you're on the river?"

"It won't. Dmitri's only come out when I was asleep or in trance. I already called Sloane's office. His secretary will tell him that I'm not coming in."

Marina did not try to argue with him; he'd made up his mind.

"All right. I'll bring the note to his office tomorrow."

"Thanks." John rubbed his temples. "God, my head's killing me again."

"Here, stretch out on the couch. Take off your shoes." She carried over a pillow from the armchair. "I'll get you an aspirin."

"No." He grabbed her arm. "No. Stay here with me. I just want to close my eyes for a while. But keep talking to me. If it looks like I'm falling asleep, nudge me. Don't let me go to sleep." He looked into her face with the pleading gaze of a lost child. "Please, don't let me fall asleep. . . ."

Sloane suddenly felt the pressure of time on him. He quickly finished checking his Friday lecture notes and reached for one of the books Basil Tillard had sent him, thumbing through it for paragraphs on Boris Godunov, the ostensible murderer of the tsarevich. He read voraciously, determined that he'd be brought around to Cy's side only if something that the hypnotized John said was inconsistent with historical fact. If he erred on some detail. So far, he'd been right on the money.

Sloane's eyes were arrested by a description of the murder/accident:

At the dinner hour, when all personnel had dispersed to the *posad* outside the walls, a tocsin sounded from within the palace and an alarm was raised.

So, as Tillard had said, the "accident" just happened to take place at the time when the palace was most deserted. He read on.

Dmitri's body was found in the rear or inner court of the Uglich kremlin, not far from the base of the Naugolania-Florovskaia tower. Almost one hundred *sazheni* (two hundred and thirteen meters) away lay the Spasskie gates. The Nikolskie gates were eighty *sazheni* to the south. Hence, Dmitri died as far away from personal contact as was possible.

Sloane reread the paragraph. It implied that Dmitri's death had been carefully calculated. Yet where was the proof of that foul play? Having witnessed Dmitri's violent epileptic fit, wasn't it possible that the tsarevich had accidentally killed himself?

Sloane found his proof from a most unlikely combination of sources, an obscure German journal translated into halting English and a book by a Frenchman enamored of games.

He read the sections marked by Basil Tillard in the German journal, and a chronology of May 15, 1591, formed in his mind. After Dmitri's death, his uncles, Mikhail and Grigory Nagoy, positive that Boris Godunov had engineered the killing, retaliated by attacking town

officials who were on Godunov's payroll. They were joined
by a mob of angry Uglich citizens who also suspected
Godunov. Many officials were killed, including Bitiagovsky, the *d'yak* who had handled the allowance of the
Nagoy family. According to Mikhail Nagoy's testimony
at the inquest into Dmitri's death, held days later, he and
Grigory planted a bloodied *nagaiskii* on Bitiagovsky's
corpse in order to hasten official inquiry into Boris' role
in the murder.

Sloane stopped reading. From the context of the passage, he divined that a *nagaiskii* was a knife. The book's
glossary defined it as a "Tartar dagger" often found in a
boyar's arsenal.

He picked up the French book. Its binding was breaking
down. No surprise, he thought: The copyright date was
1854. He shoved it under his desk lamp and read the
elaborate script of the title page. Prosper Mérimée. Damn,
the whole book was in French. He tossed it on the windowsill.

Minutes passed and he eventually retrieved the slim
volume from the sill. Conjuring up his college French, he
painstakingly translated the passages marked by Tillard.
His effort was handsomely rewarded.

In *Demetrius the Imposter*, Mérimée had written ex-
tensively about *tycha*, the game Dmitri was playing when
he died. To participate, a player had to provide his own
nojik, or *tycha* knife. It was not an exceedingly sharp
instrument, but had a pointed tip so that it would stick
to the board. When thrown it left a small hole.

Like a puncture wound.

Sloane reflected on the conversation he'd had with
Basil Tillard. Hadn't the history professor commented
that Dmitri's carotid artery was neatly severed? Clearly a
nojik could not have produced such a wound. Too dull.
And Grigory and Mikhail knew that. Why else had they

planted a sharp-bladed dagger on Bitiagovsky? They had seen the boy's wound and planted on Bitiagovsky's body the type of weapon capable of producing that kind of wound. That weapon was a *nagaiskii*, not a *nojik*. The wound was a deep slice, almost surgical in its precision. Not a jagged puncture. And yet, had Dmitri accidentally killed himself while at play, the instrument of death would have been a *nojik* and the wound would have been a puncture.

Sloane laid down the book. Mikhail and Grigory Nagoy, after discovering their nephew bleeding to death in the palace courtyard, had gone out of their way to get Grigory Nagoy's *nagaiskii* and plant it on Bitiagovsky. They had ignored the dozens of *nojik* knives that lay around the tsarevich's body. Why? Because they knew Dmitri hadn't been killed by one of these knives. And now Sloane knew. The brothers' actions on that spring day spoke louder than the hundreds of pages historians had devoted to the mystery. The inevitable conclusion:

Tsarevich Dmitri, prince of Uglich, had been murdered. In cold blood.

Chapter Sixteen

Sloane put a star by the passage in Mérimée's book and briefly outlined his conclusions on a piece of paper. His exhilaration over having discovered the means of the tsarevich's death was tempered by the sobriety of the revelation. A nine-year-old boy had been murdered, his throat slit. Sloane thought about his own nine-year-old son. What sort of monster would kill a child? What possible aim could it serve?

He gazed at the illustration on the title page of the Ian Grey book, *Boris Godunov*. Was this the man who had ordered the killing of Dmitri, the slaying of a mere child? Sloane stared at the face. It was not that of a monster. The expression on that face was kind. This was a man with two children of his own. A man who had bodily intervened between Ivan the Terrible and his son, Ivan Ivanovich, in an attempt to spare the latter's life. An ambitious man, yes— ambitious enough to banish the other members of Feodor's Council of Five and to order the trial of Ivan Shuisky, the boyar who had plotted against him. But the murderer of an innocent child?

Sloane ripped a sheet of paper from his pad and wrote

Godunov's name on the top. He arranged the books into a
stack and one by one read the sections marked by Basil
Tillard, searching for Godunov's motives for murder. He
scribbled furiously, condensing the different authors'
arguments, rejecting some as specious, accepting others
as withstanding the test of historical scrutiny.

Four hours later, his "motive" list, if that is what it
could be called, exculpated Boris. Godunov, so Sloane decided, had never considered Dmitri an obstacle in his way
to the throne. Sloane reread his conclusions:

Item Number One: Boris Godunov would not have
killed Dmitri because that in itself would not have assured
him the crown after Tsar Feodor's death. For, as the
author Platanov wrote, Godunov's authority could still have
been circumscribed by the combined forces of other
boyars. The tsarevich's murder would have assured Godunov's ascension only if it were coupled with a plot to
curtail boyar power, which it was not.

Item Number Two: It is questionable whether Dmitri
ever would have succeeded Feodor because his legitimacy
was uncertain. The marriage of Marie Nagoy and Ivan IV
was not sanctioned by the Russian Orthodox Church.
Marie was the tsar's seventh wife, and according to canon
law a man could marry only three times in his lifetime.
Dmitri, in the eyes of many, was a bastard.

His tainted birth, Sloane reasoned, explained why
foreign diplomats in Rus ignored the young tsarevich.
Leo Saphieha, the politically astute Lithuanian ambas-
sador, never even mentioned the boy's existence to his
king. This omission, this slight to a monarch's brother,
would never have occurred had the foreigners considered
Dmitri in the line of succession.

Item Number Three: Dmitri's hopes for succession were
undermined in other ways. Feodor's wife, Irina, was a
healthy young woman who had many years left in which

to bear children. Even if she bore a female, Dmitri's hopes would be dashed, since sole rule by a woman was not unprecedented. It hardly seemed likely that Godunov would kill a boy who might, in a year or two, lose all chance of succession. Indeed, Dmitri, had he lived, would have lost his already tenuous claim to the crown after the birth of Irina's daughter, Princess Feodosia, in 1592.

Item Number Four: Even if Feodor had not sired a child, Dmitri's claim to the throne after Feodor's death would have been overridden by Irina Godunov. She, after all, had been made co-ruler with Feodor, an arrangement created by her brother.

Item Number Five: The risks involved in a plot to kill Dmitri would have been far too high for Godunov. If Feodor had found out or even suspected Boris' participation in the murder, it would have caused an irreparable rift in their relationship, a rift not even Irina could patch.

Had Feodor been the ogre portrayed by Dmitri, Godunov, if he'd wanted, probably could have murdered the tsarevich without Feodor's censure. But the tsar was not an ogre trying to disinherit his brother. His relations with the Nagoy family were not as strained as Sloane had thought. Although Mikhail Nagoy complained about the meager family allowance, Feodor listened to the family's grievances through a cousin of Marie's, Andrei Nagoy. He used Andrei as his emissary so that the Nagoys would rest easy, knowing their interests were well represented by one of their own.

Nor did Feodor "banish" his younger brother to Uglich, contrary to the Nagoys' suspicions. The tsarevich had been left the appanage in Ivan's will and had been directed to rule Uglich until the time came that he might become tsar.

Item Number Six: After the tsarevich's death, Godunov, realizing that he would be accused of the murder, attempted to flush out the real assassin. After the Nagoy massacre of the Uglich officials, Godunov organized his own vigilante squad, not merely to retaliate for those deaths but to terrorize the local citizens into divulging all they knew about the tsarevich's death. As the author Stephen Graham put it: "Something was desired to be *known* from the kinsmen of the Nagoy and the people of Uglich under that torture," a torture so "out of Boris' character." Clearly, Godunov's brutal retaliation was a thinly disguised and frantic effort to find the real murderer.

Sloane clutched the list in his hand. It seemed that the Pushkin drama had greatly wronged Godunov. He sat back in his chair, satisfied with his conclusions except for the one major gap in his research:

Who the hell had planned Dmitri's murder? And who, inside those massive palace walls, had delivered the fatal thrust?

THURSDAY, MAY 13

Chapter Seventeen

✸ ✸ ✸

"Where is he?" Sloane directed his question to no one in particular. "Perry, give his room number another buzz, will you please?" Perry went out the door to the hall phone.

Zugelder yawned. "Maybe he's carrying out his threat from yesterday. He wasn't too thrilled about coming in, you know. And after yesterday's incident, I can't say I blame him."

Perry reentered the room and rolled up his sleeves. "No dice. He isn't answering."

"Damn it." Sloane thumped his fist on the back of the chair. "What's happened to him? And where's Marina?"

She rushed into the auditorium just as he mentioned her name.

"Where the hell have you been? Let's get started." Sloane began climbing the steps to the stage.

"Without John?"

"Isn't he with you?"

"No."

"Where is he?"

"Didn't your secretary tell you?"

"Tell me what?"

"Well, I stopped by your office to give you this"—she held up John's Cyrillic note—"and your secretary said you were over here. She acted as though she'd given you John's message."

"Marina—just tell me. Where is he?"

"On a river trip."

"Oh, swell."

"Before you get mad, let me explain."

She told Sloane and the others the story of her arm and what the Russian book had said about Dmitri's *svaya* bolt. Then she told them about John's note and handed the translation to Sloane. As he read it, she wished that she'd more firmly opposed John's decision to go on the trip. Though she knew he needed a respite from the study, she couldn't stop imagining that a nine-year-old Russian from the sixteenth century—ignorant of moving cars and traffic lights and freeways—was at this very moment waking up in the rear of a Volkswagen bus.

"And he was dozing when he wrote this?" asked Zugelder.

"Yes. Off and on."

"Automatic writing," murmured Sloane.

"What?" asked Perry.

"Automatic writing," said Sloane loudly. "Something written by the person without his being aware of it. The subconscious actually controls the hands. Though in this case, I'm not sure John's subconscious is responsible."

"What do you mean by that?" asked Zugelder.

"I mean that John didn't write the note. Dmitri did."

"They're one and the same, Dustin."

"You still think so? After what Marina told us?" He struck his fist on the chair once more. "Damn, I wish John had come in today. I'd really hoped to get a third video-tape of him under hypnosis for Andrew."

"Your friend at Princeton? Don't worry. He'll have

enough to work from. Besides, do you really think he can
and anything to this case that we haven't already thought
about?"

"Maybe. Maybe not. But I want to find out what simi-
larities exist between John and the woman who spoke
Egyptian that he worked with."

"Suit yourself. But I hope he's not making a special
trip. At any rate, John's absence gives us an early start on
contacting that San Mateo minister whose name we got
from the Greenes' pastor." Zugelder plucked his briefcase
from the crevice of the fold-up seat. "Are we going to consider tomorrow's session canceled unless we hear from
John?"

"What do you mean 'canceled'?" asked Marina. "We've
got to meet tomorrow. We're running out of time."

"What's the hurry?" asked Zugelder.

"Don't you understand? It's May thirteenth today.
Thursday, May thirteen."

"Perceptive, aren't you?" joked Zugelder.

"You don't understand," Marina said. "The dates all this
week have been paralleling a week in Dmitri Ivanovich's
life. The *last* week of his life. When we first started conducting this experiment, he said it was Monday, May 10.
Every day we've hypnotized him, it's been a day later. The
eleventh, the twelfth. And now today. We only have two
days left. He'll be killed on Saturday."

"Marina, be sensible." Zugelder's good humor disappeared. "The coinciding dates—that's just John's subconscious substituting today's date for the fictitious day in
the past that he's supposedly reliving."

"No, it isn't." She twisted toward Sloane. "You've read
as much about Dmitri as I have. You know the dates are
the same. He won't be around next Monday to materialize
before us. He'll have died forty-eight hours earlier."

"Where has your objectivity gone?" Zugelder fumed.

"You act as though this is the real Dmitri of four hundred years ago that you're talking with. Okay, maybe the dates are the same. Maybe John isn't just giving us today's date with a different year attached. But don't you realize the significance of that? Those coinciding dates are probably what triggered John's memory of Russian history in the first place. Deep in John's memory bank, I'm certain, is lodged the information about Dmitri that he learned as a child. That information surfaced this week merely because John's subconscious noticed the similar dates."

"No, you're wrong," Marina said. "You know that isn't true."

"I know what I believe, young lady." He pulled on his coat. "Dustin, as soon as I get a few things straightened out in my office you and I are driving to the pastor. I intend to put an end to this lunacy once and for all."

The door slammed and Marina sat down on the stairs of the stage, emotionally spent. She recognized the validity of Zugelder's argument. She had no proof that Dmitri wasn't just a memory of John's come to life. Only a few inexplicable coincidences and a burning conviction that hinged on nothing more than intuition. A feeling that Dmitri was not simply a product of John's active subconscious, not merely a bravura performance.

"Don't take Cy too seriously. He's a polemical sort of fellow." Sloane tried to prod Marina out of her dejection. "Obviously you don't buy his hypermnesia theory."

"No, I don't. It's more than that. It's like Dmitri's using John's body as a soapbox. Not reincarnation, but something else. I get the feeling that I'm talking to the actual kid. Like my voice is cutting through time to him."

"That doesn't sound very likely."

"You think I'm stupid, huh?"

"No, not at all. John's knowledge of sixteenth-century Rus and its royal family is so extensive that I also find it impossible to believe that Dmitri is simply a byproduct of forgotten history lessons. And like you, I don't believe reincarnation is involved. We can't travel backward and forward in Dmitri's life like hypnotists can with subjects who claim they've been reincarnated. We're limited to a time line that parallels our own. Each minute of his life that goes by is a minute of ours, and vice versa. I really don't know what he is."

"How do we at least prove that Professor Zugelder is wrong?"

"That this isn't hypermnesia? First we have to disprove the notion that John Greene is merely play-acting the role of a historical figure he once read about. In that respect, the work Cy's doing—probing John's past—may prove valuable to us. With any luck, he'll discover that John never learned Russian. His research will backfire on him. That'll be one point for our side."

"But you agree there's a time factor, don't you? We've got to hurry. Dmitri will die on Saturday."

"Yes, this phenomenon—even if it's just John's subconscious—that's passing itself off as Dmitri Ivanovich will most surely stop appearing after Saturday. Since it knows so much about Dmitri it must also know he was murdered on Saturday, May 15."

"Murdered?" Marina was stunned. "How can you be so sure? From the books I read I was led to believe that the Godunov murder theory was only conjecture. Just one of many theories. Like the one that says Dmitri was hidden somewhere by his mother—"

"Or committed suicide. Or accidentally killed himself. Yes, I'm familiar with them all." Sloane withdrew two folded pieces of paper from the inner pocket of his jacket, his notes from the previous night. "Here, I want you to read this."

After reading a few minutes, Marina refolded the

papers. Her face registered disbelief. "Even though I questioned the story of Dmitri's 'accidental' death I still can't believe someone deliberately killed him. How could anyone murder a child? And if Boris wasn't responsible, who was?" she asked.

"I don't know. That's where you come in."

"Me? What do you mean?"

"That time factor you mentioned? There's a chance it can be stretched. This Dmitri of ours doesn't have to die on Saturday."

"How?"

"If—through historical research—we can discover who planned Dmitri's murder and if you can warn him before one o'clock on Saturday, then he has no excuse to disappear. He'll have to stick around, for a while at least, and that gives us more time to study him."

"All right. How do I start? There's so little time."

"Try finding out if there's any written material on the people who were in the palace courtyard at the time of Dmitri's death." He fished a pen from his pocket. "Give me a piece of paper and I'll write down their names." Marina ripped a sheet from her notebook and handed it to Sloane. He drew a group of stick figures on it, three females and four males. "Okay, here's Dmitri. I'll put a big 'X' under him. Also present were his governess, Vasilisa Volokhova, and her son Iosif; Bitiagovsky's son Daniil and his friend Nikita Kachalov; and lastly, Dmitri's wet nurse, Irina Tuchova, and his chambermaid, Marie Samoylava. Now, one of these six people probably either killed the tsarevich or let the murderer through the gate. We've got to find out which one."

"Something tells me 'we' means 'me.' "

"Cyrus was right. You are perceptive."

"But why couldn't I just tell Dmitri not to go outside on Saturday? That way, he wouldn't be in the courtyard to be killed."

"That wouldn't do any good. Without the killer's name, Dmitri would be an open target all day on Saturday."

"But what if I can't find a suspect?"

"Then come Saturday afternoon"—Sloane reached for the light switch—"this apparition of Dmitri Ivanovich will vanish. And we'll be left with a lot of videotapes that don't prove a thing."

"And what about John?" The young woman's face was suffused with concern.

"He'll be fine."

"But if Dmitri dies. . . ."

"Marina, all I know is that the best way to assure John's safety is to assure the safety of Dmitri. All right?"

She nodded. Sloane escorted her to the door. Outside 130–B the skies were dark. The rain had returned.

Chapter Eighteen

He was tired of waiting. He'd stood on the spot for over an hour and she hadn't shown up. The hunt would begin any minute and he would have to go. Outside the gates he saw the riders and their horses assemble. He sensed the excitement in the air. Valets ran across the courtyard fetching cloaks and satchels, adjusting bridles and saddles and holding the dogs at bay.

Her absence disconcerted him. He wondered what had detained her. Could something have gone wrong? Had she been caught prowling around the estate? He tried not to panic. It was, after all, not a likely possibility. No alarm had sounded. Her ability to dematerialize at will would shield her from harm.

He considered the alternatives. Was she deliberately staying away? Perhaps she thought his disease was contagious. Or believed his attack was more debilitating than it really was. She might have assumed he'd be too weak for a rendezvous in the courtyard.

That seemed the best explanation. She was giving him a day of rest. What a surprise it would be tomorrow when he told her that he'd spent the day hunting! Perhaps it was just as well that she had not come. With so many hunters around the grounds, the likelihood of her being discovered increased tenfold. He prayed that he was right, that she was giving him time to recover and was not ill or injured. And he hoped that if, by some quirk, she was just now approaching the palace, she would have enough sense to retreat once she saw the cluster of riders.

He ground his buskins into the soil as if stamping out a tobacco ember. It was too bad, actually. He'd looked forward to seeing her. By tomorrow he'd forget all the tidbits of gossip about the banquet. She wouldn't get any of the roast hen he'd smuggled to his room. Nor the left-over *pirogi*. But it was more than that. Why delude himself? He missed talking with her, missed that inexplicable soothing effect she had on him. When he was with her, his frustration and anger at the world dissipated. She was a release from the humdrum existence of his life. Like Vladimir.

Vladimir. He'd nearly forgotten that his friend would be arriving to join the hunt. Soon now. In a way, the timing was odd. As though to compensate for the absence of one friend, another appeared. But he had not planned it. Nor had he told Vladimir about the gypsy. It might be better to keep her a secret. Vladimir might feel compelled to tell his old friend, Mikhail Nagoy, about her existence.

A trumpet blare signaled the start of the hunt, and glancing once more around the courtyard, Dmitri dashed out the gates to where his horse waited, pawing at the ground. Unlike their European counterparts, the horses of Rus were small, and Dmitri mounted his steed with little assistance from the groom. He adjusted his cloak over the fine saddle of Moroccan leather and velvet, and grabbed a leash connected to one of the lead dogs. The footman who handled the dogs wore leather gloves. The animals were thought unclean, and it wasn't proper that anyone, not even the lowest servant, touch a dog with bare hands. With the dog leash and reins in his grasp, Dmitri swung his feet into the stirrups and lightly tapped the horse, using a lash twined around the little finger of his right hand. On hunts, spurs were seldom used.

Though Dmitri had been on many hunts, he responded with a novice's enthusiasm to the bugler's call. The day was fine and his horse moved well, its unshod hooves clipping at a fast rate. All around him meticulously groomed horses pranced with anticipation, their riders preening and excited. He felt a part of them. Normally a hunt such as this was the highlight of the week or month in which it took place. But this week, he realized, was unusual. What with the banquet and the new falcon and Vladimir's upcoming visit and the gypsy's appearance and the hunt, he had not wallowed in his usual monotony. This week was most special. And it seemed to be building to some sort of climax. He wondered what Saturday would bring. So deep in thought was he that he didn't hear his name being called.

"Ho! Dmitri! Trying to avoid me, are you? Oh, I know— you're trying to wriggle out of a *tycha* rematch with me. And that's very sensible of you. I'll have you know I've been practicing." A young man galloped into view and laughed, exposing white teeth. He doffed his cap with a mischievous air, dismounted from his horse, and approached the tsarevich on foot, as custom required.

"Vladimir!" The boy tapped his horse and cantered to where his friend was standing, the man who was more of a brother to him than that fixture in Moscow. "I'm sorry. I . . . I was thinking about something else." He motioned the man to remount his horse.

"Getting secretive, are you? What took you so long to get here?"

"I was detained."

"Detained! Really, how formal."

"But I was! I. . . ." He longed to tell Vladimir the truth but hesitated. "I was conditioning for my rematch. I can still beat you at *tycha* any day, you know."

The man replaced his cap and scratched his short beard with an amused expression. "That you can, my little princeling, that you can."

"So how are you? Is the mare truly in foal?"

"She was. Delivered me one scrawny colt yesterday. Beautiful markings, though. Has a white star right in the middle of her forehead."

"Really? What did you name her?"

"Tamor. Short for Metamorphosis."

"Metamorphosis? How peculiar. What does it mean?"

"Well, it means to change or transform. As if by magic."

"Magic? Why did you name her that?"

"Don't know. It struck my fancy. Would you like to see her?"

"Oh, yes. Very much so."

"That's good because"—the man leaned over in his saddle close to the boy's ear—"I do believe she'll be yours soon."

"You don't mean it!"

"Yes I do. Your uncle's decided that you can't keep riding old Strepyen forever. It's about time the old girl was put out to pasture. You'll need a man's horse, and by the look of her, Tamor will be more than a handful. Sprightly, she is."

"When can I see her?"

"Now, hold on a second," he laughed. "Didn't mean to get you all worked up. She's barely standing. You don't have to worry. No one else is going to get her. I'll keep her for you." In the distance, the hunters were nearing the woods. "Come on, we're going to miss the chase!"

They raced across the field and linked up with the other

men. The dogs strained at their leashes, wild with the
scent of hares. The men looked confident that each would
fare well in the hunt. Their confidence was not misplaced.
It was no secret that the woods had been stocked with
hares just prior to the hunt. Mikhail's woodsmen had
snared the animals from nearby areas and transported
them to this site so that the gentlemen would have plenty
of game to flush. No one, the most inept hunter included,
would go home empty-handed.

The hunters divided into small groups, and Dmitri and
Vladimir joined a company of three men who carried ivory-
handled knives suspended from their girdles. All three
seemed in high spirits. Dmitri suspected they had taken
a few swigs of strong water and was proved right when
they offered the flask to Vladimir before letting the dogs
loose. A fat man in blue tucked the bottle into his satchel.

The dogs scampered into the thicket and the men did
their best to follow, but the going was not as easy as they'd
anticipated. The fat man wheezed and almost toppled
off his horse, his fleshy body jiggling in the saddle. Cries
of "Ho!" "Ho!" filled the woods around them as dogs of
other groups found their prey. A stranger might have
thought large animals instead of small hares were being
caught, so loud were the shouts.

Presently, the dogs in Dmitri's group also circled in for
the kill. A yelp and then a snapping of jaws, and Dmitri
and his companions were supplied with game to flaunt.
After the first rush by the dogs, in which the group killed
about a dozen hares, the pace of the hunt slackened. The
hares were reluctant to stir from their hiding places, and
some of the men dismounted and charged the brush in
hopes of rousing them. Dmitri carried no hares, but Vladimir had tied a few to his saddle, as many as he could use,
and called his dog back to his side. When the other men
in the group had done likewise, the group headed back to
the open field.

While the men were hunting, their servants had cleared a space in the field for recreation. Brightly colored tents with striped pennants greeted the dusty hunters as they emerged from the woods. Mikhail Nagoy had already arrived and was surrounded by his cronies. Dmitri questioned whether his uncle had actually participated in the hunt. There was not a bead of sweat on him and his clothes still hung in crisp folds. The large man waved to Vladimir and the two exchanged warm greetings.

Outside, in the bright sun, his uncle did not appear as ferocious as inside the palace walls. Dmitri watched Mikhail and Vladimir, and shook his head. He would never understand the bond between these two opposite people. One, whose every move was calculated to gain him the upper hand, who was ruthless and coarse. The other, possessed of a sensitive nature, little ambition, and a mind that explored the realms of philosophy and science. The boy supposed they complemented each other, these two. His uncle had spirit but formed hasty conclusions; Vladimir was often lax but was guided by logic and reason. Between the two of them, they always would find the best way to solve a problem.

Dmitri once asked Vladimir why he liked Mikhail Nagoy. The man replied that Mikhail had a quick and resourceful mind. "But you personally," asked the boy, "what do you get out of the friendship?" Vladimir thought for a moment and then replied cryptically, "I gain a better understanding."

Of what, wondered Dmitri? Was that why Vladimir was friends with him as well? To gain some vague understanding?

It couldn't be possible that he was one of "Them"— the sycophants who hung around his uncle in hopes of bettering their position if Dmitri became tsar. Such men were as transparent as the dew.

Dmitri curled up on the pillows inside of Mikhail

Nagoy's tent and munched on sweetmeats of coriander and hazelnuts while the men discussed the fate of a certain counterfeiter in Moscow. The man was discovered forging the tsar's coins and received a stiff sentence: The very coins he'd minted were melted down to their liquid state and poured down his throat. The conversation sparked a debate about the justice system and whether this penalty indicated a return to capital punishment. Death was not a common judicial penalty in Tsar Feodor's reign; it was normally reserved for highwaymen.

Dmitri yawned and watched the footmen prepare the areas for the archery, boxing, and riding competitions. One servant climbed a nearby tree and hung a golden ring the size of a man's fist from a branch. Although Dmitri handled the bow and arrow with some degree of skill, he'd never tried spearing the golden ring on a lance. Maybe today. It didn't look hard, but he supposed it would be difficult finding a lance light enough for him to hold.

He rolled off the pillows and walked to where the servants were marking off the distances for the archery tourney. As he approached, two of the servants dropped the quivers they held in their hands and prostrated themselves at his feet. One cracked his head loudly on the ground. Dmitri was sure the man had sustained a nasty bump on the forehead and tried not to smile. He told them to return to work and they did, one a little dizzy from his encounter with the prince.

"Care to try your luck?"

Dmitri turned and saw Vladimir sorting through the bows.

"Uh, no thanks."

"How are you feeling?"

"What?"

"The attack yesterday. Your uncle told me about it."

"Oh, better. They pass quickly." Dmitri casually picked

up a feather that had fallen off one of the arrows. Inside he was churning, wanting to tell his friend about Marina but fearful of the consequences. In the end, his need to share his secret was greater than his apprehension. "Can you keep a secret?"

"Yes, I think so. Why? Do you have one to tell me?"

The boy replied cautiously. "I have someone who wants to meet you. A woman."

"Meet me? Whatever for?"

"I've told her a lot about you."

"What about me?"

"Things."

"Who is this woman?"

"A friend."

"You are being secretive today. Where did you meet her?"

"Promise you won't tell."

"What?"

"Promise you'll tell no one. Especially not Uncle Mikhail."

Vladimir nodded his head thoughtfully. "Oh, that's what's worrying you."

"Promise?"

He knelt down and took the boy by the shoulders. "I promise. To tell no one. That's what friends are for."

Dmitri heaved a sigh of relief. "In the courtyard. I met her in the courtyard on Monday."

"In your courtyard? How did she get in?"

"Magic."

"Magic? Who is this woman?"

"A gypsy. She's visited me all this week. Except today. I waited—that's why I was late—but she didn't come. She has the most marvelous powers."

"Powers?"

"Yes. She can appear and disappear without warning."

An odd cast fell over Vladimir's face. "What does she look like, this gypsy of yours?"

"Quite queer-looking, actually. Dresses in the strangest clothes."

"And no one else has seen her?"

"No." The boy wagged his finger. "Now remember, you promised not to tell."

"You can trust me. Does she"—Vladimir forced a grin on his face—"does this friend of yours happen to have two differently sized feet?"

Dmitri was taken aback. "How did you know?"

Vladimir did not reply.

"The visions?" Dmitri asked.

Vladimir did not answer the question. "I'll meet her if you want. Let's go rejoin the others."

The rest of the day passed quickly, with drinking and bickering and rowdy wagering among the men. Dmitri wandered among the revelers and was often stopped as a kopeck or two was pressed in his palm and his head patted. He and Vladimir did not talk after the competitions began, except to tentatively arrange a boating excursion for the next day. Dmitri was surprised that his friend had not shown more interest in the gypsy. Later in the day he caught Vladimir's eye and the man answered him with a wan smile.

They rode home at dusk. The birds of the night serenaded them and their horses cast large shadows. Dmitri was dirty and tired and ready for a bath. He loosened his necklet, and as he was doing so the large center opal fell into his hands. His good-luck stone. He pocketed it and felt for the broken threads at his throat. There were none. He didn't know what had torn the gem loose.

Members of the group began to disband, each heading toward his own estate. The *krestanin* were still in the fields, laboring in the failing light. Many of them were children,

Dmitri's age or younger. Up ahead, silhouetted against a red sky, the palace appeared ominous. Forbidding.

Dmitri leapt off his horse, and without saying good-bye to the others trudged up the steps to the house.

He was not aware that he was being watched from above.

Chapter Nineteen

Marina was discouraged. She hadn't found a single lead to the six people in the courtyard. What's more, she was finding it difficult to concentrate. She could not get it out of her head that it had been a mistake for John to go on the river trip. The Cyrillic note had shaken him, more than he cared to admit. She had seen that look of panic on his face only once before, in winter quarter, a few hours prior to a particularly tough final in a class worth ten units. But even then his face had registered just a fraction of what it had shown last night. She should not have let him go.

And Dmitri, what was he doing now?

She tried to bury herself in her work, but her disappointment mounted. The pages grew indistinguishable from one another and her frustration intensified. She found few references to the tsarevich in any of the indexes.

She shook her leg to keep it from falling asleep and snatched still another volume from the rapidly diminishing pile. It was of relatively ordinary dimensions and had the kind of fresh-paper smell to it that indicated it had not been abused by an overabundance of readers. Before opening it, she looked at the cover: *A History of Russia* by Nicholas A. Riasanovsky.

One more time, she thought to herself, as she flipped it over and opened to the index pages.

To her astonishment, not only was Dmitri listed but his name was followed by a long line of page numbers. She opened expectantly to each reference. As she read passage upon passage, the slight frown which pinched her forehead deepened. Something was awry. No Dmitri, prince of Uglich, here. No mention even of that other Dmitri, Ivan IV's first son. Instead, still a third Dmitri.

Marina was confused. A third Dmitri? She read the Riasanovsky account and realized that the events he described were in the year 1605, fourteen years after Dmitri had died.

At this point rumors to the effect that [Tsar] Boris Godunov was a criminal and a usurper and that Russia was being punished for his sins began to spread. It was alleged that he had plotted to assassinate Prince Dmitri; it was alleged further that in reality another boy had been murdered, that the prince had escaped and would return to claim his rightful inheritance. The claimant soon appeared in person. Many historians believe that False Dmitri was in fact a certain Grigory Otrepiev, a young man of service-class origin, who had become a monk and then left his monastery. Very possibly he believed himself to be the true Prince Dmitri. . . .

The Jesuits received from him the promise to champion Catholicism in Russia. The role of the Muscovite boyars in the rise of False Dmitri is less clear. Yet, in spite of the paucity and frequent absence of evidence, many scholars have become convinced that important boyar circles secretly supported False

Dmitri in order to destroy Boris Godunov. Indeed, the entire False Dmitri episode has been described as a boyar stratagem.

Marina's memory was jogged. Of course. The pretender to the Russian throne whom she'd read about in the MITMA card catalogue. She was fascinated with the details of his life and skimmed ahead in the book. How intriguing. Not merely a pretender, but a successful one:

> On June 20, 1605, False Dmitri entered the capital in triumph. The people rejoiced at what they believed to be the miraculous return of the true tsar to ascend his ancestral throne. On the eve of the riots that overthrew the Godunovs, Vasilly Shuisky himself had already publicly reversed his testimony and claimed that in Uglich Dmitri had escaped the assassins, who killed another boy instead.

Marina's fascination grew. She had not known that Godunov, Tsar Feodor's successor, had been overthrown by False Dmitri. And Shuisky? Who was he?

She scanned the author's bibliography to see if she had any of the books that he'd used. She did. *Boris Godunof* by Graham. Opening it to a page following Shuisky's name in the index, she found herself back in 1591, immediately after Tsarevich Dmitri's death:

> Suddenly universal odium attached to the name of Boris Godunof and he lost in a day all the popularity he had achieved in a lifetime. . . . He did not go himself to Uglich; he sent a man who had good cause to hate him—Vasilly Shuisky.

Her confusion abated a bit. Godunov had chosen Vasilly Shuisky to head the commission that investigated Dmitri's

death in order to reassure the public of an impartial verdict. As head of the inquest, it was Shuisky who had
announced that Dmitri's death was accidental. Why then,
fourteen years later, had he reversed that testimony?

Marina thought back to Riasanovsky's description of a
boyar stratagem. Of course. Vasilly belonged to that inner
circle of boyars who by supporting False Dmitri hoped to
oust Boris Godunov. But in order to give credence to
False Dmitri's claim that he was the son of Ivan IV, Vasilly
first had to reverse his testimony at Uglich and claim that
Dmitri had never died.

One question nagged at her: What was the "good cause"
Vasilly had for hating Boris Godunov? Graham isolated
the reason. Vasilly was a relative of Ivan Shuisky, the
member of the Council of Five whom Godunov had executed, and whose family he'd exiled. Including the young
Vasilly Shuisky. Marina wrote herself a note to look up
the details of Ivan Shuisky's conspiracy later.

Another question formed in her mind: Why had Vasilly
agreed to head the commission at the request of Boris
Godunov, the man who had so abused his family? Once
again, Graham was one step ahead of her. By accepting
the chairmanship of the commission and declaring Dmitri's
death an accident, Vasilly gained an invaluable bargaining
chip. At any time he could change the verdict to murder,
a reversal which would expose Boris to countless accusa-
tions. Thus Vasilly held in his hands a permanent source
of blackmail.

Marina mused over Graham's logic. Why hadn't Vasilly
declared a verdict of murder and accused Boris? Even if
the indictment couldn't be proved, it would have blemished
Godunov's reputation. Was it so much more satisfying
for Vasilly to have the Tsar Godunov in his debt than to
have him defamed for life?

And then she stumbled upon the answer. A section at

the beginning of Philip Barbour's book, *Dimitry*, about the Uglich commission:

The depositions of everyone who knew anything whatsoever about the events were taken and duly recorded. No judgment was passed. No accusation made. . . . But for one reason or another the results of the inquiry were not fully and clearly circulated, and as a result, the people drew their own conclusions.

"The people drew their own conclusions." That could mean only one thing: They believed Godunov guilty of murder despite the official verdict by the commission. Vasilly had implicated Godunov, and in a more subtle manner than Marina ever imagined, by withholding circulation of the official report. As Platanov wrote: "It gave those who hated him [Godunov] a convenient motive for slanderous charges as to the murdering of the tsarevich."

Marina marveled at Vasilly's remarkable sleight of hand. But this was drawing her no closer to a list of suspects. On her desk she saw the note she'd written: "Find out about Ivan Shuisky's conspiracy." She made a deal with herself. She'd satisfy her curiosity about Ivan Shuisky and then she'd return to the miserable task of sifting through the Uglich commission's testimony for suspects.

Within seconds she was completely absorbed in Platanov's *The Time of Troubles*. Ivan Shuisky, she read, fearing that Godunov would try to remove him from the Council of Five as he had done with the others, decided to launch a preemptive strike. Before he could attack Godunov, however, Shuisky had to remove Godunov's sister—Tsar Feodor's wife—from the tsar's good graces. Otherwise, Boris would have the royal forces behind him in any dispute with Shuisky.

With the support of a metropolitan of the church called Dionysys, Shuisky and his family tried to persuade Feodor to divorce Irina on the grounds that she, after years of marriage, had not borne an heir. The plan backfired. Boris Godunov undermined it by maintaining that the dynastic line would continue, even if Irina was barren, because Dmitri, the young prince of Uglich and son of Ivan IV, would succeed. The Shuisky family was exiled and Ivan Shuisky was executed. End Platanov.

Marina closed the book before she realized the importance of the paragraph. Dmitri was the key to the succession after all. It was so clear now. The Shuisky plan had failed in 1587 because Dmitri was alive. Four years later, after they returned from exile, the Shuiskys developed the same plan. Those four years had convinced them of Irina's infertility and hardened them into an angry, bitter family, capable of carrying out a heinous deed. They would correct the mistake they had committed last time. There would be no Dmitri the second time around to spoil their scheme. The boy had to die.

Marina understood now. Boris Godunov's choice of Vasilly Shuisky to head the Uglich commission had been something the Shuiskys had planned. Godunov's sister-in-law was married to a Shuisky—Dmitri Shuisky, Vasilly's brother. It was she, Marina theorized, who had suggested Vasilly as the "perfect" head for the commission. The man who could clear Godunov of a murder charge. And who, at the same time, could make sure his own family was never linked to the crime.

Marina slouched in her chair, dumbfounded. Her eyes smarted. Here was the motive, the murderers. Yet she felt no relief. The terrible irony of it all struck her. The Shuiskys were never able to carry out the second part of their plan, the call for Irina's removal, because, within a short time after Dmitri's death, the tsarina was pregnant.

Their timing was off. Their four years of waiting were for naught. And a nine-year-old boy had been brutally murdered for a reason that was no longer valid.

PSYCHIC RESEARCH LAB
Manning Hall

Dus—

Where the hell did you people ever get the notion that John Greene is psychic? On all prelim tests he scored normal. Subnormal, even. Didn't even guess as many correct answers as he should have through chance.

You've been working with rats too long, my boy.

Anyway, we're discontinuing the ESP tests. Give me a call if there's any reason we shouldn't.

You going to the Peters' dinner party on Saturday?

—Grant

GT/jp

The church was modern, more like a ski chalet in Squaw Valley than a place of worship. Beams curved up to the ceiling and sunshine flooded through the skylight. The floor was pegged wood and the altar was a mass of gracefully intertwining horizontal and vertical columns of oak. Sloane and Zugelder spied the door to the minister's office in a corridor to the right of the vestibule.

"Please, come in. Sit down." Mr. Clark welcomed the two psychologists into his sitting room. "Mr. Evans explained your predicament to me. I find it quite remarkable. Not your predicament, of course, but your study. Tell me, are you still conversing with the young boy?"

"Yes, we are," answered Zugelder. "For the moment."

"We had a slight mix-up today and didn't meet with John. That's why we're here early," added Sloane.

"And what is your evaluation?" asked the minister. "Do you think he learned the history as a child?"

"Yes, I do," replied Zugelder, "but I have no proof of my belief. No proof that hypnosis has simply jogged John's memory—what we call hypermnesia. That's why we're here to see you. My colleague, Professor Sloane, has a different viewpoint. He believes that John never learned Russian. That this Dmitri is a . . . a psychic manifestation that we know very little about."

The minister lifted an eyebrow. "Possession?"

"No. Not possession as you think of it." Sloane recalled that unaccounted-for knowledge of a foreign language often accompanies so-called demonic possession. "But perhaps a form of possession. An assistant of ours likens it to a time warp. As if somehow a rupture in the time barrier has allowed Dmitri to speak through John—possess him, if you will—or has allowed John to gain access to the tsarevich's thoughts."

"It sounds rather incredible."

"I know. That's why we're checking out John's background. At the Greene house, as I'm sure Mr. Evans told you, we were shown a Russian samovar that had been salvaged from the house of John's natural parents. The discovery led us to think that whoever bought that object may have been the Russian speaker who taught John about Dmitri. You knew John's parents?"

"Yes. The Whitings, a very nice couple. Such a tragedy."

"Were they active churchgoers?"

"About average as I recall. Frankly, I don't remember either of them speaking Russian or ever mentioning anything even remotely connected with that culture. If they had once lived in Russia or taken an extensive trip there I think I would have heard about it."

"What about friends?" probed Zugelder.

"I remind you it was so long ago. I really couldn't give you names of friends. I simply didn't know them that well. All I can tell you is that I've never had a parishioner of Russian extraction."

Sloane picked up the line of inquiry. "Relatives?"

"None that I know of. That was why John was put up for adoption." He sighed. "I'm sorry I can't be more helpful. It is possible that a close friend of the family was Russian, but I'd have no way of knowing. The best I can do is refer you to the principal of John's former elementary school. Perhaps one of the teachers there remembers something John brought into show-and-tell. Or dealt with his parents in the PTA."

Zugelder seemed disappointed. "That would be very helpful, thank you."

"I'd like to see John now that he's grown up. A bright boy, a bit precocious, but all children his age are to varying degrees. I felt so bad when his parents were killed. It seemed so unfair. He'd already suffered so much. His infant sister, you know. A crib-death case. Mrs. Whiting sank into a deep depression after that. Never fully recovered."

"How old was John?" asked Sloane.

"Five, I think. Yes, about that. I remember seeing him at the baptism."

"Yes, Mrs. Greene mentioned a younger sister." Zugelder bowed his head, as if trying to formulate a thought. "You don't happen to have John's baptismal record, do you?"

"No. The family moved here when John was about one and a half. He was baptized elsewhere."

"His sister's?"

"Yes, I suppose so. We keep all of our records. Why?"

"I was thinking perhaps we could attempt to contact one of the godparents."

"That's an excellent idea. I'd be happy to get her file for you." He walked to the door. "What was her first name, do you know? Started with an 'N,' I think. Nancy, maybe."

"No," Zugelder said, "I think Mrs. Greene called her Natalie."

"That's right. A beautiful name. Natasha."

"No. She said Natalie."

"That was what the Whitings called her, Natalie. They anglicized the name for everyday use. But she was christened Natasha. I'm sure of it." He stopped in his tracks, suddenly struck by the Slavic origins of the name.

"The baby, who was she named after?" Sloane asked anxiously.

"As a matter of fact, I think she was named after her godmother. A local woman but not a member of this church."

"Does she still live here?"

"I don't know."

"What about her last name?" Zugelder interjected. "Do you remember it?"

"No, but her signature would be on the baptismal paper as a witness."

"Could you get the record for us? It's not too much trouble, I hope."

"Not at all. Please wait here."

It seemed as though he were gone for hours. When he returned, he carried a large cardboard box.

"Right, this is the file for that year. I had trouble finding it. Misplaced." He scanned the tabs attached to the many folders. "Here we go. Whiting, Natasha."

Sloane and Zugelder crowded on each side of the minister. They strained to read the small print of the church document. Zugelder frantically pointed to a name at the bottom.

"Bingo! Where's the phone directory?"

Mr. Clark glanced at the lower third of the document.

There, in neat cursive handwriting under the heading "Godmother," was what seemed to be the missing link: Natasha Tsurischeva. The woman, so it appeared, responsible for the resurrection of a minor historical figure named Dmitri Ivanovich. A boy whose second coming was already a stark reality.

He knew he was putting too much time into the project. His wife was angry. His coworker, Cyrus Zugelder, thought he was crazy. The only support he had was from Marina, the winsome graduate student who was prone to emotional outbursts.

Sloane stubbed out a cigarette in the ashtray near United Airlines Gate 23. He hadn't realized how much he'd been hoping for the impossible, that Dmitri would be a psychological breakthrough, until today. When he'd listened in on Zugelder's conversation with Natasha Tsurischeva's secretary, his dream had been nearly shattered. This Mrs. Tsurischeva was indeed the woman on Natasha Whiting's birth certificate. And she was Russian. But Sloane was not going to give up hope until the woman had been thoroughly questioned. Zugelder had made an appointment to see her tomorrow.

He was so preoccupied with his thoughts that he wasn't aware that the plane had landed. When he saw the passengers disembarking, he moved closer to the gate and searched for his friend.

Carter surfaced in the first third of the passengers, his wispy titian hair bobbing half a foot above the heads of his fellow travelers. He waved his arm in greeting.

"Well, you've finally done something to cover up that unfortunate face of yours. Good move," he remarked, pointing to Sloane's beard.

"Nice to see you, too. That your only bag?"

"Yeah. Finally have learned how to travel light. We want the Hilton. That's not too far, is it?"

"No, not at all." Sloane guided Carter out to where his car was parked. "But we're not going there. You're an official guest of the Sloane household. That is, if you'll take us."

"I'd be honored. How's Blake?"

"Fine. A bit peeved at her husband but that should pass."

"What about?"

"Mostly my involvement in this project. She thinks it reflects an 'unrealistic and lackadaisical' attitude toward getting tenure."

"Does it?"

"Naturally I want the committee to approve me, but in all truth, Andrew, this compliance study I'm doing with Cy Zugelder bores me to tears."

Carter picked an errant hair from his jacket. "I know the feeling. But I hope you're cognizant of the power of that departmental committee, Dusty. If they don't recommend you to the dean, there's no way you'll be kept on unless you've got a little something going on the side that I don't know about."

They drove on in silence for a while, Carter gazing with interest at everything they passed. Sloane knew Carter missed California even if he staunchly refused to admit it.

"So when do I see the wonder child?"

"With luck, tomorrow. Wonder child didn't show up today. Turns out he's on a raft trip. Doris, my secretary, got it confused and thought he meant tomorrow. But you can look at the videotapes today. And my notes."

"Good." Carter grew serious. "You know the odds are that this case is simply hypermnesia."

"I know."

"What information have you come up with?"

"Oh, we latched on to a Russian samovar in the Greene household and now Cy's sure he's proved hypermnesia. I thought it was a fluke until we found out about the woman from Mr. Clark."

"What woman?"

"A friend of John's natural parents. She was on his sister's baptismal record."

"What's so important about her?"

"She's Russian."

"Have you talked with her yet?"

"No, Cy's got an appointment with her tomorrow." Sloane wiped a speck of dirt from the windshield. "Looks like I may have wasted everyone's time."

"Don't be a martyr. It doesn't suit you," Carter said. "Is the instantaneous translation you arranged working out?"

"Yeah, it worked out fine on Wednesday. He'll be coming tomorrow."

"Good. Have you considered using the Hidden Observer Test in this case?"

"No. I don't see how it would be very helpful. Why do you ask?"

Sloane was puzzled. He knew Carter often employed the Hidden Observer Test, a technique used to "break through" the hypnotized part of a subject's brain and communicate with the unhypnotized part. Once, in a pain-reduction test, Sloane had seen a hypnotized subject be called upon to verify that he was feeling pain his hypnotized self was not aware of. The hypnotist activated the Hidden Observer by placing his hand on the subject's shoulder, although, Sloane knew, any other prearranged signal would have worked. When the hypnotist touched the subject's shoulder a second time, the Hidden Observer vanished and the hypnotized self took over once more.

Carter rested his arm on the back of the seat. "John hasn't been able to remember any of Dmitri's appearances, has he?"

"No."

"Well, I thought it would be interesting if by using the Hidden Observer technique you could get John to speak while Dmitri was still there. You could tap John while Dmitri was in midsentence. Maybe then John could shed a little light on this mystery."

"It might work. All right, we'll give it a try. Remind me to tell John about it before the induction so he'll know the signal."

"Okay. In the meantime why don't you start filling me in on this Dmitri Ivanovich."

As the car sped on, commuters began flooding the freeway. Buses. Car pools. Automobiles crammed with people who were chatting rapidly, unwinding from the day's work. About how cranky the boss was. How slowly the hours dragged. And in one car, the topic of interest was the life of a nine-year-old Russian with a penchant for chocolate bars. His life. Then. And now.

John wiped the sweat from his brow and took a swig from the canteen nestled between his feet. He took another swig and another, sating his raging thirst, and then offered the canteen to an oarsman behind him, who accepted it with alacrity. As John adjusted his life jacket, an invigorating spray of water blew across his face. Ahead, curving around a rocky bend, he saw the three other rafts, leaving rippling waves in their wake.

The oar slid in John's hand as he pulled it through the water. Coarse white ovals, harbingers of blisters, formed on his fingers. His arm muscles ached and the part in his hair was sunburnt, but he let none of these minor discomforts detract from his enjoyment. He breathed deeply, pumping his lungs with air redolent of the spring flowers that crowded the riverbank. Balancing his oar on his lap, he cupped a hand, dipped it into the river, and poured the icy water over his neck.

The raft moved easily in the water. Once in a while it passed other boaters; occasionally a cow or two wandered over to the water's edge for a drink, appraising the rafters with indifferent brown eyes. For the greater part of the journey, however, the raft swept by fields resplendent with crops of every imaginable variety—bursts of green and yellow superimposed on a sky seemingly anchored to the ground by a range of low mountains.

But the last mile or so, the four rafts had been surrounded by small hills of porous rock which obscured the scenery. John was not able to see over them. Nothing grew on the rocky hills, and after a short time even the formations cut into the stone by years of flowing water grew monotonous. John yawned.

At long last, he spotted a break in the rock. Pushing down on the oar, he cut through the current like a knife. As he pulled the oar through the stream he noticed a lessening resistance, and with each additional stroke the force of the swirling water declined. Gradually, the stone window drew near. John exerted more pressure on the oar. Just inches away, he craned his neck to peek through the opening. The sight was unbelievable.

Set back from the river was an enormous stone complex surrounded by a high wall. A massive granite tower pierced the sky, flanked by a gracefully curving dome whose superstructure lay within the thick walls. Inside the tower John saw the gleam of a large bronze bell, swaying slightly to and fro but not ringing. To the right of the tower was a church steeple.

John was mesmerized. What was this imposing struc-

ture? One of Father Serra's missions? No, not in this part
of California. Maybe it was a monastery. A convent. Who
knew what it was doing out here in the middle of nowhere.

John leaned back in his seat, entranced with the structure, its beauty enhanced by the crumbling hills of rock
that framed it. He was captivated by the gleaming dome.
Indescribable, really. If pressed he'd say it resembled a
rosebud. A bud nearly matured, waiting to bloom, whose
petals were sheaves of yellow metal that glittered in the
sunlight. There was something vaguely familiar about the
shape of the dome. John wasn't able to place it.

As his raft left behind the opening in the rock, he
shouted to a friend, "Hey, Stan—did you see that building?
Kind of like a cathedral."

"What building?"

"The one on the left."

"Didn't see it."

"You're kidding! Wait till we get around this corner.
The rock looks like it ends there. Then look to your left."

One of the students in the raft ahead asked them what
they were shouting about.

"A building," Stan answered. "Up ahead on your left."

The river seemed unnaturally calm as the rafts rounded
the bend. John barely touched his oar. The rocks slowly
receded and he held his breath, waiting for a reaction from
the people in the first three rafts. There was none. He was
puzzled. How could they have missed it?

The student in the raft ahead of his turned around and
yelled, "Hey, John—you crazy or what?"

As his friend Stan strained to see around the rocks, it
suddenly dawned on John what he had seen and why no
one else had seen it. It was a message to him alone. A
message from Dmitri, a vision of the palace in which the
tsarevich had died. The boy was taunting him.

Strangely, John did not feel the sense of shock that had

accompanied Dmitri's Cyrillic note. Nor was he surprised
that the boy could now make himself known to him during
his waking state. By leaving campus, John had achieved
nothing. He should have realized that he could not escape
the boy. Dmitri was inside of him, like a malignant
growth, spreading throughout his system, ready to burst
through his human casing.

John felt no panic, but a deep weariness. He was tired
of fighting the boy. There was nothing more he could do
but give in to the tsarevich's will. And so, in a strange
catharsis, John closed off his emotions, replacing his fear
with a dull numbness. An anesthetized, passionless acceptance of Dmitri's continued infringement on his life. For
if he tried to fight the boy, he felt certain that his very soul
would rupture.

The raft glided past the rocks and bobbed in the current.

The field was empty.

FRIDAY, MAY 14

Chapter Twenty

✶✶✶ ✶✶✶ ✶✶✶

"Okay, John, I want you to try something different today."
Sloane knelt by John's side. The young man was deeply
hypnotized.

"I want you to age-regress just as you've been doing and
let Dmitri talk; only, this time I want you to go back to the
month of April 7099. Not May. Or go back earlier to
March or February if you wish.

"You're breathing quite normally now. I'm going to
count backward from five, and on zero you will be wide-
awake. Dmitri will be speaking. But remember, when I
tap you on the shoulder, although you will still be in a
trance the unhypnotized part of you will be able to speak
to me."

Sloane whispered to Marina, "I'll try to give you a signal before I come back onstage for the Hidden Observer
Test." She nodded.

"Okay, John. Five, four, three, two, one, zero."

Marina moved into the boy's line of vision.

"Good morning."

"You weren't here yesterday."

Marina clenched her fists at her sides. Their trick had
not worked. It was May 14, 1591. Dmitri's time was still

paralleling their own. His death was only one day away. She frantically fabricated an answer.

"Yes, I know. I hurt my ankle."

"Twisted it?"

"Yes. I tripped over a root."

"You'll have to be more careful. There is much undergrowth around here."

"I will. It doesn't hurt much." She brushed her hair back from her face. "Dmitri, let me ask you something. Right before I visit you, do you ever feel strange in any way?" Marina hoped she'd phrased the question correctly. Carter had asked her to find out if Dmitri experienced any abnormal sensations before her visits. She didn't know why he wanted the information.

"No."

"Nothing at all? Think carefully."

"Um, maybe I do hear a ringing in my ears. A buzzing, really."

In his seat, Carter wrote a note to himself.

"Why do you ask?" questioned Dmitri.

"No particular reason." She stretched her hands in the air. "Pretty day, isn't it?"

"It's all right."

"You don't seem terribly enthusiastic. What's the matter?"

"Vladimir was supposed to take me out boating today."

"Did he forget?"

"No, he sent word by messenger that he couldn't come. He has business."

Marina wished Vladimir had paid the boy a visit. She enjoyed hearing about him, this young man she would never meet but whose life, over the past five days, had been revealed to her in glimpses.

"That's really quite understandable, Dmitri."

"I know." He did not want to dwell on his friend's

absence. "You're late today. You should have showed up earlier. I can't talk long."

"Oh, really? Why not?"

"I've got to go to church." The boy wrinkled his nose in disgust. "It's so boring."

"Why go?"

"My mother, she wants to go pray." He spoke in hushed tones. "And I know what she's going to ask for."

"What?"

"The Finn told our fortunes last night and. . . . You never read my palm! You told me that you'd teach me how."

His indignant manner surprised Marina. "I will. Tomorrow. I promise. It can't be rushed." He didn't seem mollified. "Now, what's this about the Finn?"

He refused to change subjects. "I don't think you can read palms at all."

"Dmitri!" She acted shocked. "How dare you accuse me of lying?"

"Prove it, then." He gave her his hand, palm up.

Marina gazed at the lines and creases with bewilderment. "Okay, see this line? See how long it is? That means you've got a great memory. And here? That indicates the people who are special to you. Now, there aren't many of them—there's only a few lines—but since the lines are deep it shows they mean a lot to you. Like Vladimir and—"

"Are you there?" The boy blushed as he realized the implications of his question. He tried to qualify it. "I mean, after all, you're one of the few people I know. No one else likes talking to me."

"That's not true. You just don't give anyone the chance." She smiled at the boy affectionately.

Dmitri's blush deepened, and he seemed even more embarrassed that his fondness for this strange woman was reciprocated.

"What's this line here?" he asked with false non-chalance.

"That line?" Marina paused, not wanting to discuss the only line on the boy's palm which she truly recognized. "That's your lifeline, Dmitri."

"So what does it say? I'm going to live forever, aren't I? Tsar Dmitri."

She reached over and tousled his hair. "Yeah. Forever." She took a deep breath. "All right—no more palm reading. You were going to tell me what the Finn predicted."

"That's not what I call a thorough reading," he complained.

"Later. Now, what did the Finn say?"

He withdrew his hand grudgingly. "My mother asked him how long it will be before my brother dies."

Pleasant woman, thought Marina. "And?"

"He replied that he saw the cloud of death approaching the royal family any day now. That's why my mother wants to go to church. She's praying to have his death sped up."

"That's rather an awful thing to say about one's mother."

"It's true. Why else does she want to drag me along? She wants to make certain that God knows who's next in line."

Marina laughed. "So where's church?"

"Over there." He waved a hand casually to his right.

"You've got your own?"

"Of course. What did you think that building was?"

"I don't know. I didn't notice it before. Guess I'm not very familiar with your religion," she admitted.

"If you plan to stay around here you'll have to learn more about it. I'll help you." He took her hand and sat her down on the floor. His lucid description of the official church and his disdain for it fascinated Marina. Though bright and well educated, Dmitri was, after all, only nine years old. She reckoned that his criticism was a repetition of what he'd heard his uncle say. Words memorized by the brain but not digested by the heart.

"There is supposedly one true Church and that is the Rus Orthodox Church. Two years ago the patriarch of Constantinople recognized the greatness of Rus by establishing a patriarchate here. So. . . ." He stopped, struck by a horrifying thought. "Your people do believe in God, don't they?"

Marina, like many behaviorists in psychology, was a confirmed agnostic. She decided not to push her luck. "Of course," she said.

The boy was relieved. "Good. Anyway, Job is the metropolitan at the head of the Orthodox Church. You may have heard of him. I've never seen him but I hear he wears magnificent robes of gold and silver."

"You must think highly of him."

"He would not have been my choice. Nor would the Church, for that matter. I understand he serves my brother well."

Marina had forgotten that the separation of church and state was unknown four hundred years ago. She envisioned the young Dmitri eavesdropping on one of his uncle's vituperative conversations regarding the Church and its obeisance to Feodor. Feodor—the man who, in the minds of the Nagoy family, stood between Dmitri and the throne.

"They're opportunists, you know. These 'holy men' of the Church. Hah! They do everything my brother tells them to do. They know they can be easily replaced." The boy was raging. "They've used the Church to gain power. It is no wonder that it's no longer the true Church of God."

"And what Church is the true Church?" She almost stumbled over the videotape cord. Damn engineers, she thought. Why couldn't they have installed more plugs?

"I'm not certain. Perhaps the Poles are right. Catholicism might be the way."

Dmitri's mention of Catholicism struck a chord in Marina. He had mentioned the very religion to which False Dmitri had converted; the Pretender had done his homework well. She considered asking Dmitri more about the topic but knew she would just be hearing a rote articulation of his uncle's opinions.

"Tell me about your father."

The boy did not hesitate to answer. "A great soldier." His anger abated, supplanted by a panegyrical fervor.

"Your father won many battles?"

"It was my father who routed the Tartars."

"Of course, the Mongol khanates."

"Yes, and he also destroyed the Livonian order. His might was known across the land. Along the way he acquired a nickname: *Groznyi*, 'The Awesome One.' I would like to be respected like that someday."

She winced as the boy reflected on a future that would never be realized. He continued to extol his father, the man posterity called Ivan the Terrible. A man who had ravaged the countryside with a bloody reign of terror, the *oprichnina*—the fulcrum of his depraved, autocratic rule.

Marina was appalled. To think Dmitri aspired to be like that monster. Obviously the boy had been told only of his father's military exploits, not of his domestic abominations.

"My father was a wonderful ruler. Not like my brother, Feodor. He is an imbecile. Do you know that he actually nominated himself as a candidate for the Polish throne?" Dmitri laughed. "He can't even govern one sovereignty let alone two. 'Feodor the Good,' they call him. Hah! Feodor the Feebleminded is the truth."

Marina was only half-listening. Her mind was on a more pressing issue: Dmitri's assassin. She was no closer to discovering Shuisky's agent within the palace walls than she had been when the session started. She interrupted the boy's vilification of his brother, hoping to elicit from him information that might possibly expose the murderer.

"Dmitri, do you like all the people who work here?"

"It's not for me to like them. They serve their purpose."

She knew she'd phrased the question incorrectly, so she tried another tack. "Do they treat you well?"

He appeared perplexed by her question. "Of course. They can't afford not to."

"Who hired them?"

"My uncle, I guess."

"Where did they come from?"

"Some came with us when we moved from Moscow. Others were already here."

"Are any of them new? Just arrived?"

"Of course. We always have a few new workers. They replace the ones that run away."

"Run away?"

"Yes. Sometimes the overseer will stop by the fields and an entire family will have left."

"Your servants work in the fields?"

"Well, not our personal servants. The rest do. The *krestanin*. According to the laws of the state they're not supposed to be able to leave until the nationwide census is complete. But many disobey and run off."

The census. Marina had read about it earlier. A survey conducted from 1581 to 1593, the period called "The Forbidden Years" because peasants were forbidden to switch jobs and move to different estates. The tsar had ordered this restriction not to facilitate the count of citizens, however, but to halt the flow of peasants hired away from the gentry by the wealthy boyars.

The tsar's motive for helping the gentry class was to build a counterweight to the boyars. The gentry, living on plots—*pomestie*, or service estates—that the tsar gave them, were obliged to serve him in any capacity as he saw fit. The boyars, on the other hand, lived on *votchina*, lands they had inherited from their fathers, and thus were not obligated to the tsar.

"Why do your workers leave? Aren't they treated well?"

The boy's temper flared. "Of course we treat them well."

"How much are they paid?"

"Paid?"

"Yes. Their salary. Money."

"We give them food and shelter. Clothes. A comfortable life. What do they need wages for? We take care of them."

Marina began to comprehend what a desperate existence the serfs of Rus led. Through her reading she knew that the peasants had been legally bound to their employer's land even before the census, by the 1497 *Sudebnik*, or Code of Laws. They were permitted to leave only during the two-week period celebrating the November holiday of St. George's Day, after the fall harvest had been reaped. Few actually were able to leave. Landlords no longer accepted payment for the year's rent by *obrok* (in kind) or *barshchina* (in labor). Only cold, hard cash would suffice. Cash no peasant had.

Concomitantly with the stiff rental fees, the peasants were faced with departure fees and oppressive government taxes. Soon these serfs—as the indentured peasants were later called—would be little more than baptized property. Many fled.

"Where do they go?" Marina asked.

"The runaways? Many go to live with the Cossacks."

"Don't they ever return?"

"I really don't know. None of my personal servants has ever left me."

"Those personal servants. The ones who come in contact with you every day. Are any of them new?"

"No."

"You haven't had any problems with them? None have ever displayed signs of animosity to you or your family?"

"No, they know they are lucky to be here."

Marina felt she'd reached a dead end. His answers were leading her nowhere. As a last effort she asked: "Have you ever met a man named Shuisky?"

The boy bridled. "The regent's brother-in-law."

"No, not Dmitri Shuisky. I mean his brother Vasilly."

"No. At least not that I recall. I've probably just forgotten. One of the house servants comes from the Shuisky estate and might have mentioned him."

"Which one?" Marina had to restrain herself from pouncing on the boy.

"Why are you asking all these questions?" She'd triggered his curiosity.

"Dmitri, just answer me!"

"Not until you answer me first."

She sought a reply that might quickly end the stalemate. "I may want a job here. We don't seem to be pulling in much money in town."

"It's no wonder. Your friend gives the impression of being a lunatic."

"Yes, I know. So I wanted to see if I'd qualify for any job. In fact, I was just talking to two of your servants, both former Shuisky employees. They told me about a job in town that I might investigate. Only I don't remember the job and I didn't ask their names. Who were they?"

"Two people? I don't remember two personal servants of mine from the Shuisky estate. There's only—look!" The boy pointed to the right. Marina whirled and saw Sloane mounting the steps to the stage. Damn it. What poor timing for him to try the Hidden Observer technique. His headphones were off. Obviously he'd removed them just seconds earlier and didn't realize what he was interrupting. Marina tried to wave him away but without success.

"What's he doing here?" the boy asked.

"I don't know. Stay here." She ran over to Sloane.

"You can't interrupt," she said through gritted teeth. "He was about to tell me who Shuisky's agent is."

"Well, I can't turn back now, can I? He's seen me. Sorry. I was afraid he'd leave for church before I could get to him. Relax. You can ask him after I leave. I'll make it fast."

Sloane walked over to Dmitri and without a spoken word placed his hand on the boy's shoulder, the prearranged signal to tap John Greene, about to emerge as the Hidden Observer. The boy stared blankly into space for a split second and then rubbed his face. When he removed his hands, his expression had changed to one of wonder.

"Oh, wow, you should see this!" John spoke rapidly in English, excitement spilling from his lips.

"What do you see, John?" Sloane removed his hand.

"It's incredible. It's this huge walled-in courtyard with all these trees and shrubs around." John turned his body slowly and tilted up his face toward the ceiling of the auditorium. "There's this totally bizarre tower over there. And that"—he pointed to the air—"that looks like a church." He lowered his head. "Look at these clothes. Jesus. How do you suppose they get in and out of them?"

"Do you see any people?"

"Yeah. Over there. There's this kid waving." He laughed. "This is such a trip. You can't believe this mansion. And the dome." He stopped, his face tilted upward. "I've seen it before. I've seen this whole setup before."

"What do you mean?" asked Sloane.

"The other day. Yesterday when I was rafting with—"

Without warning, John was cut off. His body jolted. Dmitri had retaken control.

"So"—the boy's Russian sounded menacing after John's spurt of English—"what's he here for?"

Sloane involuntarily retreated a few feet, numbed by this unexpected turn of events. Marina stumbled over her words.

"Sloane? I think he just came by to pay his respects."

The boy glanced over his shoulder. "Maybe some other time. They're signaling me. I'm late for church. I shouldn't have talked this long to you."

"No, Dmitri. Wait. You can't go."

"Sorry. I've got to."

"Then just answer a question."

"Can't. My mother will scold me as it is. Come later tomorrow. That way you'll catch me after church." He walked a few paces, then stopped and held out his hand. "I almost forgot. I brought this for you. My uncle gave it to me for good luck when I was born. He got it in Poland. Dubnik, I think. I hope you like it. Good-bye."

The boy pressed the object into her hand, and before Marina was able to say anything, he had gone.

"Dmitri, don't leave. Dmitri!" She stamped her foot in frustration.

Slowly she opened her hand. Dmitri had given her a stone. But no ordinary stone. Its polished exterior revealed a kaleidoscope of sparkling colors. The simple beauty of it staggered her. She shifted her gaze from the stone to the face before her. It was calm, completely reposed. Halcyon. A faint bridge of freckles crossed the nose.

She knew the stone did not belong to John—at least she'd never seen it in his possession. There seemed only one explanation, staggering though it was, for its appearance: It was indeed a gift from Dmitri Ivanovich, having been sucked through the same time warp as he. Physical proof of his existence in the twentieth century.

"Okay, John," Sloane said to the mute figure, "I'd like you to rest for a minute and then we'll start to bring you out. That's it. Keep breathing normally."

The young man's chest rose and fell in an unhurried rhythmic pattern.

"I didn't get the name," Marina said. "I didn't have a chance to get the name of Shuisky's contact."

"It's not that important," Sloane said. "There's always tomorrow." He noticed the stone in her hand but said nothing.

"All right"—he turned to John—"I'm going to count backward from five to zero. As I do, you'll wake up. At first you'll feel a slight tingling in your limbs. By three your mind will be alert and you'll feel energetic. By zero you'll be fully conscious. Five, four, three, two, one, zero. Fully awake now."

The young man did not immediately snap out of the trance. Several minutes passed before he appeared able to speak. Sloane shook his shoulder, puzzled by his slow response.

"How are you feeling?"

"Kind of groggy."

"Just sit there for a while." Sloane waved to the dark-haired man in the middle of the auditorium. "That was great, Charles. We'll see you again tomorrow. Make it a little later. Twelve-thirty or so."

Charles, the interpreter, rose from his seat and collected his gear. He gathered the headphones worn by Perry and the three psychologists, unplugged his microphone system, and exited through a door in the side wall. Marina had not explained the experiment to Charles, and Sloane preferred to keep it that way.

"Rally round, gang." Sloane flipped off the videotape machine and headed into the conference room. Carter whispered in his ear.

"Uh, John?" Sloane patted the young man's arm. "Could you wait outside for a minute? We'll call you."

When Marina, Perry, and the three psychologists had

assembled in the room, Carter closed the door and spoke. "Have you noticed that each day that John's been hypnotized, he's had a harder time coming out of trance?"

"What do you mean?" asked Zugelder as he pulled out a chair.

"Maybe I've noticed it because I just finished watching those two videotapes of him. At any rate, each day it's taken John a longer time to wake up."

"What do you infer from that?"

"I'm not sure. It's as though he's having a hard time shaking off Dmitri. He looks tired, drawn out."

"Are you suggesting that this experiment is endangering John's health?" asked Zugelder. "If that's the case, we should drop it immediately. I don't want any sort of lawsuit on our hands."

"I don't think we'll have to worry about that, Professor Zugelder. I was merely making a simple observation. Perhaps he just hasn't been sleeping well."

The group sat in glum silence for a moment. Carter's words had unsettled them. Especially Marina, who knew that John was suffering from more than lack of sleep. She had noticed a change in him—as if his energy were being sapped by Dmitri, as if a merger between the two were occurring. When John had called her last night and told her about seeing the Uglich palace, she didn't know what to be more worried by: the actual incident or John's passive account of it. He was no longer questioning what was happening to him, no longer caring.

"We've got to look at this case as a puzzle," said Carter, breaking the silence, "and take each piece of information we have and try to fit it into a larger scheme of things. Like that stone Dmitri gave Marina. Put it on the table, will you please?" he asked her.

She reluctantly placed the stone before Carter.

"Have you seen it before?"

"No," she answered softly.

"Looks like an opal to me," said Perry. "You don't suppose Dmitri actually—"

"I'm sure John had some reason for carrying it in his pocket," said Zugelder impatiently. "He might have brought it in subconsciously. Perhaps he once read that the Russian royal family doted on opals."

"But an opal that large would be expensive. What's John doing with that kind of money? And don't you think it's strange that it's loose and not in a setting?"

"Well, we'll just have to ask him when he comes in, won't we?"

"I'd brace myself if I were you, Professor Zugelder," said Carter. "I fully expect that John will deny he's ever seen the stone. In which case I recommend that we have it analyzed."

"This is preposterous!" said Zugelder.

"Not really. Not if you analyze this case as I do," said Carter.

"And how do you analyze it? What's your explanation?" asked Zugelder.

"I've narrowed it down to one of two possibilities. First, it could be a manifestation of a second personality. A personality created perhaps as a result of some recent trauma in John's life. It's possible that John's forgotten history lessons—if indeed he ever did learn about Dmitri—have formed the basis of this personality, but subsequent learning, perhaps unconsciously repressed, must also have taken place."

"And the second explanation?"

"You won't like it, Professor Zugelder," warned Carter.

"Try me."

"The second explanation is that we're communicating with the actual Dmitri Ivanovich."

Sloane was startled by his friend's statement. When

Marina had suggested that she was in communication with the actual tsarevich, Sloane had dismissed the notion. How could Carter really present the theory as a viable explanation?

"You must be joking." Zugelder's voice was laden with sarcasm.

"No, I'm quite serious."

"But on what do you base such a belief?" asked Sloane.

"On a theory that's held by a number of scholars. Not quacks, Dustin. But reputable men and women from the academic world."

"And what is this theory?" asked Zugelder irascibly.

"Time dislocation. It's nicely explained in an article I took the liberty of bringing with me: 'The End of Time,' by an author named Joan Forman. The article's an excerpt from a book, *The Mask of Time.*"

"You still haven't explained what the theory says."

"The article defines time dislocation as a slippage in time in which information from one time bracket, be it past or future, becomes superimposed on that of the current time bracket, the present. I first heard about the theory in Egypt while hypnotizing that American woman. It's the only theory that's ever come close to explaining why she started speaking ancient Egyptian."

"Why did she?" asked Marina.

"Because, over two thousand years ago in that very area of Egypt, a young princess had a conversation with her handmaiden. That conversation was played back to us in the present through the American's voice. You see, her Egyptian speech was merely a projection from the environment. My colleagues and I heard that voice because energy waves generated by the princess were absorbed by the surroundings and then 'rebroadcasted,' as Forman would say, through the American thousands of years later."

"But why that particular American? Why wasn't the

princess's voice heard years earlier through someone else?" asked Perry.

"No one can answer that. Somehow the American woman possessed the criteria needed to serve as a broadcaster."

"Like John," said Marina. "He's the broadcaster for Dmitri."

"No, not like John," said Zugelder, "because we're not in Russia. Dmitri Ivanovich never came to America. His so-called energy couldn't be stored in our environment."

"You're quite right," agreed Carter. "Dmitri's case is different from that of the Egyptian princess, but it still falls within the definition of time dislocation."

"How?"

"It'll take a bit of explaining."

"I can't think of a better time to hear it," said Zugelder.

Carter reached for his briefcase and withdrew the Forman article. "All right. To begin with, as anyone with a science background knows, the conservation of matter and energy is a basic law of physics. Each may change but not disappear. They are two inextricable components of the same system—the atomic structure of the universe.

"Man, like the world around him, is atomic in structure, and like all matter he produces electromagnetic fields, giving out and receiving information. In fact, this world of ours is apparent to us only because information about every part of it is continually being sent out into space."

"I knew I should have taken physics in my freshman year," whispered Perry to Marina.

"Now, although information generally propagates from the present to the future, occasionally the move is in the opposite direction. No law in physics prohibits information from being transmitted from the future to the present. Indeed, quantum mechanics tells us that the atomic particles known as electrons move backward and forward with equal facility."

"This is all terribly fascinating but what does it have to do with Dmitri?" asked Zugelder.

"Just one minute. Time dislocations, such as this appearance by Dmitri, are quite possibly the result of the brain's interpretation of information fed to it from a different time and then translated into audiovisual terms. Information delivered not through any of the five senses that we're familiar with, but via the human force field."

"I don't understand," said Perry.

Carter rephrased his explanation. "As I see it, John's electromagnetic field has picked up Dmitri's—for want of a better word—'signals' from four hundred years ago, signals that were sent into space but never dissipated. His brain, in turn, has interpreted the signals and translated them into the audiovisual display that we've been watching each day."

"But why were Dmitri's signals picked up?"

"Forman has some ideas about that. Although she can't explain why a person like John can receive such signals when others can't, she does suggest why the signals from someone like Dmitri are more apt to be picked up than others. She writes:

'An arresting feature of this type of case is that the apparent previous existence has usually ended in a violent death. It is as though the forgoing of the normal and gradual preparation for death had deprived the individual of forgetfulness!' "

"So," ventured Marina, "Dmitri's anguish at dying intensified the signals he sent out and made them easier to pick up."

"Precisely. Now, you must not make the mistake of thinking that these signals are like taps of a telegraph. These are not messages that Dmitri sent out, but rather the basic components of Dmitri himself, only scrambled in a form we do not recognize. Thus, you're able to communicate with him. Marina, remember I asked you to find out if Dmitri ever experienced any strange feelings prior to your visits? I wanted that information because often in time dislocation the participants receive preliminary notice. Like the advance warning that occurs to individuals who can sense an impending earthquake or thunderstorm. And Dmitri fits that pattern. The buzzing in his ears is his clue that he is about to slip into a time warp."

"This is ludicrous!" said Zugelder. "I can accept your first theory that Dmitri might be a second personality formed by John, but this time-dislocation stuff is strictly in the realm of science fiction."

"Regardless of which theory you accept," Carter said curtly, "you must treat Dmitri as a separate entity from John. Even if he is merely a second personality, he has his own desires, his own life-style. And judging by the manner in which he cut off John in midsentence today, he has more power than John. Far more. At any moment he could dominate John, breaking through into the real world. Rather, our world."

"And what's that supposed to mean?" asked Zugelder.

Sloane intervened in the conversation. "I hate to interrupt but we'd better bring John in. He probably thinks we've forgotten him. Perry, can you call him?" Sloane hoped that the two men's tempers would cool once John entered.

The young man entered the room and smiled at the psychologists. The bags under his eyes were pronounced and he shuffled rather than walked, confirming Carter's assessment of him.

Sloane nodded toward Carter. "I don't think you two have met. John Greene, Dr. Andrew Carter."

They shook hands.

"Glad to meet you, John. I'm sure Professor Sloane has told you how interested I am in your case."

"Yeah, it's a real winner, isn't it?"

"I know it must be strange for you. We psychologists often get a little carried away with what we're studying. I hope you don't mind another body."

"Not at all. The more the merrier. I figure my salary goes up with each additional observer."

Sloane winked at John. "Don't count on it."

"So what's your professional opinion, Dr. Carter? Got any new theories to add to the pot?"

"As a matter of fact I do, but I've got to be honest with you. It'll take some time before any of this makes much sense."

"As long as it's sometime this quarter. After all, it's easier earning money this way than by scrubbing pots in the dorm kitchen. But I'm not too keen on spending my summer vacation in this room. I'll never be able to stand. . . ." John's voice suddenly faltered. He put a hand to steady himself against the door frame.

"What's wrong?" Sloane grabbed John's arm to support him.

"God, I still feel so groggy. Dizzy." He slumped against the door frame. Sloane tried to hoist him to his feet, but he wasn't able to get any leverage.

"Marina," he said, "bring that chair over here, will you?"

She did not stir from her seat.

"Marina? Get the hell over here!"

But the young woman remained in her seat as if glued to it, her face a mask of disbelief, eyes focused on John's reflection in the long mirror opposite the doorway. Had she not been wearing her contacts she would have sworn her eyes were playing tricks on her. Above her, a fluorescent light was flickering, threatening to burn out. She supposed it was this flickering that was creating the illusion before her now. The mirror seemed to be glowing, generating sparks that crowned John's head in a radiance of shimmering gold light. An iridescent nimbus.

The others were all focused on John and had not noticed the mirror. As if in a dream she saw Carter drag the chair beside her to the doorway. A sense of déjà vu took hold of her. Where had she seen this before? The glow, the limp body suspended in the strong arms of another, the sightless blue eyes. This image. It gnawed at her. Time froze as she tried to place where she'd seen it before.

And then she remembered. Remembered the print in one of her Russian history books.

The picture: An icon painting of the martyred Tsarevich Dmitri. St. Dmitri.

Chapter Twenty-one

By talking with Marina, he'd made himself late for church. He hurried across the courtyard to the entrance of the great house, hoping his mother wouldn't lecture him on punctuality. Tardiness, she often told Dmitri, has been responsible for the fall of many great men. He hoped she wouldn't retell the story of his father's enemy, the Crimean Tartar, who lost a crucial battle because he delayed issuing orders. Once, when Dmitri was four, he interrupted the story to ask, "But Mother, if the Tartar hadn't delayed, Father would have lost the battle and I wouldn't be here. So isn't tardiness good?" His mother tried to explain that she was speaking from the point of view of the Tartar, but the boy remained unconvinced. At that stage in his life his values were absolute. Anything that benefitted the tsar was good. Anything that did not was bad. Therefore, tardiness was good.

As he crossed the yard, Dmitri looked over his shoulder and observed that Marina and the man had left. Slon? That was his name? The boy wondered why she'd brought him along today. Perhaps the halfwit really had learned to speak a couple of sentences in their language. It didn't matter. Even if the man spoke fluent Russian, Dmitri wouldn't trust him. There was something about the way Marina acted around him—as if Slon had some sort of power over her. It bothered the boy. He was convinced that no good could come from her association with the man. He must remember to tell her that. Tomorrow.

Dmitri was equally disturbed by what had happened when the man placed his hand on his shoulder. An odd sensation. Like being whisked through a dimensionless corridor filled with haze. At the end of the corridor, Dmitri had been held paralyzed—for just a second—and then he'd felt a surge of energy and been jerked backward, as if dangling from a rope. And then the corridor was gone. He was back talking to Marina.

Had the man worked a gypsy incantation on him? He was not sure.

And yet, in that half-second of immobility, he had seen the most wondrous sight. Above him, a row of miniature suns suspended in a black sky, and stretching before him a vast ocean of seats, closely grouped together, in three sections. The seats were unoccupied. Hundreds of them. Empty. Waiting for him.

That was all he remembered. The image was blurry and it faded before he was able to bring it into sharper focus. Though he'd not mentioned the strange vision to Marina, he suspected that she would know what it meant. She might have seen it, too. Or was that shocked look on her face attributable to something else? Something he hadn't seen.

Had Vladimir not been detained today, Dmitri would have aked him about the image. He, too, would know what it signified. For Vladimir occasionally spoke of visions that flashed into his mind one second and out the next. So real that once or twice he had tried to speak with the people who appeared in them. Often the images made no sense to him,

as the field of chairs meant nothing to Dmitri. But sometimes, a day or a week or even a year later, something
would happen that would trigger the memory of the dream
and he would understand.

Vladimir did not mention the dreams to many people.

Dmitri reluctantly put aside his reflections as he entered
the house. He found his mother downstairs. She was im-
patient but did not rebuke him, and they walked to the
church in silence. A large number of people were inside
the building, and they bowed low at the sight of the
tsarevich. He barely acknowledged them as he made his
way to the front of the church. His mother remained in the
back with the rest of the women. In the back, near the
doorway, where their unpure female bodies could not defile
the house of God.

The priest, called by many names—"guardian of the
great light," "orthodox doctor," "ghostly father"—entered
the church from the rear. He was dressed simply in black
and wore his thinning hair long. Unlike boyars, for whom
long hair was a symbol of disgrace, holy men were en-
couraged to grow theirs. The priest's was red, and it
streamed down his back in a stringy mass.

The ghostly father reached the middle of the aisle,
crossed himself, and in a loud voice began his ritual:
"*Blagoslovi vladyko . . . O Khristu.* Bless us, heavenly
pastor. Bless us, Christ." The man's movements were
slow, less an infirmity of age than an attempt to heighten
the solemnity of his position. His gait was steady as he
approached the tsarevich. "*Godpodi pomilui. Godpodi
pomilui.* Lord have mercy on us. Lord have mercy on us."
He reached the altar and there he recited the Lord's
Prayer. The congregation chorused "Amen."

As the priest read the Psalms, Dmitri's mind wandered.
He was hungry, and he hoped his stomach would not
start rumbling as it had last Friday. He gained little solace

from the fact that no one else in the church had eaten. Fast days were stupid. If his uncle could throw a banquet on Wednesday, one of the two days of the week reserved for fasting, why couldn't he sneak a chicken wing? His mother would be shocked. Her brother already had strayed from the fold. She would not lose her son. Christ was betrayed on Wednesday; Christ suffered on Friday. They would fast.

Dmitri thought back on all the Fridays he'd spent in church. One stuck out in his mind—the last Friday of Lent. After existing on a diet of bread and salt and water, he'd nearly passed out. He'd had to be propped up in order to participate in the Release of the Easter Birds, a traditional ceremony. He recalled opening the latch to the cage and standing feebly as his bird spread its wings. This ceremony was stupid, too. He doubted that God would liberate him from his sins just because he'd freed some damn bird that had been captured in the first place.

"Oh, come let us worship and fall down before the Lord."

Dmitri joined the others in kneeling before the icons on the wall. As the ghostly father read the Ten Commandments, the boy busied himself by playing with wax drippings from a nearby candle. He pulled the candle closer to him, and there, at the front of the church, hidden from the rest of the worshippers but in plain sight of the priest, he poured some of the hot wax into his hand and molded it into a soft ball. He pressed his left thumb into the ball and the wax hardened about it. Pulling it away, he gazed with pleasure at the image. A perfect cast. Every line of his thumb reproduced exactly. He admired the cast and then held it over the candle's flame. It turned black and melted, drop by drop, into the candleholder. Gone. Something so tangible one minute, verifying his very existence, that was gone the next. He supposed nothing of a person's life was permanent. Nothing remained after death. Except another's memories.

He recalled a funeral held in the church a few months previously for one of his relatives. Even his memories of the girl were fading. She had been laid on a slab, her feet shod in brand-new buskins to help her on her journey, with a certificate from the ghostly father to St. Nicholas in her hand. St. Nicholas, the chief mediator to God, revered by all the people of Rus. Did the saint ever receive this confirmation of the true faith of the girl, her passport to heaven? Dmitri did not think so. It was written on paper, paper that could no more withstand the elements than his ball of wax had withstood the candle's flame. As the girl's body decomposed, so the paper would deteriorate. Only the soul was indestructible.

"Praised be the Trinity—the Father, the Son, and the Holy Ghost—forever and ever."

It had been wintertime, he recalled, and the ground had been frozen. They hadn't been able to bury the girl, so they'd moved her to the *bozhedom*, God's house, on the outskirts of town. She'd been placed next to other corpses, all as hard as stone, piled high like logs on a wood stack, and had spent the winter there, waiting for the spring thaw. He wondered if she had been robbed of her jewelry by the thieves of the dead, loathsome slime who wandered from *bozhedom* to *bozhedom*, pillaging the deceased. And he wondered if St. Nicholas had waited, too, leaving her soul standing at heaven's gate until she was interred below the rich Rus soil.

"My soul doth magnify the Lord."

She had been buried just a month ago. No holy water had been sprinkled over her grave because her body itself sanctified the earth. The priest had prayed for her soul that day, just as he had every day since her death. He did it not out of a sense of duty, however. He did it for money. Her family had paid him. They were not willing to gamble. Should the girl's soul be on the second level of heaven and not on the first, she would need the ghostly father's intervention to move up a notch. So they paid. All families did. And the church grew fatter.

"Blessed is the man. . . ."

Dmitri was sure that the girl was in heaven's first tier by now. The priest prayed daily to St. Nicholas, and St. Nicholas, it was well known, liked attention. There was a battle once between the Russians and the Tartars in which a Muscovite soldier, chasing a Tartar infidel on horseback, asked St. Nicholas for assistance. The Tartar, who was only a little farther up the road, overheard this plea and raised his head to heaven and said, "Nicholas, if he catches me with your help it will be no miracle. But if you save me, who do not know you, then great will be your fame, and your name will be praised in both our lands."

The Russian's horse got stuck in the mud and the Tartar escaped. So much for St. Nicholas' modesty.

The priest, leaning heavily on his *posokh*, or staff, launched into a legend about the saint for that day. Dmitri paid no attention. He spent the time analyzing the *posokh* for dents. It was rumored that when the priest's wife got mad, she hit her husband over the head with it. Priests' wives were part of a special class of women, like his mother. Without being married, a man could not be a priest, and the women took advantage of the edge that gave them. Dmitri found no dents. He went back to playing with the candle wax.

He poured a thin layer of the wax into his palm, and when it hardened, he was careful not to crack it. A fine impression of his lengthy lifeline formed, and for the first time he noticed that the line was broken in the middle. A slight fissure separated it into two unequal parts. Using his fingernail he scratched the surface of the wax and extended the line across the gap. It made more sense that way. How could one die and be reborn?

"Yea, Lord have mercy on us."

The priest had ended the legend and was repeating his earlier chant. The congregation joined him, and together they said the phrase forty times. The boys in the church answered the chant as though they were one voice, rolling their tongues as fast as they could go: *"Verij, Verij, Verij, Verij.* Praise, Praise, Praise, Praise." Forty times over, so quickly that the word became indistinguishable and only the sound remained. Guttural. A sound not quite human that sent shivers through Dmitri.

When the priest started reading from the Gospels, Dmitri sighed. It would be over soon. Indeed, it was not long before they were all bowing and repeating "Alleluia," and the service, all two hours of it, had ended.

Dmitri stopped at the door to accompany his mother out of the church. Though he had not liked leaving Marina in the middle of a conversation—particularly when she was so agitated—the relief in his mother's face, knowing her son had been prayed for, convinced him that he had done the right thing. He supposed his mother wouldn't be so adamant about going to church if, according to tradition, the priests of Rus were allowed to pray for Dmitri, the brother of a tsar. But because of an ordinance sent to the higher ecclesiastics—prompted, he suspected, by Boris Godunov—prayers for him were banned. His mother had taken to her bed when she'd first learned of it.

It was his mother, too, who had pleaded with him to write the note to Feodor. A reminder that they shared the same father. A subtle suggestion that since Feodor was sickly, his younger brother should be trained in courtly manners and skills to relieve the tsar of some of his more strenuous tasks. Not that Dmitri believed he would learn anything from his brother. So inept was Feodor at social functions that he was the butt of many jokes among the foreign ambassadors. Still, no one hated Feodor. No one except Dmitri and his uncles. Though the man was undeniably simpleminded, he was considerate and kind and warm. He was Feodor the Good.

Dmitri's mother was never able to hate Feodor as her brothers did. He was, for a period of time, her stepson, and she had loved him and cherished his antics. She could not believe that his outrageous treatment of her son was an action of free will. He had to be under the influence of the potions and spells of the warlock Godunov. And so she urged Dmitri to write one more time to Feodor, to reach the core of him that was untouched by the devil. The boy had done as she requested and received no reply.

Dmitri left his mother at the entrance to the palace and walked the length of the western wall to the northern side. As he rounded the corner, he observed the Finn emerging from the pantry with a chicken leg in his mouth. He laughed at the sight of the shabbily dressed old man, scampering through the garden. Like all prophets, the Finn maintained that he required no sustenance, neither meat nor drink. God would provide. Pretense of such great austerity seemed to increase his credibility. But here he was, carrying stolen food, as he did every day, to a little sheltered area under the fruit trees. He would be shocked were anyone to call him a hypocrite, just as Mikhail Nagoy would be shocked by the idea that the Finn should be reprimanded. In Rus it was an honor to be robbed by spiritual men.

Dmitri suspected that the Finn's spirituality derived more from opium than from divine inspiration, but even so, he didn't dismiss the man's predictions. Last night, when the Finn predicted the cloud over the royal family, Dmitri felt a chill go up his spine. It had to mean the tsar's imminent death; Dmitri would finally battle the warlock Godunov face to face. He was scared—scared and exhilarated and filled with new purpose. His cause was just.

The presence of the gypsy assured him that he would

win. Her power would counteract any magic the warlock tried to use against him. Dmitri fingered his necklet and the spot where the opal had been. He was not sure why he had given the stone to the woman. He had done it on an impulse, and that was surprising. It was the first present he'd given anyone in the nine years he'd been alive.

His mother reacted differently to the prediction. She feared the tsar's demise would instigate a rash of plots against her son. She spoke again of hiding Dmitri, of putting a substitute in his place, and asked the Finn the best way to defeat Dmitri's enemies. The seer replied that they must gather dirt from his enemies' estates and throw it into a fire. The men would be doomed. Dmitri then inquired what the meaning of the buzzing in his ears was, without mentioning Marina. The Finn referred to the *Rafli*, the literature devoted to the interpretation of portents, and said that a buzzing in the ears, like an itching finger and the cracking of a wall, presaged a journey. The tsarevich was to go on a long trip.

Dmitri sat down amid the flowers that had survived the winter's frost and sighed. He had not needed the Finn's prophecy to know that he would be leaving this place soon. He felt it in his bones. Perhaps that was why he'd given the gypsy his stone, parted so easily with it. His luck was changing, and he no longer needed the comfort of the opal. The world was in transition, and he would move right along with it. To a new life. The life he was meant to lead.

He thought back to his first recollection as a child. He was three or four, and his mother was showing him a small engraving of Moscow which she cherished. She showed it to him often, stealing into his nursery two or three times a week to dandle him on her knee and point out the places she used to go. She talked about the people she'd known and said if he were very, very good, he would live in

Moscow someday. In the city of his birth, where his glorious ancestors lay.

He remembered asking his mother how he could be
good, and she replied that once a month they would send
the tsar presents and good tidings. Gradually the tsar
would take notice of them. When the boy asked to be
reinstated at court, his brother would welcome him with
open arms.

One night his Uncle Mikhail burst into the room and
took the engraving out of his mother's hands. He slashed
it with his knife, defacing the wooden buildings and the
hauntingly beautiful St. Basil's Cathedral, and tossed it
into the fireplace. His mother tried to pluck the engraving
from the flames but his uncle kicked her away. He lifted
Dmitri in his powerful arms and shook the boy, repeating
over and over, "You are the right heir to the throne. You
will never beg to get to Moscow. You will conquer and
vanquish, but you will never beg." He dropped the boy
and left, and Dmitri moved to his mother's side. She said,
"My picture, my beautiful picture. My beautiful Moscow."
Dmitri watched as the paper caught fire and the paint
smoked and the buildings dissolved, working from the
edges of the picture to the center. To the center of Moscow,
where his brother's palace lay. Finally, the palace itself
burned, leaving crumpled black ashes that settled lightly
on the stone.

He remembered that night and his uncle's words. He
would vanquish his enemy and ride gloriously into Moscow. His foes would fall into charred bone that he would
grind into dust to be scattered by the wind, cleansing the
tainted city of Moscow. And he would be tsar.

He would be tsar.

At last.

Chapter Twenty-two

"I can't believe we're really talking about this." Sloane pulled a napkin from the dispenser on their table. "I've been watching it unfold for the past five days and I still can't believe it."

"I know. It was the same way with me, having that woman suddenly start speaking Egyptian. It was like . . . like nothing I'd ever encountered." Carter tapped the side of his plastic cup. "I was positive I wouldn't run into anything like it again. Until now."

"You're sure that it's time dislocation?"

"As sure as I'll ever be. Dmitri's memory is simply too complete; his archaic Russian is spoken with too much finesse. And the other pieces of the puzzle: the automatic writing, the opal, and that river trip he just finished telling us about. There's no room for disagreement anymore, Dusty. I brought up the multiple-personality explanation as an alternative mostly to appease Zugelder. But you two are ready to handle the idea of time dislocation."

Marina stared at the tables in the engineering-division patio. She saw people laughing, eating. Some bickering. But none who had the slightest awareness of the kind of problem that confronted the three of them. A problem not only difficult to fathom but one that should never have arisen: how to prolong the visit of a boy from the sixteenth century.

"I'm sorry I didn't arrive here sooner. When he dies tomorrow this experiment will be finished," said Carter, interrupting Marina's reflections. "The time corridor will close again."

"We just can't stand by and let him be killed," said Marina. "What if something happens to John?"

"Marina, there's nothing we can do about it. He's dead. He's been dead for four hundred years," said Sloane.

"We can save him!"

"Marina, you're not being realistic." Sloane clasped his hands and spoke softly to her. "Somehow—God knows how—we've been in contact with a young Russian boy who lived before the turn of the seventeenth century. But he's dead, Marina. Chances are he was brutally murdered. I don't like it any better than you do, but we can't help him. It's out of our realm, out of our capabilities."

"You're wrong. We can do something." She visualized the scene in the conference room just minutes ago, so coincidentally like the icon painting of Dmitri, and she reflected on other coincidences of the last five days. Coincidences that she felt, however fantastically, she now was able to explain. "You concede I've been talking with the real Dmitri Ivanovich, right?"

"Yes. . . ." Sloane rubbed his temples.

"Then if I'm talking with the real Dmitri, I can prevent his death. I can warn him that someone is going to kill him. I can change history."

"What?" asked Sloane.

"Change history?" echoed Carter.

"Yes. Dmitri doesn't have to die. I can make sure he lives."

"But that's impossible. That can't be done," Sloane said.

"What do you mean?" she said. "On Wednesday you said that if we discovered the identity of Dmitri's murderer, we could 'stretch the time limit.' We could warn Dmitri and extend his life."

"On Wednesday I believed we were dealing with a psychic reproduction of Dmitri, not the real prince. I wanted more time to study him. But now the picture is different. Dmitri is real and we can't change history."

"Why not? I can tell him to stay inside tomorrow. Or go out boating with Vladimir. It's that simple. I'll tell him about Shuisky. He can take it from there."

"I think you're serious," remarked Sloane.

"Totally."

Sloane looked to Carter. "Can it be done?"

"I don't know. It's never come up before in cases of time dislocation. But then there's never been a case this extensive. Theoretically," he admitted, "she should be able to do it."

"What if I told you that I've already changed history?" Marina asked. "Three times, in fact. Would that help convince you?"

"What do you mean?" asked Carter.

"Exactly what I said. I've already changed history."

"How?"

"Hand me that book I gave you." She gestured to the Russian history text that Carter had been reading before the hypnosis session.

"On Tuesday, May 11, 7099, Mikhail Nagoy doubled the number of guards at the two palace gates. I'm not making this up. It's written right here." She pointed to a passage.

"Yes, I remember that," said Sloane. "The guards were reinforced because of a rumored attempt on the tsarevich's life."

"And on Wednesday, May 12, 7099," Marina continued, "the day Dmitri had his epileptic fit, his mother rushed to his side and later reported that she heard him talking to 'spirits.' This upset her so much that the very next day, Thursday, she contacted her most reliable soothsayer."

"Yes. So what's your point?"

"Don't you understand?" She tossed the book back to Carter. "*I* was the reason why Dmitri's uncle reinforced the security. It wasn't any so-called attempt on Dmitri's life that scared Mikhail. It was me, a foreigner on the Nagoy estate whose appearance Dmitri naturally reported to his uncle.

"And on Wednesday, when Dmitri regained consciousness after his epilepsy attack? It was *me* he was talking to, not 'spirits.' It only seemed as though he was talking to ghosts because his mother couldn't see me.

"And just today, Dmitri told us that his mother consulted with her astrologer, the Finn. Why? Because she believed that her son's conversation with the spirit world was an omen of some sort.

"That book also says Dmitri was late for church on Friday. He was detained by us. Just seconds ago. Think of it.

"Can't you see what's happening? I've been directly responsible for events that happened nearly four hundred years ago!"

"It can't be," Sloane said. "It just can't be."

"Believe it. All along we've been directly affecting the course of history."

"But we can't be sure," said Sloane slowly, trying to grasp the situation. "Marina, even if you were responsible for causing the reinforcements, history had recorded it before you were even born. Your actions are in some way predetermined."

"Maybe so. But I can still try to save him."

"I just don't believe this is happening."

Carter spoke to his friend, weighing each word carefully. "We've got to face the facts, Dusty. It seems we may be playing a part in history whether we like it or not, predetermined or not. You've been a goddamn psychologist too long. You've run people through tests knowing how they'll react and what they'll say. And when one person performs differently than you expected, you label him the freak in the bunch. The nonconformist. Isn't that what we call them, nonconformists?

"This is what we've spent our whole lives waiting for, Dustin. We've broken all the old conceptions about the human brain, those artificial boundaries of what the mind can and cannot do. We can throw away all our old statistics now. Instead of limiting our studies to that ten percent of the human brain that we know people use, we can focus on the other ninety percent, because, for the first time, we've got an inkling of what it can do."

"What right do we have to interfere? To tinker with history?"

"Every right in the world. The human brain—it's our field of study, for God's sake. I can't explain exactly how Dmitri came to be here but I can't deny he is here. Re-created in John's brain. Can you let him die on Saturday? Can you afford to pass up this opportunity to enrich our knowledge of the human mind?"

"Andrew, we're not just talking about one man's psyche here. We're talking about altering the natural stream of history, or have you forgotten? All right, say we are changing history. That our actions today are having ramifications four hundred years ago. I don't think you really comprehend what you're saying. You're advocating an incredibly reckless, even dangerous, course of action. If we save the boy, we may unintentionally change the shape of the world as we know it."

"Oh, c'mon. You sound like the Bradbury story in which the time traveler steps on the prehistoric butterfly, setting off chain reactions that eradicate modern life. But Dusty, we've already stepped on our butterflies. We've already interfered in history. And yet the world is still the same."

"It's one thing to cause a reinforcement of some guards," Sloane said. "It's quite another to save a boy who would have become tsar of Rus had he lived. We'll be altering the entire royal lineage. The Russian crown will never pass into the hands of the Romanovs. Peter the Great won't exist. Nor will Catherine. God only knows if the Russian revolution will still occur." He thought for a moment. "Or if any of us will be born. I don't care if I'm missing some grand opportunity by refusing to save the boy's life." He turned toward Marina. "Tomorrow, when you talk to Dmitri, you can't divulge anything you know. If you do, I'll personally come up on that stage and drag you off."

"I'll feel like an accessory to the murder!"

"You will be, if you save him. An accessory to a very different murder. Your own. If in some later war Dmitri wages as an adult, in some battle, one of your ancestors dies, just one, you'll be killing yourself."

"What about John? What happens to him if Dmitri dies? He and Dmitri are fused in some way. Can you assure me that he'll be safe? Can you live with your conscience if anything happens to him?" She was close to tears.

"Marina, we have to—"

"Let him die if he has to. That's what you're saying, isn't it? I'd like to see you say that if it were your wife at stake. Or your child. Maybe then you'd know how I feel. Let's save history, by all means. Let's make sure nothing is altered so that Stalin can have his pogroms and Hitler can have his concentration camps and America can invade Vietnam. And for this, for this great act of keeping history on course, we let John die. We let them both die."

"You're getting hysterical."

"Good, at least that proves I'm human. Not like you. You can talk in abstracts of time and space but you can't operate on the level of human lives. All right. Stay detached. But I won't."

"Marina, it's too big a risk. Listen to me. Dmitri must die. And he must die tomorrow, Saturday, May fifteenth. If you can't handle that, we won't meet tomorrow. It'll be called off. The session canceled. And then John will really be in danger. Which is it?"

"I've got to leave." She stood and started to walk away.

"It's your choice," he said. "Just say it."

Her pace slackened but she did not turn around. "I'll see you tomorrow," she said. And then she was gone.

Chapter Twenty-three

"Mrs. Tsurischeva, thank you so much for taking the time out to see me."

"My pleasure, Professor Zugelder. Do sit down. I'd love to hear about John. I lost contact with him so many years ago, you know." The woman behind the desk rose and offered her hand. "If I'd known he lived so close I would have given him a call."

The psychologist lowered himself into one of the two chairs before the desk.

"Now, what can I do for you?" she asked.

"Well, it's rather difficult to explain. I'm a psychologist at the university and John Greene is in one of my classes. This last week he's been a subject in a hypnosis study we've been conducting."

"Subject?"

"Just our terminology, Mrs. Tsurischeva. A figure of speech. We haven't dissected him, if that's what you were wondering."

She smiled, and Zugelder responded appreciatively. She was a handsome woman. Although her hair was flecked with gray, her face was remarkably unlined.

"What exactly has John been doing in this study of yours?"

"We're still trying to figure that out. You see, John was age-regressed—uh, given a suggestion to behave as he did when he was nine years old."

"And?"

"Instead of regressing to his own life at nine he apparently regressed to someone else's life."

"You must be kidding."

"Yes and no. That's why I need your help."

"I don't understand."

"John started speaking in Russian. He told us he was the Tsarevich Dmitri Ivanovich."

The woman laughed. "Who?"

"The Tsarevich Dmitri. He was the son of Ivan the Terrible. The heir to the throne of Rus."

"Yes, Professor Zugelder, I know who he was. I'm just surprised John should remember him after all these years."

"Remember him?"

"Yes. When John was little I used to baby-sit him all the time. Carol Whiting was working and I hadn't yet embarked on my career." She waved a hand over her spacious office. "One of John's favorite bedtime stories was the tale of the brave little Dmitri."

Zugelder gripped the armrests. Here it was, his proof that John had learned about the Russian prince. He proceeded with caution. "Isn't that rather an odd choice as a bedtime story, Mrs. Tsurischeva? After all, the boy is savagely murdered in the end."

"Oh, no. I can see we're dealing with two different stories. You're relying on historical fact. My story is rooted in folk legend. Like the stories told by the wandering minstrels of medieval times. They were called *byliny* in Rus. In my tale, Dmitri doesn't die; he escapes at the last moment. Some benevolent monks take him in, and for ten years they teach him all he needs to know to be a wise and just tsar. Then, when Dmitri has reached manhood, he leaves the monastery and battles the wicked Boris Godunov for his title. You see, the story actually evolved to support the legitimacy of a later tsar, the False Dmitri. I assure you, truth and goodness triumph in the end."

"Isn't that soft-pedaling history a bit?"

"It happens all the time, doesn't it? And not just in Russia. Take a look at your English nursery rhymes: 'Ring around the rosies; pocket full o' posies; ashes, ashes, we all fall down.' Good God. That poet was soft-pedaling the Black Plague. The distinctive red rings on the victims' faces and bodies; the flowered funeral wreaths; the crematory pyres that were constantly burning in hopes of stopping the disease."

"I see your point."

"Indeed. We do go to considerable lengths to shield our children, don't we? Although I suspect it's harder to do now that a child can turn on the TV and watch World War III unfold."

Zugelder steered the conversation back to John.

"Mrs. Tsurischeva, when you baby-sat John did you ever speak to him in Russian?"

"Yes, often."

"And he spoke Russian back to you?"

"I believe so. He was just at that age where children pick up languages so effortlessly."

"When did you stop baby-sitting John?"

"He was around five. Soon after Natalie was born. Carol thought she should be home with the children."

"And did you still visit?"

"No, I didn't. My husband and I moved to Europe. We've only been back in California a few years."

"Then you never talked to John in Russian again?"

"No. As I said, I lost contact with him after the fire."

Zugelder crossed his legs. "Did you ever give Carol Whiting a samovar?"

"Why yes, yes I did. I'd forgotten all about it. How did you know?"

"John's adoptive parents have it. They found it in the rubble of the house."

"Oh." Her face darkened. "Carol was a nut about anything made out of bronze. She had loads of it around the house. I remember how thrilled she was with the samovar."

"I'm sorry if I'm treading on painful ground."

"That's all right. It happened so long ago."

"There's one more thing that puzzles me. John has an extraordinary memory for all sorts of details and facts pertaining to Dmitri's life. Beyond anything he would have picked up from a folk story."

"I can't be of much help there. I do recall sending him a book on Russian history when he was a little older. Carol wrote later on that he was still enthralled with it. But I haven't the vaguest notion whether he read it—it was rather advanced for a child of his age. It probably was destroyed in the fire."

"I'll ask him about it." Zugelder jotted down a note. "You've been a great help, Mrs. Tsurischeva. I know you're a busy woman, so I won't take up any more of your time. However, I'd like to send you a form to fill out that would help us further."

"I'll be glad to help, Professor Zugelder. Say hello to John for me. Tell him I'd like to get together with him sometime."

"I will. Thank you again."

Zugelder left the office elated, positive that his instincts had been correct from the start. Hypermnesia, no doubt about it. As the elevator descended he tried to imagine the looks on the others' faces as he told them what he'd discovered. The whole rigmarole could finally be laid to rest.

John could go back to his classes and Dmitri could return
to his stone sepulcher. He hoped.

Perry began to think he'd lost his mind. This was his
third time around the outside of the geology building and
he still hadn't spied the entrance to Sutter wing. It was
getting embarrassing. He stopped and sat on the edge of
Bracker fountain and studied the map in the back of the
student directory one more time. He was surprised to see
the fountain running.

Bracker fountain was a recent addition to the university
grounds. At a cost of nearly one million dollars, it combined the worst features of a Hawaiian waterfall with those
of the ancient Roman baths. The students agreed that it
resembled an oversized washing machine in the rinse cycle.
Mr. Bracker, a wealthy businessman from Akron, had
donated the money, stipulating that it be used to build a
fountain. He hadn't cared that California was in the middle
of a drought at the time. No fountain, no money.

The student body reacted negatively to this personifica-
tion of Mr. Bracker's ego at the expense of conservation
measures. The fountain was the focus of so much derision,
in fact, that it had lain dry for two years. But now, with
the arrival of the rain, it apparently was welcomed into the
community.

Perry refolded the directory and resolutely strode toward
the building. To his delight, he accidentally found the
entrance to Sutter wing. He twisted through the corridor
and entered the office of Tomás Martínez, associate professor of geology. The geologist happily dropped what he
was doing to analyze the stone that Perry produced from
his pocket.

"It's an opal, all right."

"That's what we thought. Then it's valuable?"

"Of course. It's a semiprecious stone. I happen to think they should charge more for them. So many of our semiprecious stones are far more alluring than their precious counterparts." He held the stone to a light. "Beautiful, isn't it? What did you want to know about it?"

"Whether it came from Poland or not."

"Poland?" The professor was clearly taken aback.

"I know it sounds like an odd request."

"Well, sure, there are always ways to determine the origins of a stone. Naturally it'll have to be run through a lot of tests." He picked off some grit from the back of the gem. "You know, Poland isn't exactly famous for its opals."

"Then it couldn't have come from there?"

"I didn't say that. It's just that opals are pretty synonymous with Australia these days. Over ninety percent of them come from there." He sensed Perry's disappointment. "But that isn't saying this particular opal is Australian."

"What about before Australia was colonized? Which regions supplied opals to the world?"

"To tell you the truth, I'm not really sure. You think this opal is that old? Sure is in fine condition." He handed the stone back to Perry. "It's easy enough to check where the main supply was. I've got books here on practically every stone you'd ever want to know about. And then some."

Perry sat down as the geologist tugged a binder from the shelf and spread it across his desk.

"What do you know. You're not too far off. Seems the major opal deposit was in what's now eastern Czechoslovakia. Right on the southern slopes of the Carpathian mountains. Near a place called Prešov. See? Look on this map. What made you guess Poland?"

"A friend told me. Go on, what else does it say?"

"The area was the main supply of opals for two thousand years. Even the Romans mined it. But its location was a well-kept secret, so well kept that many Europeans in the Middle Ages referred to the stone as 'oriental,' thinking it came from the Far East."

Perry made a swift calculation in his head. In Dmitri's time Czechoslovakia had not existed and Poland had been a larger state than it was now. He visualized the geographical area around the Carpathian range. Yes, eastern Czechoslovakia could have been a part of sixteenth-century Poland.

Perry rubbed the gem between his hands. Could it really have once belonged to the Tsarevich Dmitri?

"Do you mind if I look at that map?"

"No." Martínez turned the binder to its side. "Not at all."

Perry scanned the brightly colored map, not really looking for anything in particular. Small dots, located within the red area that designated the opal reserves, marked the largest mining settlements. A name popped out at him. Dubnik. Dmitri had called out that name before he left for church. Goosebumps formed on Perry's arms.

Something in the back of his mind nagged him. Something about the stone. Why an opal? Why hadn't Dmitri given Marina a different gem, perhaps one more likely to have been found in Rus? He had said it was lucky for him. Why? What was special about it?

The stone sparkled in Perry's hand and suddenly he understood. The opal, whose luminescence had been coveted for thousands of years. Glowing but without heat. Milky white, but a panoply of colors.

And also the October birthstone of Dmitri Ivanovich. It had heralded his birth. And now his death.

SATURDAY,
MAY 15

Chapter Twenty-four

卐 卐 卐

Marina woke with a tight, dry throat and an uneasiness gnawing at the pit of her stomach. Her hand trembled as she turned on the bathroom faucet and filled a glass of water. Swallowing was difficult.

The luminous dial of her digital clock read six-thirty. The darkness outside her window seemed more like two-thirty. Either way, too early to get up.

Crawling back between the sheets, she tried to still her racing mind. No use. Her thoughts darted in wildly scattered directions, reverberating in every fiber of her body. They ranged from planning her weekend to washing her hair to doing assignments for various classes, but always they returned to the same locus: Dmitri and John.

Scrapping the idea of sleep, she eased herself out of bed and ransacked the kitchen. In the refrigerator she found a tube of ready-made biscuits. While they baked she cracked two eggs in a bowl.

She pulled back the breakfast-nook curtains, faded by years of morning sunrises, and thought about the young tsarevich. All she had to tell him was "Don't go outside today. Get inside right now." She'd explain that she'd read his fortune and it was dangerous for him to venture into the courtyard. He trusted her now. He'd listen to her advice and follow it.

What if he did follow it? she asked herself. Would the killers enter the palace and murder him there? Would they wait a day? Her head spun. It was all so crazy. For years her father had urged her to "Take some math, Marina. It'll teach you to think logically." She'd waded through geometry and trigonometry and calculus. And for what? Logic couldn't help her now. She was dealing with the illogical, the irrational. The impossible.

What would happen if he lived? Would all of Sloane's dire predictions come true?

And there was John to consider. Could he survive the tsarevich's death? Hour by hour the lives of the two grew more inseparable. John had become steadily more withdrawn until he was now totally without expression, seemingly resigned to whatever happened. Last night, though Marina hadn't told him of her talk with Sloane and Carter, nor revealed that Dmitri was to be killed today, John had acted strangely, as if somewhere deep inside of him he sensed the coming of his own personal Armageddon. He had not spent the night with her but had instead returned to the dorm, displaying an uncharacteristic solitariness that alarmed her.

She wished she could rid him of his melancholy. But she was certain of only one thing: She could not risk his life. He would be safe as long as the boy was safe.

If she warned Dmitri, he could tell his uncle, and the family could seek asylum. Yes, John would be saved. But Dmitri, would he really be saved? Chances were, she knew, he would be killed later. A year, maybe two. What was it that Queen Elizabeth's envoy had heard? That Dmitri was "not safe from attempts" on his life by those "that aspire to the succession, if this emperor [Tsar Feodor] dies without issue." If it wasn't Shuisky who killed Dmitri, someone else would. And for similar ambitious reasons. Perhaps not during the short lifetime of the Princess Feodosia—Feodor's daughter—since she temporarily would void Dmitri's claim to the throne. But after she died as an infant? Would the assassins gravitate to Dmitri once more?

Marina whipped the eggs and poured them into a skillet. Light streamed in the open window and illuminated the old tablecloth.

If she didn't warn him, he would die. Did she have the strength to stand by and watch him be murdered? She didn't know. Though the worldwide changes predicted by Sloane should the boy live were abstract and difficult to envision, she had no trouble visualizing Dmitri's death. What should have been intangible to her, a murder committed four centuries earlier, was imbued with a startling reality.

What if Dmitri had survived the attack, as some scholars suggested? Grigory Otrepiev—the *razstrign*, or unfrocked monk, who became False Dmitri—could he have been the tsarevich in disguise? He knew every intimate detail of the real Dmitri's life. His likes and dislikes, his habits and idiosyncrasies, the names of Dmitri's friends and pets. In Poland False Dmitri even recognized and conversed with a former servant of the tsarevich called Petrovsky.

But Marina knew it could not be so. False Dmitri's appearance contrasted sharply with that of the tsarevich. Although blond and blue-eyed, he lacked Dmitri's facial features and physical attributes. His bones were too large, his waist too short.

Marina placed the food on a plate but was not able to eat. Descriptions of False Dmitri lingered in her mind. She remembered passages in Philip Barbour's book, *Dimitry*:

> First of all, as more than one writer has pointed out, it is improper to call False Dmitri an "imposter"

or a "pretender." He was convinced that he was the son of Ivan.

The man who was crowned tsar [False Dmitri] by all accounts and signs firmly believed that he was heir to the throne. Therefore, if he was not the tsarevich, he can also hardly have been a deliberate imposter.

But if False Dmitri was not the tsarevich, and not an imposter, who was he?

Her thoughts turned to John. She and he had begun to make plans, far-reaching plans, to carry them through the coming years. What if there were no years to come? If—after today—all that remained of the man she loved were memories? Those plans, those hopes, would be cruel reminders of what she had lost. And she would seethe with the knowledge that she was responsible.

She didn't know why she tortured herself with such thoughts. There was no choice to be made. It had been made a long time ago when she'd first discovered that she loved John Greene.

She would not give him up without a fight.

Marina raised her right arm above her head and stretched it. The six-sided scab on her forearm itched. She recalled the agony Dmitri had endured that morning three days ago during the epileptic seizure. His face had been contorted in pain. His body, a mass of tremors. No, she couldn't watch him suffer again. She couldn't be the witness to his murder, to the end of that vibrant life.

If she had a wish, it would be that Dmitri's life was not in danger today. That his mother would kidnap him and that history would plod along its course.

But if that were not the case and she took action against

his death, she prayed that she would still be born, that the world would not be too different, and that somewhere, in time and space, she would once again find John Greene, and he would be waiting for her.

"Good morning." Carter, dressed in a pair of bermuda shorts and a T-shirt, having acclimated quickly to the California weather, appeared in the doorway of the Sloanes' kitchen. The red stubble on his chin was dotted with white—a pattern, Sloane knew, that dismayed Carter as much as it did Carter's three-year-old daughter, who had expected the beard to turn pink as he aged.

"Morning, Andrew." Blake smiled at him. "What say I fix you an omelet? Cheese and bacon okay?"

"That's fine. Thank you."

"You want some coffee, old man?" Sloane rose from the table.

"No, thanks. Can't seem to handle it on an empty stomach anymore. Water's fine."

"So how far did you get in the books?"

"Far enough to realize that there aren't very many other cases like this one." He took a sip of water. "But I think you knew that already."

"It did cross my mind."

"Frankly, I'm disturbed by the turn of events this case has taken."

"What do you mean?"

"Dmitri's hold on John. It's as though he's taken over John's body. Look at the long periods of time it's been taking John to emerge from trance. Or his fainting spell yesterday. I don't like it."

"What do you think accounts for it?"

"I don't know."

Blake set Carter's steaming omelet before him, and

Sloane retreated as the two engaged in conversation about Karen Carter's new job. He walked to the kitchen counter and ruminated about Carter's time-dislocation theory, about the give and take of time, energy, and matter.

Sloane gazed out the kitchen window and admired his grapefruit tree, the only survivor of a harried summer three years earlier when he'd tried his hand at what Blake facetiously termed "therapeutic farming." The tree was in full bloom, its limbs bowed with sprays of flowers, its roots deeply sunk in ground where an oak had once stood. The oak had deteriorated long ago, returning to the soil what it had taken in life.

That was how everything worked in the world, Sloane supposed. In cycles. The oak, now in an unrecognizable, decomposed form, enriched the grapefruit tree, which in turn would age and decay, ultimately replenishing the soil with the life-giving nutrients needed should another seed fall on that spot.

Maybe John Greene was just such a seed. Not merely receiving Dmitri's "signals" from across time and space, but actually absorbing the tsarevich, a boy who had somehow escaped the burial of his earthly body and was now embodied in a new, but no less real, form in the corner of John Greene's mind. A form assumed, like that of the mighty oak, through death.

Sloane turned around as Carter unfolded the newspaper. From where he stood he could read one of the headlines on the third page.

Dmitri, the Moscow panda, had died mysteriously in the night.

Zugelder mailed the appropriate forms to Mrs. Tsurischeva and hopped back in his car, clutching a stream of stamps commemorating extinct animals, among them the dodo bird, remembered chiefly for running toward its attackers instead of away from them. A genetic boo-boo in the parade of evolution.

Eyeing the dashboard clock, he was disheartened to learn that he was due at 130–B in less than two hours. What a rotten way to spend a beautiful Saturday. He and his wife had had it all planned. They were going to drive to the beach, have lunch at their favorite seafood restaurant, then go sailing. He didn't know why he'd let Sloane and that grad student talk him into showing up on a Saturday. Must have been his exuberance at having tracked down the Russian link in John's past. He'd not yet told the others of his visit with Mrs. Tsurischeva but planned to spring it on them during today's session. In the meantime, he delighted in the knowledge that was his alone, the "truth" behind Dmitri's presence in the twentieth century.

Zugelder drove slowly down Ashley Street and waved at the cop parked near the corner. The policeman was there, ostensibly, to catch speeders. In reality, he'd long since abandoned his idling motorcycle, devoting most of his day to exchanging "hellos" and "so-longs" and occasional neighborhood anecdotes with pedestrians and slow-moving motorists.

As Zugelder drove past campus, he remembered that he hadn't picked up the analysis of John's voiceprints. Maybe Roger would be in his lab, he mused. He knew that the technician, a conscientious man, often toiled on weekends.

Sure enough, Roger was hard at work.

"This is criminal. Do you realize what a gorgeous day it is outside?" asked Zugelder.

"Yep. Problem is it was a gorgeous day yesterday and I took the day off. I cut out and went waterskiing." He patted the pile of work on his desk. "So now I'm paying for my frivolity. Penitence, you know. Good for the soul."

"I should have known."

"So to what do I owe the honor of this visit?"

"I forgot to collect the results of those voiceprints." Zugelder smiled and folded his arms. "Not that it would have done any good had I shown up, since you were out being decadent."

"Don't get nasty. You're just trying to conceal your senility. Memory's the first thing to go, they say." He pulled a rubber band off a roll of white paper. "What did you want these done for, anyway?"

"For a hypnosis experiment that Dustin Sloane and I are conducting."

"What about?"

"Oh, we age-regressed a student to nine and he started talking Russian. Says he doesn't know it. So one tape is of him speaking while hypnotized and the other is him reading Russian phonetically."

Roger appeared surprised. He stopped unrolling the sheets of paper. "You mean it's the same kid speaking on both tapes?"

"Well, sure." Zugelder was flustered. "Isn't that what you came up with?"

"Hell, no. These two voiceprints are as different as night and day. No way it could have been the same person."

"Are you positive?"

"See for yourself." Roger swiftly unrolled the prints, laying them side by side. He pointed to the graphs. "Time is plotted along the horizontal, frequency along the vertical. Those black lines you see are the amplitude of the speaker's voice. When a person speaks he gives his own characteristic reading of each word. The configurations that result are as reliable as fingerprints in identifying people. Compare these two. They're totally different. You must have gotten your tapes mixed."

Zugelder's pulse raced and he sat down, reeling from the news. It just couldn't be.

"Roger, that's impossible. I only had two tapes."

"Let me double-check, then. Maybe I goofed some-where."

He played the first tape for the two of them. John Greene's phonetic Russian filled the room. Zugelder chewed on a nail as Roger loaded the next tape.

It was the right tape, all right. Dmitri's voice, loud and clear. High-pitched, harsh. A note of trepidation under-lying every word. A voice from the grave.

Dmitri was to die today. No one had told John; he'd read it in their faces yesterday. In the way Marina looked at him, as though he were rappeling down a steep precipice with a rope of questionable fiber. In the way the atmos-phere was scored with a brooding sense of doom, of impending blight.

Yes, Dmitri was to die today.

John wheeled his bike across the dorm patio. He was not frightened. He was relieved. Today would bring an end to his nightmares, a resolution to the conflict within himself. He would wake up after the session and the boy would be gone. Forever.

Only the induction bothered him now. To know that he would lose control of his body once more, vacate it. To lose track of time. Maybe Dmitri was like that. Maybe there was no one around to tell the tsarevich that time had passed, that he had lived beyond his era.

John coasted to the stop sign, and whipping the bike around the corner, changed gears on the small incline. From far off he heard drumming. He guessed the school band was practicing for a rally but he didn't hear any music. Funny. Just the beat. He strained to hear the other instruments.

The noise intensified as he pedaled. It wasn't drumming exactly. More like an abnormally loud heart palpitation.

A throb. Rhythmic but with variations in pitch. It irritated him and he stopped the bike.

The sound was directionless. He cocked his head to one side but couldn't isolate its origins. It was just there, droning on and on. He mounted the bike again.

John stopped by the student store for a soft drink. Cut off by the concrete walls, the sound declined in volume. He asked the cashier if she heard it, but she shook her head.

Wonderful, he thought as he rode toward the quad—killer bees have attacked campus and the administrators are waiting to sell the movie rights before they do anything about it. The sound grew louder, less muffled. His temples ached.

John entered Hester quad, and for the first time was able to pinpoint the direction from which the beat came. He decided to follow it. The psychologists were not expecting him for another ten minutes. Coasting by Jackson Hall and 130–B, he cycled in a straight line across the quad. He discerned words within the noise. Like a chant.

It was very loud now. He could distinguish a man's voice speaking in a rapid, clipped manner, almost as if reciting a litany. But instead of an audience's response, there was only that vexing din. John got off his bike and walked it along the corridor. He followed the staccato tones to their source: Hester Memorial Church.

The background cadence accelerated, drowning out the man's voice with its heavy, pulsating beat. John stood outside the carved oak doors, hesitant to enter and disturb the liturgy in process. He wanted to look through a window, but there wasn't one accessible. The pace of the beat inside increased, threatening to sunder the very walls that contained it. John could stand it no longer.

Gripping the handle, he thrust open the doors. The noise ceased abruptly. The church was empty.

Chapter Twenty-five

"Hi."

"Hello." The boy smiled and touched Marina's hand. "Your sling's gone. How's your arm?"

"Much better, thank you."

"I'm sorry I hurt it. You believe me, don't you? That I'm sorry I hurt you?"

"Yes, I believe you." She spoke softly. "You didn't have to give me the opal, you know."

"I know. It wasn't just because I hurt you." His face brightened. "You like it, don't you?"

"It's beautiful, Dmitri. I'll treasure it."

"I'm glad you came today. I've got most of the afternoon free now that church is done with."

"That's right. I forgot you had church today. How did the services go?"

"Tedious as ever. We got another sermon on sinners. That's the fourth in the last three weeks. I think he needs to expand his repertoire."

She smiled weakly.

"You seem unhappy today."

"No, just tired."

"Your friend, you're worried about him supporting you, aren't you?" the boy guessed. "He hasn't come up with any money."

"Yes, we are feeling the pinch."

"I never much liked your friend. I hope you don't mind if I'm so candid, but he never seemed to me much of a provider."

"No, that he isn't."

"Good. Then we'll have no argument. You'll stay here."

"Stay here?"

"Yes, my nurse is leaving. Uncle Mikhail is looking for a new one. You were inquiring about jobs, weren't you? I'll simply select you."

"But I thought you hadn't been telling him about me."

"I haven't. But I can pretend that I've never seen you. When I tell him that I've taken an 'instant' liking to you, he'll listen to me."

"I don't know if I can." A lump formed in her throat. How much she wanted to tell the boy the truth about who she was and where she came from.

He responded with a mixture of anger and hurt. "Why not?"

"It's just that I've got responsibilities to think about, my family, my friends. . . ." She realized there was no point in wounding the boy. "I guess I'm not used to such generous offers. I'd be happy to be your nurse."

His face beamed. "I'll take you to meet the others."

"Now? I couldn't possibly."

"Of course you can."

"Isn't this a little premature? I haven't got the job yet. Besides, I've got things to clear up first." She reached over and squeezed his arm. "Don't worry. I'll have plenty of time to meet them."

In the audience, Sloane touched his headphones and looked sideways at Andrew. What could she be thinking?

"Plenty of time"—was she seriously contemplating saving the boy? Carter returned his look with a shrug. It was all up to her now.

"Especially Vladimir. I want you to meet Vladimir."

"He'll be the first person you'll introduce to me." Marina grasped the boy's hand. "Dmitri, there's something I must tell you."

Sloane started to his feet. He was prepared to stop her if she warned the boy. Marina noticed him stand and she glared at him, resenting his attempt to control her actions onstage.

Zugelder poked Sloane in the side. "Don't get so worked up. This isn't for real, you know."

"It is now, Cy. You don't know what you're talking about."

"Oh, don't I?" Zugelder had wanted to talk about his conversation with Natasha Tsurischeva at the beginning of the session, but Sloane had been anxious to start the induction. Now seemed as good a time as any to break his news. "John Greene knows all about Dmitri."

"What are you talking about?" Sloane was trying to listen to both Zugelder and Marina. He kept his eyes on the stage.

"He had a Russian baby-sitter when he was a kid. She taught him the language." Zugelder slipped off the headphones and hung them around his neck. "And she told me John's favorite bedtime story was about the brave prince Dmitri Ivanovich."

"What?" Sloane turned to his colleague. "I don't believe it."

"She even sent him a book on Russian history. See for yourself." He handed Sloane the preliminary report he'd compiled on Mrs. Tsurischeva. As he did, Zugelder's hand shook. He did not mention the voiceprint analysis. Though he'd tried to convince himself that a mechanical error accounted for the configurations of the graphs, still his hand shook.

From her vantage point on stage, Marina was able to see the two men conferring. She figured Zugelder was persuading Sloane not to interfere with her actions onstage. Good for him, she thought.

"What were you going to tell me?" The tsarevich tugged at her hand.

"Oh"—she rested her eyes once more on the boy's face—"that I'm, um, not really a fortune-teller. To tell you the truth, I don't know anything. I sort of made up that spiel about your palm yesterday."

"I figured as much. I've seen all my mother's soothsayers and you didn't act a bit like them."

"You knew?"

"It's all right." He smiled at her with an impish, forgiving look. "I rather enjoyed it."

"You little rascal"—she tweaked his nose—"letting me make a fool of myself like that. I can see I'm going to have to be more careful around you. Hey, what say we celebrate my new job?"

"Great."

"What do you feel like doing?"

He sat down and hugged his knees to his chest. "I'd like to go out on the river, but that would entail getting past the guards. How about a game of *tycha?* I could teach you." He jumped up enthusiastically.

Panic seized Marina. Her knees nearly buckled and a vertiginous haze enveloped her. With effort, she answered as calmly as she could. "No, I don't want to do that."

He sensed the fright in her voice and backed off from her. "What's wrong?" he asked.

"Nothing." She detected his bewilderment and held out her hand to him. "I'm sorry. I felt weak for a moment."

"Should I get you something?"

"No. I'll be fine."

"Maybe you should sit down." He stooped and swept the ground. Suddenly he rose, his eyes fixed on a point in the distance. He waved his arm and yelled, "Just a minute!" He touched Marina's hand. "I'll be back in a moment."

"Where are you going?" Her heart strained against her breastbone. She sensed the time had come.

"Iosif, he wants something."

Iosif Volokhova, the son of Dmitri's governess. Was he Shuisky's agent? He was merely a child. Yet children are easily duped, and Marina was certain that Iosif's appearance at this moment was no coincidence. Her intuition told her that he'd admitted a man into the courtyard. A man who, with a single plunge of the knife, would deliver Rus into the throes of an era known simply as the Time of Troubles.

Marina frantically pulled on the boy's hand. A hot flush spread up her neck to her face, where it clustered in great pink blotches. The sweat streamed under her clothes.

"Ignore him, Dmitri." Her breathing was rapid. She was alarming the boy. For his sake, she tried to regain control. "C'mon, let's go over there." She hoped she sounded casual. "I don't want to meet anyone yet."

"No, he's coming over here." The boy took two steps toward the invisible assailant.

"Dmitri, no!" Marina choked on the words. Her eyes were wide with terror.

"What's the matter?" The boy turned to her. "Are you sick?"

"Dmitri, we must leave." She tried to push him in front of her, shield him from the deadly thrust that she knew was coming.

"What are you doing?" He tried to break her hold.

"We can't stay here. You're going to get hurt."

"By Iosif? Don't make me laugh. He's as timid as

Daniil." The boy waved his free hand in the air. "Look, there's Vasilisa."

Vasilisa. The woman in John's dream. It was all coming true.

"Not by Iosif but by a man he's bringing to you."

"I don't see a man."

Marina continued to steer the tsarevich to the edge of the stage. Sloane, who realized what was taking place before the translation reached his ears, left his seat and moved toward the stage stairs.

Carter caught his arm. "Dusty, let them be. You don't know what you're doing. Your actions could have a more devastating effect than hers."

"She's the one who doesn't realize the enormity of what she's attempting to do. That boy simply cannot live." He tried to march toward the stairs, but Carter held him fast.

A few feet away, Zugelder whispered to Perry, "Honestly, I don't know why they're taking this so seriously. It's just like play-acting, that's all." His hand had not stopped shaking.

"Dmitri"—tears ran freely down Marina's face—"believe me. Do what I say. Flee! Run!" She tugged at his sleeve. He moved in her direction. She pulled harder.

"Marina! Don't do it!" Sloane had broken free of Carter and gripped the edge of the stage. He knew he couldn't let her reach the stairs.

"I have to!" she yelled at him, her hand firmly clenched around that of the bewildered boy. "I can't let him die!" She ran with the boy to the end of the stage.

Sloane grabbed the videotape cord in front of him and gave one hard tug.

In later years, looking back on that moment, Sloane wondered what would have happened had he not tripped Marina. What would history have been like? So different, he imagined. He liked to think that his world, with history as it had always been, was preferable. But he did not linger on the thought. He never regretted the action he took that day.

The taut cord caught Marina squarely across the right ankle. She tripped and crumpled to the floor. The boy bent over her.

"Don't wait for me. Run! Hurry! Go out that way."

The boy did not move. He squatted next to her.

"Dmitri, listen to me. Your life is in danger. I'll be all right. Now please, run. Go and hide." She clutched him in her arms, then forced him to stand. He stood over her, torn as to whether he should heed her warning. Confused, he did as she asked but stopped within a matter of feet. This was his friend. The only person aside from Vladimir who ever had shown him love and affection. How could he abandon her? He retraced his steps.

Instantly his body snapped back, jerked by some unseen power. The boy ripped at the phantom limb pinned across his chest. His ribs pushed into his lungs and he gasped. Marina let out a cry. The boy struggled, feet moving in all directions, arms flailing about helplessly. Sloane stood by horrified, rendered immobile by the ghastly tableau. The boy levitated a foot in the air, arms outstretched, hovering above the ground in the strong arms of his killer.

He gazed in terror above him, his eyes riveted on the spectral dagger. Fighting with every ounce of strength he was able to muster, he thrashed wildly in his captor's grip. His lungs grew more constricted and he panted while clawing at the arm around him until his fingernails were torn.

And then, from the boy's lips, came a scream of agony. His head snapped back and the cry was cut short by an ugly gurgle. A death rattle. His legs collapsed and he doubled over in a heap, weltering in a pool of unseen blood.

Near the steps Marina was screaming and trying to

scramble to where the boy lay. Her body shook with great heaving sobs. Sloane rushed to her, taking her by the arms, but she clawed at him and lashed out with her fists.

"You killed him! You killed them both! Get away from me!" She pushed away from Sloane and slid over to the boy. "Oh God, John, I'm sorry. I shouldn't have told you to go along with this. I'm sorry, I'm. . . ." She held one of his lifeless hands in hers.

Zugelder remained in the semidarkness of the auditorium repeating over and over to himself "This isn't real, it isn't real," until finally he screamed it to the inanimate body onstage, as if trying to wake it from its final sleep.

Perry scurried up the steps and checked the boy's pulse. He administered cardiopulmonary resuscitation as the tsarevich's life ebbed away.

It was precisely one-fifteen.

The hospital emergency waiting room smelled of antiseptic, bleached uniforms, and coffee. Marina, Zugelder, and Carter sat on the lounge sofas. Sloane stood. Perry was at a public wall phone calling John's parents.

Marina's face was puffy. Her eyelids were rimmed with red and her face was mottled with pink patches. She looked exhausted. Her backpack rested on her lap and her ankle was bound in an Ace bandage. She'd ridden in the ambulance with John. The young man had not regained consciousness.

In the ambulance, one of the paramedics had pinched John's arm, and when he had not responded to the pain the paramedic had termed him comatose. He had shined a penlight in John's eyes to make sure his pupils weren't fixed and dilated, an indication of brain damage. The paramedics praised Perry's quick reactions on the stage. All of John's vital signs were normal.

A doctor approached Marina and the three psychologists. Perry returned just as he was asking the group what had happened.

Sloane cleared his throat. "He was under hypnosis and, uh, he must have seen something that frightened him because he passed out."

The doctor raised his pen from the clipboard. "He passed out? That's all?"

"No, he seemed to go into some kind of . . . fit. He started shaking."

"Did it start from any particular part of the body?"

"No, all over. And he gave this sort of high-pitched scream."

"Did you happen to notice whether his eyes rolled back in their sockets?"

"Yeah, I think so. And he was clenching his teeth. Then he—"

"Levitated," said Marina softly.

"He what?" asked the doctor.

Perry put his arm around Marina. "She's not thinking clearly. That's her boyfriend in there."

"Okay, so what happened next?" resumed the doctor.

"He passed out," answered Sloane. "And Perry administered CPR."

"He'd stopped breathing?"

"Yes," said Perry.

"And his heart?"

"I didn't get a pulse. Or else it was too weak for me to feel it. I didn't waste any time searching for it."

The doctor clicked his pen on the clipboard. "Sounds like a tonicoclonic seizure. That just means a motor seizure, one with convulsions. Must have been a particularly bad one to stop his breathing. He have any other seizures like this?"

Sloane and Zugelder gave simultaneous and conflicting answers.

"No."

"Yes."

"Which is it?"

"He had a seizure similar to this one on Wednesday," said Zugelder, "only not as severe."

"Why didn't he seek medical help then?"

"You'd have to ask him."

"Anything else?"

"Yes," continued Zugelder, ignoring the disapproving stares from the others. "He was complaining of disturbances of sleep, and of . . . hallucinations."

"Cy!" Sloane whispered hoarsely, pulling Zugelder to one side. "Those weren't hallucinations and you know it."

"I don't know any such thing. You're going to risk John's life just because you're convinced about time dislocation? Dustin, we've got to give this doctor all possible symptoms. Remember that palace John told us about on Friday morning after his fainting spell? The one he'd seen on the raft trip? That palace could have been a hallucination." Zugelder turned back to the doctor. "Yes, hallucinations. And he fainted once."

"Well, if I had to guess I'd say he's going through some kind of withdrawal. Does he use drugs?"

"No!" Marina answered.

"You sure?"

"Of course, I'm sure."

"What about alcohol? Is he an excessive drinker?"

"No," she declared.

"It has to be something else," Sloane interjected. "What else causes seizures?"

"All sorts of things. Tumors. Trauma. Metabolic disorders."

"He was stabbed," Marina said.

"What?" asked the physician.

Perry tried to stop her from talking. "Marina, maybe we better get you some fresh—"

"He was stabbed. In the neck," she insisted.

"Lady, there's not a mark on his body. Maybe you'd better lie down."

"No, I'm telling you the truth." She stood before the doctor. "We all saw it. They're just afraid to tell you."

"Sure—" The doctor was interrupted by a young intern. "Excuse me for just a second." The two physicians conferred in low tones a short distance away.

"The guy's lucky," said the intern. "For a while Nigel thought he might be hemorrhaging and wanted to take a spinal tap. But we got the first tests back. It's his glucose count. Down to thirty-five milligrams per one hundred ccs."

"Hypoglycemic, huh? Hmm. I've never known one of those seizures to be this bad. What's Nigel done?"

"Put him on an IV of D_5W at one hundred ccs per hour and given him an amp of $D_{50}W$."

"Fifty percent glucose? Good. That'll bring him up to a seventy-five count before long. Okay, get back to Nigel." The doctor smiled. "Tell him I'm gonna let him come out here and talk to relatives and friends for a while. We got a woman out here who claims the guy was stabbed."

The intern made a swirling motion next to his head with his right hand. "Time for the crazy bin. I'd move her out when she asks to see George Washington."

"Yeah." The doctor clipped his pen to his jacket pocket and walked back to the anxious group. "You're in luck. He's pulling out of it."

Marina bit her lip to keep from crying.

"Thank God." Sloane wiped his forehead. "What did you find wrong?"

"He's hypoglycemic. That means his blood sugar is way down. When it's as low as his was, it can produce seizures."

"And hallucinations?" prodded Zugelder.

"It might. Although that usually is only found with

seizures of the withdrawal type. It could cause a person to be jittery, or break out in a cold sweat for no reason. To feel weak."

"What made his blood sugar drop?" asked Sloane.

"I don't know. That's what we're gonna have to find out. He's not diabetic, is he?"

"No," Marina answered. She realized now why the others hadn't mentioned the stabbing. The doctor thought her crazy, and skeptical of her credibility, looked to Sloane for confirmation of her answer. "Look," she backtracked, "I didn't mean what I said before. I was upset and thinking about something else. But believe me: I know John isn't diabetic."

"All right." The doctor frowned thoughtfully. "I'll take your word—for now. The tests will decide the matter."

"Why do you ask?" queried Sloane. "I thought diabetes was the opposite of hypoglycemia."

"It is. But occasionally diabetics will overdose on their insulin. You know anything about the family's medical history?"

The five people shook their heads from side to side.

"Well, if he's just developing a diabetic-like condition, then this seizure might indicate what we call reactive hypoglycemia. That's where the body overcompensates for a high level of blood sugar. What about his eating habits? Normal? Does he get good nutrition?"

"Yes," Marina replied.

The doctor marked a few notes on the paper in his clipboard. "This doesn't give us much to go on. Could be any number of things. Hormonal imbalances. Liver-enzyme deficiencies. Pancreatic disease. We're going to have to run him through some tests."

"Where is he now?" asked Marina. "Can we see him?"

"Sure. They'll be rolling him out any minute. That glucose takes effect immediately. He'll be moved up to the neurology ward." The doctor rocked back on his heels and peered down the corridor. "Yeah, here he comes now."

The visitors got to their feet as the gurney was wheeled toward the elevator. John lay on it, his head propped on a pillow. He opened his eyes and the expression on his face resembled that of a trapped animal.

Spotting Marina, he clutched the bed sheet tightly in his hands and asked, "Where am I? What is this place? Marina, who are these people?" His voice trembled. But the boyish pitch, clarion and intense, was unmistakable, rising as it did with each word he spoke. The language was Russian.

Marina shrank against the wall. Dmitri had been saved after all.

Chapter Twenty-six

"Look, I don't know. I don't know! You can't expect me to come up with all the answers." Sloane paced the lounge. "Jesus Christ!" He crushed the paper cup in his hand and tossed it among the refuse of the trash can.

Carter repeated his inquiry. "Well, what are we going to do? We can't let that boy take over John's body."

"Terrific idea, Andy. What do you suggest we do? Call our local exorcist? Christ, he's just a little boy and he's being asked to believe the unbelievable. Poor kid doesn't even know what's going on." Sloane angrily stubbed out his cigarette in the ceramic ashtray, openly displaying his frayed nerves.

"Sit down, Dus. We've got to calm down before we start discussing tactics." Carter's equanimity prevailed. Sloane stopped pacing.

"Tactics?" Perry laughed feebly. "Sounds as though we're about to enter into battle."

"That's about the size of it." Carter wiped his neck with a handkerchief. "Once our friend Dmitri understands the predicament, I doubt he'll want to release his hold on John. It means almost certain death for him if he does. Off to oblivion. Moreover, he may not be able to leave John's body even if he wants to. He may not know how."

"Then it's all over." Perry's words conveyed a fatalistic appraisal of the situation. "John's lost."

"What's wrong with you people? Didn't you hear the doctor? It's his blood sugar. He's been hallucinating. It probably triggered this whole make-believe world of his," said Zugelder, but without the fervor of conviction.

"Cyrus, a person doesn't levitate from low blood sugar. Nor produce stones out of thin air. I don't think even you still think this is a case of hypermnesia, now do you?" said Sloane.

Zugelder did not answer.

"I know there's an explanation for all of this," said Marina. "The solution is right in our grasp, I can feel it. Staring us in the face. It's got to be right here, right. . . ."

As Marina turned to look out the window, a cloud of butterflies caught her eye, their dark, dappled wings merging with the trees around the patio. Something clicked in her mind.

These butterflies were mutants, descendants of cream-colored insects which over the course of time had foiled avian predators by adapting to the environment around them, gradually assuming variegated hues which allowed them to blend in with the surrounding tree bark. Through evolution, their color had changed, but inside they remained the same—as if they had merely been transferred to more durable host bodies.

What if this were the case with Dmitri?

Was it possible, she mused, that Dmitri, at the moment of his supposed death, had discarded his earthly body and projected himself centuries ahead and into John's mind? Could he, like the dappled butterflies, have escaped his predator? Certainly his and the butterflies' ultimate goal was the same: survival. Why couldn't it be that just as the insects slowly evolved, exchanging their light-colored bodies for ones progressively darker, Dmitri also was evolving? Using John as a "temporary" form, one to be vacated when he found the form he was meant to assume permanently. But what might that form be?

Another click and the answer flashed past her mind's eye like a bright neon light illuminating a dark and hidden corridor.

Grigory Otrepiev. The False Dmitri, tsar of Rus.

"We've got one last chance."

"What do you mean?" asked Zugelder. "What last chance?"

"We can convince Dmitri to take over someone else's body."

Zugelder looked at her as though the ordeal had snapped her mind.

"Don't stare at me that way. I'm fine. What if you were right"—she pointed to Sloane—"and this was all destined to happen? What if we're playing the exact role we are intended to play in history? If, somehow, our actions are predetermined. We're fulfilling only what history has already recorded." She noted their skeptical looks. "Just listen to what I'm saying before you pass judgment. What if, furthermore, you accept the hypothesis that somehow a person's essence, his soul if you will, can on certain rare occasions be picked up like radio waves by another person, providing that person possesses the particular criteria needed to house the essence."

"What criteria?"

"I don't know. That's not important to us right now."

"This all sounds pretty much off the wall to me." Zugelder leaned against the window.

"Just wait a minute. John is one of those people. He has whatever combination Dmitri needs to manifest himself. But there's another man who has that same combination. Someone who can house Dmitri as well as John. Better, in fact."

"What good does that do?" asked Zugelder. "You'd be wiping out a different person, taking over his body instead of John's. You can't play God, you know."

Marina cornered Zugelder against the tinted windowpane. "But what if it was supposed to happen? What if this whole insane mess occurred because it was necessary? If history, as we know it, couldn't come to pass without our intervention."

"Just what are you saying?" asked Carter.

"Dmitri is to become Grigory Otrepiev. The False Dmitri."

Perry rose from his seat. "Who?"

"He appeared on the scene about ten years after Dmitri's death, claiming to be the tsarevich."

"But everyone in Rus knew Dmitri was dead."

"Yes, but he convinced them otherwise."

"This is absolutely preposterous," said Zugelder.

Carter felt a chill travel up his spine. He knew what the young woman was driving at. "It could work," he said. "It just might work."

"What the hell are you two talking about?" asked Zugelder.

"A man, a former monk, mentally deficient, who woke up one day believing that he was Dmitri Ivanovich." Carter spoke rapidly. "He wasn't faking it for the money or the power. He honestly believed—with heart and soul—that he was Ivan IV's son, the rightful heir to the throne. And he managed to persuade many others of his legitimacy."

"How many?" asked Perry.

"Enough to eventually become tsar. Even Dmitri's own mother, Marie Nagoy, acknowledged him as her son."

"He recognized all of Dmitri's old servants," Marina

said excitedly. "He knew everything about the tsarevich. He even converted to Catholicism, detesting the Church of Rus as much as Dmitri did. Everything fits."

"Grigory is a receptacle for the real Dmitri to use," added Carter. "A shell that Dmitri can fill and then maneuver to realize his great dream, becoming the tsar."

"How nice for Grigory. His body gets to be tsar and his mind is displaced." Zugelder spoke harshly.

"That's where you're wrong," said Marina. "Grigory Otrepiev had lost his mind. He was a vegetable. There's no mind in his body to replace!"

"And how, may I ask, does Dmitri get into Grigory's body? Answer me that one, huh?"

"Just give me twenty minutes with him."

"Why? What do you plan to do?"

"I'm going to send him back the same way he came."

Marina moved quickly to the boy's door, instigating the second stage of the most arduous journey of Dmitri's life. Once again no longer merely fording the shallows of the Volga or threading through the Uglich woods, but crossing an ocean of time. And she was an essential part of the journey. The guide for the return trip.

Even after she'd spent thirty minutes talking with Dmitri, he seemed no more reconciled to what had happened than he had been upon first waking in the hospital. He returned again and again to the one concept he could not accept, the termination of his life as the nine-year-old Dmitri Ivanovich.

"Dmitri, believe me. There was nothing we could do."

"What do you mean? You could have warned me."

"I did."

"I mean earlier. Before today. You wanted me dead."

"You know that isn't true." Marina lost her temper. "We

were afraid. We didn't know what would happen if we interfered."

The boy stared out the window.

"Dmitri. You know me. I wouldn't trick you."

"If you *had* interfered, if you had warned me"—he shut his eyes and lay back on the bed—"I wouldn't be here right now. I'd still have a chance of being tsar."

"No, you wouldn't have." She remained firm with the boy. "Can't you get that through that thick head of yours? There were dozens of plots against you. You would have been killed in any one of them. Besides, to have saved you would have meant altering history."

"What's wrong with that?" He opened his eyes and looked at her. "How much could change?"

"Everything. Dmitri, I'm not denying that you were destined to become tsar. But not as you expected." She knew he was listening to her even though his face was tilted toward the ceiling. "There is still a way you can be tsar. The way you were intended to follow. Without your mother or your uncle."

"Oh, please, not this Grigory Otrepiev nonsense again."

"I know it sounds impossible, but you are to become him. He didn't mistakenly believe himself to be the true heir. He believed it because you had taken control over him. Just as you've taken control over John."

"John! Who is this John you keep talking about?"

"I've explained this all before. He's the person whose body you are inhabiting at this very moment. Look at your arms, your legs. They're too big to be yours. And here"—she took a mirror from the table near the sink—"look at your face. Go ahead. Look!"

The boy gazed in disbelief at his reflection. "A trick. Why would you favor my displacement of one person and not another? Why am I to be Grigory Otrepiev and not John?"

"Because Grigory has lost his mind. If you don't assume his role he'll be locked away in a corner of the monastery and looked after as the vegetable he will be. But if you return to that time, he'll become tsar. You'll become tsar. And most importantly"—she sat down on the edge of the bed—"you'll have set history on the right course again."

"I don't understand."

"Dmitri, if you don't become False Dmitri then someone else will succeed Boris Godunov as tsar. Someone who will start a dynastic lineage in Rus unknown to my people, the people of the twentieth century. That man will change the whole shape of the world I live in. I may never even exist."

Her last remark clearly affected the boy. "But what if it's a mistake? What if I'm not meant to become this False Dmitri?"

"It's no mistake. Who else but you would have known those details about your life or recognized your old servants? And who else would have deserted the Church? Surely not someone as devout as a monk, which Otrepiev was. It's you, all right. I'm willing to bet my life on it."

"What about me? What happens to my life if you're wrong?"

"You're taking a risk, I know. But if I'm right and you were meant to return to the past, then you will become tsar. I can't make that decision for you, Dmitri. It's your choice: Stay here in a world you don't know or gamble a return to the one you do."

"All right. Say I accept your insane theory. That I am to become False Dmitri. How do I get back? I don't even know how I got here in the first place."

"Leave that to me. All I need is your cooperation. Okay?"

"All right. What is it?"

"First, sit back and relax. Close your eyes."

"What for?"

"Just do as I say." She waited for the boy to lean back on his pillow. "I want you to take a couple of deep breaths. That's it. Clear your mind. I don't want you to think about anything."

He popped open his eyes. "This is ridiculous. What's it all about?"

"Dmitri! Close your eyes. You've got to promise to relax and concentrate on what I'm saying."

"I knew I should have called the guards when I first met you," he grumbled as he closed his eyes.

"Silence! Good. I want you to put your arms out in front of you. Stretch them as far as you can. Harder. Feel your muscles pull. Now relax them. That's it. Do the same thing with your legs."

Marina proceeded to relax the boy's whole body, frantically trying to remember the basic steps of hypnosis, copying Sloane's techniques. She wished she could call Sloane into the room, but she knew his presence would unnerve the boy.

"You're very relaxed now. Your head is resting comfortably on your chest, and your eyes are so heavy that you couldn't open them even if you wanted. I want you to imagine that you're on a lake. On a raft in the middle of a calm, peaceful lake. You find yourself growing sleepy. As the waves gently bob and the sun warms your face, you find yourself falling asleep. Deeper and deeper asleep. You don't have a care in the world. All you want to do is sleep."

She paused to see if her induction had worked. It had.

"You're deeply asleep. But even though you're asleep, you can still hear me and answer me. Do you understand?"

"Yes."

"Good. Now I want you to go back in time. Let your mind go. To the year 7109. Any month or day you want, but it must be in the year 7109. Perhaps you feel a floating sensation, as if you were traveling through space without

weight or dimension. Farther and farther back in time.
Your mind is reaching back. Nearly four hundred years
back. Things are beginning to crystallize now. Your body
feels solid. The blur around you is sharpening. You're now
in the year 7109. You can see and hear perfectly. Open
your eyes."

The boy slowly separated his lids and then blinked them
a number of times.

"What is the date?"

"January 10, 7109."

"What do you see around you?"

"I'm in a room. It's dark but there's light outside."

"Describe the room."

"It's small. Very small. I feel cramped. One door in
front of me. Sparsely furnished. Just a cot and a desk and
a chair."

"What else?"

"There's a book and a bunch of papers on the desk. A
candle. An inkwell. I see some clothes." The boy wet his
lips. "And a crucifix. There's a crucifix on the wall."

Marina sighed. She'd guessed correctly. Dmitri had
found Grigory Otrepiev.

"Wait a minute. There's someone outside my window."
The boy squinted. "It's Vladimir! I can't believe it! I
thought I'd never see him again. He looks . . . older. He's
motioning me to go outside."

Vladimir, Dmitri's ubiquitous guardian angel. There
in a sixteenth-century palace; here in a seventeenth-century
monastery. The man with the visions.

"He's holding two horses. I think he—" The boy gasped.

"What is it?"

"One of the horses. It has a white star on its forehead."
The boy murmured to himself, "He kept Tamor for me.
Like he promised."

"And do you want to go?"

"Yes, but. . . ."

"But what?"

"I'm scared." He grabbed her hand. "Come with me!"

"I can't."

"He's asking me to come. He says we have to hurry."

"Then you must go."

He jumped off the bed, still holding her hand in his. "There's so much I wanted to ask. So much I wanted to know about this world." He laughed. "Will anyone believe this in this twentieth century of yours?"

"Probably not."

He let go of her hand. "I—I won't forget you. Will you remember me?"

"Always."

"Then I suppose it's good-bye." He hugged her, this woman from the future.

"Good-bye, Dmitri." She kissed his cheek. "And good luck."

The young man blinked his eyes. He wriggled from her arms and tugged at his hospital gown, which had gathered to one side and separated.

"Shit. What happened this time?" He glanced around the room. "A hospital? I had one of those fits again? Hey, you can tell Sloane that I'm quitting this study. I don't care if he pays me a million bucks." John started to leave and then remembered the split in his gown. "Would you mind telling me where my clothes are? Or maybe what the hell I'm doing here?"

Marina opened her mouth to explain but couldn't think of anything to say. He'd never believe a goddamn word of it. She started to laugh.

John muttered to himself and bunched the gown at the side. "God, I'm dropping this class. Bunch of crazies in this field."

The next thing he knew she had pounced on him, toppling the two of them onto the bed, and was showering him with kisses.

His parents rushed in the door.

He supposed it would be best to begin by explaining who Marina was. . . .

On July 21, 1605, False Dmitri became tsar. His coronation was lavish, and his people ecstatic over having found their true monarch.

In 1606 he married. The union was notable because, unlike most royal marriages of the day, it was not arranged for political ends. The bride was a Czech girl who offered no strategic alliance, no monetary support, no stockpile of arms. But Dmitri loved her. Her name was Marina. Marina Mniszech.

Kismet, perhaps? Or something infinitely more complex. The simultaneous existence of that which we call the past, present, and future—each transmitting to the other, each a part of a greater, indivisible whole. Time.

Epilogue

To my knowledge, Dmitri Ivanovich has never left the sixteenth century. The incident in 130–B is one of fiction. This is not to say the foregoing story could never happen. Countless sightings of visitors from the past and future have been reported, and though many, as with UFO spottings, are optical illusions or honest mistakes, there remain those inexplicable few. Time dislocation is an actual theory.

I've attempted to be fairly accurate in rendering history, though I've no doubt let slip a few anachronisms or downright errors. The authors and books mentioned can be found in most metropolitan libraries with the exception of the nonexistent *Bartrell Encyclopedia*. All of the major historical characters lived but one, Dmitri's godfather, Vladimir. Their personalities are, for the most part, contrived, but some of their traits are historically factual, such as Marie Nagoy's nervousness and dependence on fortunetellers and Mikhail Nagoy's ambition and quarrelsome nature.

The descriptions of food, drink, dress, and customs are all based on fact. The religious service that Dmitri attends is a construct of services described by Queen Elizabeth I's envoy, Giles Fletcher, in his book, *Of the Rus Commonwealth*, and may differ from what Dmitri actually attended on Friday and Saturday. It is unlikely that Mikhail Nagoy was as irreligious as I've portrayed him. Yet it is true that superstition infiltrated Muscovite religion. Spirits were believed in, the Finnish were regarded as mystics, and the *Rafli*, the literature of portents, was consulted.

It is also unlikely that Mikhail would have wooed or thrown a banquet for local boyars in support of Dmitri, no matter how ambitious he was. Such acts easily could have been interpreted as indictments against Feodor's government. Nor would Mikhail have held the banquet on a Wednesday, a fast day.

On Monday, May 10, the Uglich palace guards were indeed reinforced. Moreover, on Wednesday, May 12, Dmitri did suffer an epileptic attack. His mother was cut by the *svaya* bolt during an earlier fit, however—on Easter. And though she testified before the Uglich commission that her son spoke to "spirits," she did not pinpoint May 12 as one such instance.

There is no conclusive evidence that Vasilisa Volokhova or her son had anything to do with Dmitri's death. She is a victim of the author's license. Similarly, none of the historians I read implicated Vasilly Shuisky in the murder. However, George Verdnadsky, in an article in the *Oxford Slavonic Papers*, "The Death of the Tsarevich Dmitri: A Reconsideration of the Case," stated that the German author Karl Stählin once suggested the possibility.

The twentieth-century characters are fictitious.

I'd like to thank Dr. David Sato for devising a disease to fit John's symptoms and Tim Ruttman for supplying the Russian spoken by Dmitri/John. For simplicity's sake, I've updated Dmitri's speech to modern times.

For further information on hypnosis technique, I refer

the reader to two books: *Hypnosis for the Seriously Curious* by K. Bowers (Monterey, CA.: Brooks/Cole Publishing Co., 1976) and *The Experience of Hypnosis* by E. R. Hilgard (New York: Harcourt, Brace and World, 1963).

Lastly, I would advise anyone who has a buzzing in the ear, or an itching finger, or who hears a wall cracking, to think twice about it. Especially if he or she sees a man dressed in medieval clothes coming down the street. For you see, I omitted telling you that there was a second False Dmitri. And a third. And a fourth.

And they all wanted one thing.

To be tsar.

ROYAL FAMILIES OF RUS

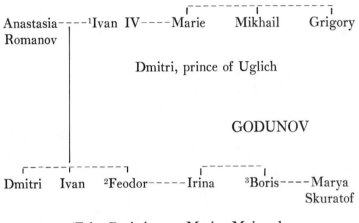

IVANOVICH

Anastasia - - - -¹Ivan IV - - - -Marie
Romanov

Dmitri, prince of Uglich

NAGOY

Mikhail   Grigory

GODUNOV

Dmitri   Ivan   ²Feodor - - - - -Irina   ³Boris - - - -Marya
                                                        Skuratof

⁴False Dmitri - - - - -Marina Mniszech
(Grigory Otrepiev)

SHUISKY

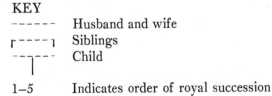

Ivan   ⁵Vasilly   Dmitri - - - - -Sister of
                                          Marya
                                          Skuratof

KEY

- - - - - -   Husband and wife
┌ - - - ┐   Siblings
- -┬- - -   Child
   │

1–5   Indicates order of royal succession

The Background: A Bibliography

Barbour, Philip L. *Dimitry*. Boston: Houghton Mifflin Co., 1966.

Dmytryshyn, Basil, ed. *Medieval Russia, A Source Book, 900–1700*, 2nd ed. Hinsdale, Ill.: The Dryden Press, 1973.

Fletcher, Giles. *Of the Rus Commonwealth*, ed. Albert J. Schmidt. Ithaca, N.Y.: Cornell Univ. Press, 1966.

Graham, Stephen. *Boris Godunof*. New Haven: Yale Univ. Press, 1933.

Grey, Ian. *Boris Godunov: The Tragic Tsar*. London: Hodder and Stoughton, 1973.

Koslow, Jules. *Ivan the Terrible*. New York: Hill and Wang, 1961.

Mérimée, Prosper. *Demetrius the Imposter: An Episode in Russian History*, trans. A. R. Scoble. London: R. Bentley, 1853.

Platonov, S. F. *Boris Godunov*, trans. L. Rex Pyles. Gulf Breeze, Fla.: Academic International Press, 1973.

———. *The Time of Troubles*, trans. John T. Alexander. Lawrence, Kans.: Univ. Press of Kansas, 1970.

Riasanovsky, Nicholas V. *A History of Russia*, 3rd ed. New York: Oxford University Press, 1977.

Verdnadsky, George. "The Death of Tsarevich Dimitry: A

Reconsideration of the Case." *Oxford Slavonic Papers*, V, (1954) 1–19.

Von Hernerstein. *Description of Moscow and Muscovy, 1557*, ed. Bertold Picard, trans. J. B. C. Grundy. New York: Barnes and Noble, Inc., 1969.

Waliszewski, K. *Ivan the Terrible*, trans. Lady Mary Loyd. Hamden, Conn.: Archon Books, 1966.

Wilson, Francesca, ed. *Muscovy: Russia Through Foreign Eyes, 1553–1900*. New York: Praeger Publishers, 1970.